ALSO BY

CARLO BONINI & GIANCARLO DE CATALDO

*Suburra*

GIANCARLO DE CATALDO

*The Father and the Foreigner*
*Romanzo Criminale*

# THE NIGHT OF ROME

Carlo Bonini & Giancarlo De Cataldo

# THE NIGHT OF ROME

*Translated from the Italian
by Antony Shugaar*

Europa
*editions*

Europa Editions
214 West 29th Street
New York, N.Y. 10001
www.europaeditions.com
info@europaeditions.com

Copyright © 2015 Giulio Einaudi editore s.p.a., Torino
First Publication 2018 by Europa Editions UK
This edition, 2019 by Europa Editions US

Translation by Antony Shugaar
Original title: *La notte di Roma*
Translation copyright © 2018 by Europa Editions

Library of Congress Cataloging in Publication Data is available
ISBN  978-1-60945-536-1

Bonini, Carlo & De Cataldo, Giancarlo
The Night of Rome

Book design and cover illustration by Emanuele Ragnisco
www.mekkanografici.com

Prepress by Grafica Punto Print – Rome

Printed in the USA

# CONTENTS

To Tiziana and Giulia, who never led us astray.

To Massimo, who explained two or three things about politics that we still didn't know.

# THE NIGHT OF ROME

Sebastiano Laurenti was contemplating the spectacle of chaos from behind the tinted windows of the black Audi A6.

Rome was burning.

For five days now the city had been on its knees. Immobilized by a wildcat public transportation strike. Submerged by the total cessation of garbage collections. Suffocating from the stench of the bonfires that the enraged citizens were setting on street corners.

It had all begun when a young girl in Tor Sapienza filed a criminal complaint, stating that she'd been attacked by two negroes. The outlying areas had immediately burst into open revolt.

Rome was burning.

The revolt had exploded against the welcome centers for immigrants. In the grim subdivisions known as *borgate*, gypsies became the targets of vigilante squads. Young Roma children stopped attending schools. There were checkpoints established around the gypsy camps. There was a smell of pogrom in the air.

Press from around the world descended on Rome. In the dispatches they filed, a nine-column nightmare. A criminal blockbuster that filled prime-time television screens. The memory of Naples buried in garbage during that city's recent strikes paled in comparison. In his Easter homily, Pope Francis had issued a heartfelt appeal to mankind's sense of mercy. And even more than that, an appeal to its sense of humanity, if such a thing still stirred. The prime minister had formed a standing crisis unit at the Palazzo del Viminale, headquarters of Italy's Ministry of the Interior and therefore of its national law enforcement agencies. The unit included representatives from emergency management, police, firefighters, and the armed forces.

But there wasn't a bulldozer, garrison, armored van, or street patrol capable of reversing or even halting the collapse.

It was as if the city had decided to curl up and shut itself off, swallowing everyone and everything up in a subterranean miasma of resentment, hatred, and misery.

Gangs of ultras put aside their mutual hatreds and set out to wreak systematic devastation on Italy's capital. The metro station of Vigna Clara had blown up, a strategic location for the imminent inauguration of the jubilee of mercy, proclaimed just the month before by Pope Francis.

Anarchist graffiti appeared, taking credit for the explosion. Nobody believed them.

The authorities, with the mayor out front, wandered list-lessly from one garrison to another. The authorities spoke optimistically, reassured the populace, and made promises they would never keep. The authorities didn't understand. What was happening in Rome eluded any logic.

And *he* had been the engine driving all of this. Sebastiano.

A tall, restrained, sober young man. Destroying Rome hadn't been his purpose, it had only been a means to an end.

Deep down, he just hoped it would all be resolved to everyone's best interests.

The bonfires, glowing dirty red in the sunset, gave him no pleasure, no pride. If anything, a faint, unpleasant annoyance.

Sebastiano didn't love war.

Sebastiano was a builder of peace.

He dialed a phone number in London.

He'd been little more than a child when he'd had his life stolen from him. He'd learned early that there was only one way to take back possession of his life.

Violence.

On the fourth ring, a woman's voice answered. Alex.

The accounts had all been transferred to the new branches of various banks on the Turks and Caicos Islands. No snafus or problems. The woman from Rome had phoned Alex. She was upset about the sudden, tragic death of Frodo.

"So what did you say?"

"I told her that you were very angry at her, Sebastiano."

"Thanks, Alex."

"Seba . . . "

"Yes?"

"Don't hurt her, okay? Not unless it's strictly necessary, I mean."

Sebastiano said nothing. *That's not the point, Alex.*

*The point is how badly she hurt me.*

ONE MONTH EARLIER

# I.
## THURSDAY, MARCH 12TH, 2015
### *Saint's Day: Pope St. Gregory I*

VIA SANNIO. ST. JOHN'S BASILICA. SIX IN THE MORNING.

The sign stated: "Public Works Contract for Station, Rome Metro Company. Contracted Company, Mariani Construction s.p.a., Member of the Metro C Consortium. Project for the Construction of the C Line. T3 Lot. Line Running from Piazza San Giovanni to the Imperial Forums."

The man pulled the woolen watch cap down over his ears, shivered slightly in his gleaming black bomber jacket, and impatiently scanned the flashing stoplights that illuminated the deserted expanse of Piazza San Giovanni. At his side, his buddy, a mountain of muscles with a neck set deep between his broad shoulders, shook his head. He pulled his smartphone from his jacket pocket and checked the time. Six AM. Not so much as a whiff of this asshole's stench. At least it had stopped raining.

The arrival of the red Fiat Panda compact driven by the construction supervisor Lucio Manetti was blanketed by the screeching passage of an empty trolley. Manetti parked in the usual place. And then, as he did every morning, he hovered for a moment inside the car, performing his odd, neurotic ritual dance around the car. Doors locked, check. Headlights off, yes. Running lights, likewise. Then, with a light tap of his forefinger, he shoved the heavy frame of his Coke-bottle eyeglasses back onto the bridge of his nose, patted his leather portfolio binder, and adjusted the long, pointy umbrella that hung over his forearm. He was late. He didn't need to glance at his watch to know that. It was enough to see the first slanting shafts of daylight over St. John's basilica and the accompanying view, which he'd grown to detest in all those years of construction. The view of the cathedral's dome was blocked by the gigantic support structure for the mole, the tunnel boring machine that rested a hundred feet below ground, where it had sat idle for God knows how long. Months? No, years. He'd lost track. First they'd hit the ruins of a Roman villa. Then pools of water, so that you'd have thought they were digging in the Karst region, with its porous limestone subsoil. Then the protracted holdup with the money. The bulldozers had stopped working. The Calabrian and Neapolitan construction workers hired by the subcontractors had vanished. The only one left watching over the Big Hole now was him. He was the supervisor of a ghost construction site. If for no other reason than that—he thought—he might as well get himself a nice hot espresso before starting his long day of doing nothing. To hell with the schedule. What could five minutes change in the face of that eternally unfinished project?

He walked into the café.

Five minutes later the two men—leaning idly against the rolling shutter gate of the construction site—finally saw him reappear.

"We're in no hurry, you piece of shit, after all, where do you think you're going to go?"

The construction supervisor crossed the street with a brisk step, one hand rummaging in the pocket of his raincoat for the keys to the construction site. The morning ahead was packed with things to get done. First off, make a call to the Prefecture. He needed to get new anti-Mafia certificates for two companies being added to the list of subcontractors. Dottor Danilo Mariani had insisted on bringing them into the earthmoving team. Right, of course, anti-Mafia certificates. That was a mouthful, considering. Those guys practically had "Camorra" stamped on their foreheads. Still, the "*dottore,*" as he insisted on being called, didn't want to hear any objections. In fact, he'd been pretty brusque.

"Just mind your own fucking business, supervisor. I pay you to do what I tell you. I'm the head of this company. And if you don't like it, I've got lines of construction supervisors out the door who'd be glad to take your job. So pick up your phone, call the Prefecture, and ask for Signora Giada. She's already been briefed."

He opened the gate to the construction site. He didn't even have a chance to hear the two men come up behind him.

They were already lunging at him with all the fury of two rabid dogs.

The first blow hit him on the temple and made his eyeglasses fly off.

The second one shattered his incisors, flooding his mouth with blood.

The third one smashed straight into his left eyeball, practically making it explode.

The pain was so sharp and intense that he was unable even to scream. The two men lifted him up bodily and dragged him toward the large yellow bulldozer at the center of the construction site.

They tied him to the scoop of that monster machine, like a Christ on the cross. That's when the supervisor Manetti, with his lone right eye, managed to make out the silhouettes of his attackers. They were scrabbling around, retrieving something from the ground.

*Sweet Jesus . . . No, not me. Why? Why?*

The more heavily built of the two had picked up a bundle of iron rebar. He clutched the sheaf of rods in his right hand as if he were waving a pack of spaghetti. He was laughing. And getting closer. Closer and closer. Until the supervisor was able to catch a whiff of the man's pestilential breath, which reeked of nicotine and words that betrayed a faint Slavic accent.

"All right, then, Dottore . . . Don't you have anything for us? Because you know, you filthy faggot, that the money belongs to *us*, don't you?"

Spitting blood, he managed to mumble out something that resembled a last plea, as desperate as it was useless.

"Please . . . I'm begging you . . . The cashbox . . . It's in the office booth . . . But there isn't much money in it . . . "

The ogre clutched the iron rebar with both hands and raised it level with his nose.

It was only then that the supervisor Manetti noticed the faded blue tattoos that marked those hands. One letter for each of his ten fingers.

F-R-I-E-N-D-L-E-S-S.

He tilted his head back and looked up. His only remaining eye focused on the mole.

The merciful dome of the basilica.

The gray glow of dawn.

The blow slammed home with all the violence in the world.

He could no longer feel his legs. But he still managed to understand the animal's words.

"With Fabio's best regards."

S ebastiano was feeling nauseated. The real estate developer couldn't stop sniffling and he was dripping sweat
onto the rainbow onyx surface of his conference table.
That's an ugly beast, cocaine. That shit'll fuck you up.
Sebastiano threw open the large window that gave onto the
terrace looking out over the elegant neighborhood, the Rione
Ludovisi. Clinging to the white gazebo was a blaze of climbing
mimosa in spectacular bloom. With studied leisure, Sebastiano
went over and sat down on the far side of the large oval table.
And then he started staring hard at Danilo Mariani. The man's
hands wandered from the espresso demitasse to his iPhone.
The uneasy redness coloring his cheeks contrasted with the
more general unhealthy yellowish hue of his face. The merino
wool suit could scarcely contain a body mass rendered flaccid
by years of abuse. The puffy face was framed by a head of pre-
cociously gray hair which, in spite of the fact that the man was
in his early forties, aged him by a good ten years. There he sat,
heir to one of the most venerable dynasties of Roman builders.
Completely debauched. Someone, just three hours ago, had
beaten the man's construction site supervisor to a bloody pulp,
in Piazza San Giovanni.

Sebastiano wanted to understand why.

"Sebastia', I . . . "

He'd made him wait long enough. With a weary gesture,
Sebastiano authorized him to tell all.

"It's all that son of a bitch the German's fault . . . "

Young Mariani was a member of the consortium of companies that, in 2006, had won the three-billion-euro contract to build the C line of the Rome metro. The biggest infrastructure project of the third millennium. "General contractor," is what the so-called "Objective Law" had called him. Legally required to deliver a "turnkey project," finished and ready to run. The kind of horseshit that was perfect for suckers willing to guzzle it down. In nine years, the project had wasted away, shrinking from forty stations to twenty, while the costs, of course, had skyrocketed into orbit. From three billion euros to the universe, and beyond. Just like in those movies about toys that come to life. And after all, what was the metro, if not a great big toy? Everyone knew how these things worked. The fact that his name was Mariani wasn't just an accident, you know. You win the contract without so much as a penny set aside for prefinancing to get construction started. And the day after winning the job, you already start bitching and moaning and demanding arbitration. You upbraid and dress down those idiots at City Hall, insisting that the public works contract stipulated entirely different conditions. That you haven't even started and there are already unlooked-for variants. That the dirt under this blessed Rome is an unbroken field of ancient crockery and who knows what other fucking archeological finds they'll come up with. So you just make it clear to them they're going to have to pull out their checkbooks. And you ask and ask and ask. Ask, and you will be given. And if you're not given, then you don't work. The Romans will curse and the Big Hole will never get filled back up.

It had always worked before. Until that demented mayor had showed up. Martin Giardino, known as "Er Tedesco," or the German.

"I don't accept extortion," he'd proclaimed.

Just for starters, he'd blocked all payments for "construction progress benchmarks." And so they'd come, with clenched teeth, to a final and definitive agreement. In practical terms, he'd liquidated them with pennies to the euro. Even so, damn him, the German wasn't paying.

"The German doesn't have anything to do with it anymore. The matter is in the government's hands now."

"Oh well, that doesn't make any difference. The point is I'm out of pocket."

"By how much?"

"Not much. Five hundred or so," Mariani exhaled.

Sebastiano turned icy cold. Then he said, deliberately:

"Five. Hundred. Thousand. Euros. Clever!"

Danilo abandoned himself to a rushing river of justifications. Half-finished phrases, streamers of drool hanging off the corner of his mouth, drenched with sweat, self-pity by the bucketful.

"The payroll for the subcontracting firms. The workers' salaries, the suppliers' bills, damn them, and the increase in VAT that's just killing us . . . I've had a liquidity crisis, the cash flow went to hell, you understand, things that happen . . . "

"I'd say that calling it a respiratory crisis would be more accurate," Sebastiano whispered, icily. And he sniffed loudly and mockingly.

Mariani threw his arms wide, helplessly.

"Oh, all right, you know how it is, every so often I snort some of the shit, how bad could it be, everyone does it, Sebastia', don't tell me that you don't . . . "

"No. I don't, Danilo. I don't."

Ah, good old coke! The Queen of the Night, with its entourage of pussy! The eternal Petronian bacchanal of the unredeemable Suburra. The Capitoline Triad: coke-pussy-gambling . . . pa-pa-rah-pa, sound a fanfare . . . you could write a ditty about it, the anthem of Rome, the Eternal Capital . . . Everything's so obvious, it's all so predictable. When he'd chosen

Sebastiano over all the others who gathered, tails wagging, around him, Samurai had been categorical: vices are for other people, what *we* have is control. Vices make you lose that control, and if there was ever any meaning to the distinction between man and superman, well, vices mark that boundary line. There'd been no reason to insist on the point, anyway. Sebastiano carried an innate sense of restraint within him, and always had. It was his father who'd inculcated it in him. His poor, honest father, who died of honesty.

"Sebastia', do you hear me?"

"You still haven't explained why they beat your project supervisor black and blue like that. Most important of all, you haven't told me *who* did it. Because you, and only you, can tell me that, Danilo. You know very well that hitting that construction site meant hitting you, and hitting you meant hitting me, and hitting me meant hitting Samurai. So . . . "

"Fabio Desideri," Danilo exhaled. He stuck his hand into his breast pocket and pulled out a small silver case.

"Not at my house," Sebastiano said in a chilly voice.

"Oh come on, just a quick line . . . I need it . . . "

"First, finish your story."

"What's there to tell, haven't you figured it out? I needed cash, I went to Fabietto, I hoped I'd be able to pay him back in time, I couldn't do it, and now that asshole's pulled this Apache dance."

"Why didn't you just come to me, you tremendous dick-head?"

"For a couple of bucks I didn't want to give you extra headaches, with everything you've got going on . . . and after all, Fabio is our man to handle, isn't he? At least, that's how I thought of it . . . Now can I?" he begged, clicking open the lid of his silver case.

"Get out."

"Sebastia' . . . "

"Get out."

Sebastiano was afraid the other man was about to start cry-ing. If he did, he wasn't sure he'd be able to control his reac-tions. But Danilo got the message. He put the silver case back into his pocket and backed out the door, freeing the room of his bitter emanations.

A large gate loomed up before the Audi A6. Sebastiano gestured to his driver, Furio. He got out and headed for the booth, which was manned by a heavyset guy who had, at the very least, a semiautomatic, locked and loaded, under his large bulletproof vest.

"I'm Sebastiano Laurenti. I need to see Fabio."

"I recognized you, Signore. Don't you remember me?"

Sebastiano scrutinized the man. Early forties, corpulent, big black handlebar mustache. A vague recollection stirred in his mind.

"Bogdan?" he tossed out.

The mustachioed man smiled, flattered.

"My compliments for your memory, Signore. Let me walk you in."

"I know the way, thanks."

"As you prefer, Signore."

The gate swung open on its hinges, Sebastiano got back in the car, and the Audi rolled up the broad asphalt-paved driveway, lined with imposing pine trees. Bogdan Adir, or something like that. Yeah, now he remembered. Albanian, from Fier. Primitive and ferocious, an adept of the code of Kanun, the bible of goat herders with twisted daggers.

Fabio Desideri relied on a battalion of Albanians to provide protection to his clubs and bars, and of course to right the occasional wrong. In fact, it might have been one of Bogdan's brothers or cousins who did that job on the poor miserable construction supervisor. A couple of years ago, Bogdan had gotten a little too smart for his own good, setting aside a modest batch of cocaine and arranging to move it independently, pocketing the proceeds. Samurai had found out about it, though who the hell knows how. And he'd ordered Sebastiano to cover it up. So now Bogdan owed him a favor.

They had arrived in a large parking circle, bounded on one side by the mansion. A late-nineteenth-century villa that Fabio Desideri had purchased at a discounted price from the morphine-addicted heir to a bitter English old maid, her nephew or something. He climbed the stairs, surrounded by elegant flowerpots.

Why had Fabio, a guy who until then had been loyal to Samurai, broken the rules?

He didn't understand, and that made him uneasy.

Much like Sebastiano, Fabio Desideri was not descended from criminal loins. He claimed, indeed boasted, American origins, and in fact he had studied for a few years in some bilingual school, where he'd managed to squeeze out a certificate that was designed to parrot the graphics and appearance of a U.S. college diploma. His parents were honest folk, middle middle-class, you might once have called them, and it was a safe bet they had no idea at all of the kind of things their bright young son was getting up to. But whatever traits Sebastiano might share with "Fabietto," as he was known in their circle— Little Fabio—ended there. Fabietto had become a criminal by choice. And from day one he'd displayed an unquestionable talent for his calling. He'd gotten his start peddling Samurai's cocaine in Rome's VIP soirées and salons, to overstate the social level a bit. In just a few years he'd become the top dog in coke dealing to the well-born and well-to-do of Rome. The kind of people you ran into in the city's historical center. He'd even been sent off to enjoy a brief vacation at Rome's Regina Coeli prison, in the aftermath of a brawl. He'd kept his lips stitched and he'd emerged from criminal "finishing school" with a certificate of good manners. With the passage of time, he'd diversified his activities. Now he was the owner of a chain of clubs and restaurants scattered strategically in all the key locations of the Roman *movida*—Prati, Trastevere, Testaccio, Ostiense, Ponte Milvio, Parioli, Flaminio—and he'd kept the coke at arm's length. He limited himself to supplying substantial quantities to a few select customers, using the Albanians and other select operators as the "mules" shuttling around his network. For the most part professionals with dusty white nostrils, whose pay for guarding and peddling was the occasional free line to snort. If anyone had come up with the bright idea of searching Fabio's villa or any of his establishments, they would have found nothing but an assortment of handsome antique vases, fine paintings by big-name artists, antique weapons—legally registered of course—and legitimate cigarettes with authentic tax stamps. What Sebastiano remembered about him were giddy, bubbly evenings out with fashion models, wealthy fat cats, movie starlets, and famous soccer players, as well as Samurai's cautious, wary opinion: "He seems like he's having fun, but he's really just a cold bastard."

Fabio Desideri was in his early forties, tall, fair-haired, with the carefully tended body of someone who's spent a lot of time at the gym and is an adept of the zone diet. He wore an ultrasoft sky-blue cashmere light sweater over a cream-colored polo shirt, trousers the same color, and a pair of suede shoes without socks. A good-looking man, extremely sociable and well connected, his address book dense with names, in love with life and unfailingly good humored. *Smart*, he would have said of himself, using the English word even when he was speaking Italian. Skillful at speaking the brutal language of the streets and disguising himself as a high-spirited fellow partier. As confirmed by the vigorous handshake he displayed. Fabio ushered his guest into a living room whose furniture and interior decoration, distinguished by subtle, pale color tones, bespoke the work of expensive architects. A tip of the hat. Two outstandingly beautiful young women got to their feet as the men arrived.

"Cheryl, Fionnula, this is Sebastiano. Practically speaking, one of the masters of Rome."

Cheryl was a black fashion model, who stood six foot one, with the physique of a gazelle, long slender arms, fleshy lips, and a blank look in her eyes. She was in Rome for a private runway presentation for a Russian billionaire. Fionnula was a redhead with stunningly white skin, almost translucent, with a broken gaze and perfect breasts, which you could just intuit, braless, under a silk blouse. She sang in a pop band that was pretty well known, and after the runway presentation she was scheduled to perform for a small, lucky audience in one of Fabio's clubs.

Sebastiano said hello to the girls, polite but chilly, and after a quick exchange of courteous chitchat, they left the two men alone to talk.

"Can I offer you anything, Sebastiano?"

"No thanks. I'm here to talk."

"I know, I know, but first . . . I need to ask your advice, Sebastia'."

"My advice?"

"Yeah, it's about those two girls, the redhead and the black girl. Which one do you prefer?"

Sebastiano suppressed the urge to tell him to go fuck himself. That's just the way Fabio was. He was going to have to give him some rope. The master of the house settled onto a horsehide chaise longue and set forth in a frivolous tone of voice the existential doubt that had been tormenting him. The black girl was undoubtedly the winner if you were taking about sheer physical beauty, but years of hard experience in the field of fashion models had warned him not to trust physical appearances: there could be a lot of ice beneath that façade, too much. In that case, he ought to choose the redhead, but there too he feared certain contraindications. Fionnula, like so many of her people, for that matter, liked alcohol, a lot, even too much. And the sexual performance of drunk women can frequently be quite disappointing.

"Certainly, I could always suggest a little threesome action, but you never know how they'd take it. All they'd have to do is get offended, and the next thing you know I'm high and dry. Don't you think, Sebastia'?"

He'd had enough. With a decisive gesture he put a halt to Fabio's word-vomit and told him again that he was there for a specific reason. Danilo Mariani.

"Why don't you relax, Sebastia', you're always worrying about work."

"Was there any need for such extreme violence? You should have just come to me."

Fabio's voice become even more cordial, if that was possible.

"Yes, that's true, I could have. But I said to myself: You need to send a very clear message, Fabio. Our friend Danilo has been telling me to go fuck myself for months now. He refused to come to the telephone, there was no discussion of payment, you can't even begin to guess the kind of excuses he'd come up with, and in the end, instead of paying what he owed me, do you think he didn't just ask for another shipment? On credit! I have to say: too much is too much, no? I don't like violence one bit, Sebastia', but there are times when there's no other option. You wouldn't want me to be taken for the kind of guy who lets other guys run up lots of debt and eat out at his expense."

Fabio admitted it, then. As if it stood to reason. Obvious and unavoidable. Nonchalantly, he took responsibility. The uneasiness increased in the back of Sebastiano's mind.

Danilo had been a pretext. The message was for him and for Samurai.

"Sure, I could have done that," the asshole had said.

"I could have." He hadn't said, "I *should* have."

The two men eyed each other for a few seconds, then Sebastiano said that he'd arrange personally to honor the debt.

"You'll get your money, Fabio. If I'm not mistaken, it's five hundred . . . "

Fabio smiled, as if a great burden had just been lifted from his soul.

"There's no hurry, my friend."

"I'll see to it personally. Shall we say . . . in a week's time?"

"Oh, take all the time you want, perish the thought!"

Sebastiano stood up suddenly and held out his hand.

"Then we're agreed."

The other man grabbed Sebastiano's hand and gripped it hard.

"You feel like coming to the party tonight? We're going to have fun."

"Some other time, Fabio."

"Sebastiano Laurenti, the tireless protector of the peace. Give my regards to Samurai."

After seeing Sebastiano to the door, Fabio Desideri came back to the living room. He lit a Cohiba cigar, poured himself a dollop of chilled white wine, and waited a few minutes until he felt perfectly calm. Calm and full of energy. In contrast to the confidence he'd displayed in the presence of Samurai's lieutenant, he'd actually looked forward to that meeting with abject fear, more than anything else. An unusual response for him, but such was the situation. For some time now he'd been nurturing an ambitious project. More or less since the German had taken up a permanent spot in the city council and the grand maneuvers had begun to renegotiate all the long-standing pacts and agreements. More than once, he'd been on the verge of taking irrevocable action. But if there was one reason he'd hesitated, it was an exceedingly clear one. Such a step meant there would be no turning back, and it might have meant the end of him. All the same, you can't dither eternally, or else the magic moment turns into a poignant and pointless instant of regret, and the whole magnificent castle you've erected over the years collapses into sand. Therefore, when Danilo Mariani had offered him that priceless opportunity, he'd seized the day. No more waiting, or he'd never be anything more than good old Fabietto. The winds were in his favor. With the old guard decimated by waves of arrests and Samurai behind bars, a young man with the right temperament saw the highway in front of him in his hand. The more time Samurai spent waiting for the special detention provisions of Article 41-bis of the criminal code to time out, and the weaker his grip on the city became: sooner or later a king in exile just becomes an exile. Either the exile comes to an end or the king dies, and once the king is dead, long live the king.

The new one, that is.

The wild card was, of course, Sebastiano. That's why this meeting had filled him with such dread. But in the end, it had turned out to be a successful bet. After watching him lower his feathers, apparently placated in the presence of Fabio's bemused and friendly demeanor, Fabio had come to realize that Samurai's heir apparent was actually, deep down, just a straw man. None of what he'd feared—a spectrum of criminal possibilities that ranged from a violent verbal set-to all the way out to immediate and permanent payback—had happened. If he'd been dealing with Samurai instead of the young man . . . Well, then that meeting would never even have taken place. And Fabio would have come to bitterly regret his audacious move. Sebastiano had raised an eyebrow and then, once and for all, he'd submitted to the state of affairs. He lacked the balls, as his Albanian friends would have noted. Sebastiano was not now, and never would be, Samurai. Which meant that he, Fabio, would not only be popular, indispensable, and respected. But also feared. Feared and venerated. The alternative was clear now.

So either the youngster comes around, or we have to wipe him out.

Little Fabio is dead, long live Big Fabio.

## II.
### Friday, March 13th, 2015
### *Saint's Day: St. Agnellus of Pisa*

Rome, St. Peter's Basilica. Six in the morning.

Sebastiano Laurenti stared for a moment at the silhouette of Castel Sant'Angelo. The intermittent hypnotic sweep of the windshield wipers and the warmth emitted by the heater vents did nothing to help him wake up. Dawn, which consisted of inky blackness veering into a dull gray, a dawn gleaming with rain and wind, only made the hulking structure look sinister. The thermometer read 42 degrees. Too low a temperature for a winter that seemed determined not to die. Too high to hope for an unseasonable snowfall that would have filled him with a giddy euphoria—like the boy he'd ceased being, far too young. He was gripped by the memory of his father's smiling face, filled with pride, in the gardens of Castel Sant'Angelo where he'd taught him to ride a bike without training wheels. His first achievement. He pulled up the collar and lapels of his overcoat, catching a fleeting whiff of the scent of his citron aftershave, and remembered slowly massaging it into the skin on his face after a shave that had seemed endless to him. He felt a shiver of melancholy run through him, whereupon he ordered his chauffeur to join the column of SUVs and dark-blue government limousines that were moving up Via della Conciliazione at walking speed.

The procession reminded him of a funeral. It had the color and the solemnity. It had the chill of the halogen spotlights illuminating Bernini's colonnade. St. Peter's Basilica loomed before him in a spectacle that had something surreal about it. But no, this wasn't a funeral. This was the second anniversary of the election of Pope Francis to the papal throne and the fiftieth anniversary of the end of the Second Vatican Council. At least, that's what had been written on the parchment invitation that announced the extraordinary Mass to be celebrated that morning by the pontiff. It had been hand-delivered to him two days ago. And he shared that invitation with only a very select crew of high muck-a-mucks from beyond the Tiber who were now here, alongside him, crossing themselves with a slight genuflection as they entered the nave of the cathedral.

He observed the magnificent twisted Solomonic columns that supported the monumental processional catafalque of the Baldachin, the baroque altar built at the behest of the Barberini pope, Urban VIII. His thoughts turned once again to his father and the words with which he had whispered in his ear the secret of that architectural revelation, as little Sebastiano stood looking up in astonishment.

The way they'd built it was by plundering the bronze statues of the Pantheon. Learn this, son: *quod non fecerunt barbari, fecerunt Barberini.*

What the barbarians didn't do, the Barberini did. This time the memory of his father brought a smile to his face.

The barbarians and the popes. Rome. Yesterday. Today. And for all eternity.

With a reflexive instinct, his gaze shifted rapidly from above to below. He recognized the mayor Martin Giardino and his deputy, Temistocle Malgradi, in the little knot of people taking their seats in the central pews that faced the altar. Malgradi was Samurai's man in City Hall. The physician who had gone into politics. The "Tarzan" of the second Republic. From the clerical right wing to the Government of the Best to the new Italian Democrat Party that was recycling the old scrap metal of the political class. An accomplished acrobat. He had renamed his clinic on the Via Flaminia, once a haven for moneyed criminals and the venue for reckless orgies, La Casa di Vicky—Vicky's House. Vicky was the Slavic whore who'd died of an overdose in the arms of his brother Pericle. Pericle Malgradi, the great disappointment. La Casa di Vicky had become a medical and diagnostic center for immigrant women. All services, free of charge, in theory at least. In actual fact, City Hall kicked in the fees. It really is true that you can make more money with charity than with drugs. Then he'd set up his nice big Foundation with its very own hashtag— #WhatYouCanDo—and he'd had no trouble making his way through the ranks of the all too malleable Roman Democratic Party. After all, if there were bones to be cracked, then those guys could take care of it. Sebastiano and Samurai. His dream was to become mayor. Samurai had prohibited him from pursuing that dream: enough is enough and too much is too much. Why didn't he just tend to sticking to his man, Martin Giardino? The alien who'd landed here from Brunico (also known as Bruneck, in the South Tyrol of Switzerland) and didn't know the difference between the Roman beltway, Grande Raccordo Anulare, and the Aurelian Walls, mixing up Tor di Nona and Ponte di Nona, and who, for this reason among others, had been rapidly categorized and digested by the rest of Rome, and dubbed with the nickname he deserved, "*er Tedesco*"—the German. A respectable individual, make no mistake. Honest as a Franciscan monk. A supreme environmentalist. Politically hypercorrect. A concentrate of the worst habits of the left. He'd gotten an overwhelming majority of the votes and, narcissist that he was, he was convinced that it was to his own credit. Temistocle was his shadow, his guardian, his mentor.

In the pew where he'd taken a seat, Giardino was conversing animatedly with Malgradi. Who, after a nod of understanding with Sebastiano, moved over to greet him.

"Mamma mia, what an earache this German . . . This morning I just can't take him . . . "

He raised one hand to his mouth, unable to repress an acid belch.

"Why is he so excited?"

"He says that . . . "

He belched again. This time he was unable to restrain the blast of hot breath, and it popped the bubble of citron fragrance wafting around Sebastiano's face.

"Temistocle, a little self-control, we're in St. Peter's!"

"Sorry, it's because of the fritters I ate at the party in the club."

"What club?"

"Yesterday evening I inaugurated the Democratic Party club in Parioli. You wouldn't believe the quantity of pussy. It's clear that we've become the governing party."

"So am I going to be able to find out what the mayor has to say?"

"He says that he's heard there's big news."

"About what?"

"Apparently the pope is going to make an announcement."

"What, is this pope going to resign, too?"

"If only God were so kind . . . We'd finally get this Tupamaro out from underfoot."

"The Tupamaros were Uruguayan. The pope is Argentine."

"Whatever, they're both still Communists."

"Temistocle, you're seeing Communists in too many places."

"That's why I joined the DP. Come on, let's go hear what's going on . . . "

Sebastiano nodded. Out of the corner of his eye, he noticed the hasty step of the late arrival who was just making his way to the front pews of the mother church of Christendom. Jabba, with his hunchbacked posture and pallbearer's face, formerly the bagman and treasurer of the former majority and the ex-mayor, was oozing with sweat and obsequiousness. Sure, because the right wing had still been included in the coalition. No one had ever dreamed of doing without it. Much less he and Samurai. And not because of the Idea. The Idea was dead, bullshit from the last century. The question was a much simpler one. There were still too many mouths to feed. Too high a risk of finding themselves surrounded and besieged. If they wanted to do business, it was necessary for everyone to have a seat at the table. As the saying goes: One hand washes the other, and both hands wash the face.

The organ pipes started vibrating with deep bass notes, annihilating the buzz of waiting people. The odor of incense and the voices of the choir announced the pope's entrance.

In the name of the Father,
the Son,
and the Holy Spirit.

In the solemnity of his liturgical vestments, Pope Francis brushed for a moment the white woolen pallium wrapped around his shoulders. The sheep on the shoulders of the Shepherd of Souls. Then he made the sign of the cross on his forehead and opened the Book of Holy Scripture.

"From the Gospel according to Luke . . .

"A Pharisee invited him to dine with him, and he entered the Pharisee's house and reclined at table . . . "

Sebastiano soberly listened to the words of the pope. But when Francis mentioned loving one's fellow man, he clutched the seat of the pew with both hands until his knuckles turned white.

"And forgive us our debts, as we also have forgiven our debtors. Love your neighbor and you will be loved in return."

No one had shown mercy to his father. And after all, what is mercy, anyway? You only show mercy to those you fear. That was the law of men he had learned to understand. And if men were the children of God, then that too must be the law of God.

Francis bowed before the Book. He brushed it with his lips in a kiss. He gestured for the congregation to be seated. He approached the microphone on the altar.

"This year, once again, on the eve of the Fourth Sunday of Lent, we have come together to celebrate the penitential liturgy. Confession is a gift from God . . . "

Sebastiano's smartphone vibrated. A text message from Danilo Mariani. With all the mess he'd brought down on himself and others, he still felt like cracking wise.

"Sure, confession! This guy's been smoking something! I'm going nowhere without my lawyer. Let's hear it for Saint Denial!"

Sebastiano slowly swiveled at the waist, looking behind him for Danilo's silhouette. He was at the far end of the nave, near the colonnade. Not far from Monsignor Mariano Tempesta.

Strange, he thought. Why does the bishop seem as if he's trying not to be seen?

Francis went on speaking, his arms extended outward slightly, as if trying to clutch close to him those who were listening, unraveling the meaning of the parable of the Pharisee and the prostitute.

What would he have thought, if he'd had any idea of how little his flock gave a damn about the words he said? His flock, in those solemn moments, was losing all restraint.

Another vibration. Another text message. Malgradi.

"Love is fine with me. Judgment though, no, just look at this Tupamaro!"

Jabba had stirred from his slumber. He typed a text for Malgradi.

"The sinful woman and the Lord. If I think about that power drill of a brother of yours, I have to laugh. Come on!"

Malgradi scanned Jabba's text message and, smiling broadly, decided to take his revenge on Sebastiano.

"Hey Sebastia', whose side are you on? With the fat cat Pharisee or with the slut?"

Sebastiano turned off his cell phone. Malgradi and his people: a filthy crew, but necessary.

Francis paused, a pause that stretched out. Sebastiano understood.

Now maybe we'll find out why you made us get up at dawn today, Your Holiness.

"Beloved brothers and sisters, I have thought long and hard about how the Church can make it more evident that its chief mission is to bear witness to mercy. This is a journey that begins with a spiritual conversion; and we must all make this journey. That is why I have chosen to announce an extraordinary jubilee that is focused primarily on God's mercy. This will be a Holy Year of Mercy. We want to live this year in the light of the Lord's words: 'Be merciful, even as your Father is merciful.' And this applies especially to the father confessor! So much mercy! This Holy Year will begin with the upcoming solemnity of the Immaculate Conception and will conclude on November 20, 2016, the Sunday of Our Lord Jesus Christ, King of the Universe, and the living face of the Father's Mercy. I entrust the logistics and organization of this jubilee to the Pontifical Council for Promoting the New Evangelization, so that it can be set forth as a new step along the journey that the Church is taking in its mission to bring the Gospel of Mercy to one and all."

The mayor was excited. Malgradi had finally turned serious, asshole that he was. Even Jabba was now fully awake.

Well, well, Sebastiano said to himself. How very nice.

The Jubilee of Mercy.

Our Jubilee.

Pontifical Council for Promoting the New Evangelization. Sebastiano furrowed his brow.

What about Tempesta?

Amen.

Francis's solemn benediction came with the liturgical formula of dismissal.

The Mass has ended, go in peace.

The mayor grabbed Malgradi hastily.

"Come on, Temistocle. Come on! We need to put together a brief press release immediately, for the wire services. I want to be the one who wakes the city up with the news!"

Malgradi shook his head, holding up his smartphone with a sardonic smile.

"What is it? What do you want me to look at?"

"Twitter, Mayor. Twitter."

"Well?"

"The pope. Pope Francis, @Pontifex_it. He already announced the news twenty minutes ago."

"But he was saying Mass . . . "

"I'd post a nice selfie right here in the basilica," his deputy observed sardonically.

Malgradi shot an ironic glance at Sebastiano, who disengaged without giving it a second thought. He was still nauseated by those irreverent text messages and, what's more important, he had better things to do. And they were urgent.

Tempesta was waiting for him in the most out-of-view corner of the nave. Sebastiano walked toward him, gesturing as if to kiss his ring. The monsignor skipped the preliminaries. They wouldn't be necessary. Both of them knew that.

"I'm out of the running, Sebastiano. The pope informed me last night that on Monday I'm going to be on a plane to Washington. He's sending me to the Apostolic Nunciature. More or less a latter-day Saint Helena. So forget about the

2000 Jubilee. This is going to be a horse of a different color. This is a very different pope."

"You're kidding, aren't you? You know, don't you, that unless we control that herd of cardinals of the Pontifical Council on the jubilee, nothing doing. We won't be able to install so much as a park bench. Do you at least know who's going to be taking your place?"

The monsignor joined both hands as if in prayer and raised them to his lips.

"He chose the worst replacement he could have, as far as we're concerned."

"Who?"

"Officially I will have no successor. Officially. In reality I've been informed by a reliable source, let's say, an intimate source, that my 'shadow' successor will be Monsignor Giovanni Daré."

"The youngest bishop in Rome? The one who was appointed a few months ago and is at St. John Lateran?"

"Exactly. A Communist."

Here was another one who was obsessed with Communists, thought Sebastiano. As if there were still any of them around . . . Tempesta went on, with a sigh.

"It's all the church's fault, Sebastiano. We've become too tolerant. Anyway, don't waste time on Daré. He's unapproachable. Or rather: he's a true convert. The worst kind. He took his vows later in life. They use him for the real Missions Impossible, like cleaning house, moralizing, and all that stuff . . . Oh, by the way, he's hand in glove with the Community of Sant'Egidio."

"Worrisome."

"You can say that again. Francis elevated him from the exile to which he'd been relegated under Pope Benedict, some low-end *borgata* diocese. And now he owes everything to this pope. Unfortunately, the two of them get along famously. They're on a first-name basis. Why do you think I'm to be shipped off across the ocean? And what's worse, I have to pretend I'm a personal envoy of Francis, so I can't even complain."

"I never thought the South American could be so pitiless."

"He knows how to be ruthless when it comes to redesigning the Curia. I'll tell you, I've even thought of throwing in the towel."

"If you tell me you're giving up on the divine mission, I might believe you. But not on life."

Tempesta pulled out from under his cassock a velvet bag that contained a visibly oblong object.

"Yesterday evening, while going through my things, look what I found. I thought of giving it to you. Maybe you can use it, sooner or later. And anyway, it's the Year of Mercy."

Sebastiano undid the silk cords that fastened the top of the sack. He looked inside. A magnificent silver stiletto with an inlaid handle.

Tempesta smiled.

"They called it the Mercy. They used it on the field of battle to administer a quick death to those gravely wounded. Those who couldn't be transported. To eliminate the excess ballast of disfigured humanity. Of course, only after receiving orders direct from the bishop. To make sure that death was administered in God's name. To ensure it was . . . *merciful*. A single blow. Amen."

Padre Giovanni Daré was afraid.
Francis had appointed him the sole supervisor of the Jubilee.

Giovanni had objected, argued, done his best to get out of it.

"But why me of all people?"

"Because we need the right shepherd to guard the flock, *hermano*. A shepherd who knows how to keep the wolves away from the fold."

He'd obey, of course.

But he was afraid.

Pope Francis had alerted him that he would receive a visit from a young brother. A young priest about age thirty did in fact show up. Don Paolo. Sky-blue eyes, ruddy skin all over, small, fragile looking. Soft as a young girl, Monsignor Daré decided; he was well aware of certain rumors that circulated. Impossible not to be if you worked in those Vatican palaces. And yet, his unquestionable physical beauty caught him by surprise, when he saw him come toward him where he stood at the front entrance to the Vicariate.

"I've counted the minutes, Your Eminence . . . "

"Let's not exaggerate. Don Giovanni will do fine. Come with me."

They walked along an airy corridor. The young man trotted along next to him. He emanated a faint wake of flowery scent.

"His Holiness asked me to look after you. Apparently I'm supposed to . . . protect you. I don't know from what, but you'll be the one to tell me that."

"Your Excellency . . . "

"Don Giovanni."

"Don Giovanni, I need to confess."

Sebastiano Laurenti was sitting in the waiting room. He'd arrived a few minutes early. It had just been a few hours since the announcement of the jubilee, and already the big maneuvers were under way in Rome. From the haste with which the appointment had been arranged, Giovanni understood that the guy must be a person of a certain importance. In any case, he had good connections. Let's see what we have here, he told himself, while the other person, a wiry young man who gave the impression of being perfectly comfortable in his fine tailored suit, leapt to his feet and prepared to kiss the prelate's ring. Annoyed, Giovanni reached out and gripped the young man's hand, giving it a vigorous shake. Young Laurenti smiled and returned the handshake. Well, if nothing else, the young man was receptive.

The bishop threw open the doors to his office and gestured for him to enter before him.

"We'll see each other later," he said, turning to say goodbye to Don Paolo.

The young priest stood there, ashen and pale, in the center of the waiting room, swaying on his legs, a lost expression on his face.

"You understand? Wait for me here."

Don Paolo pirouetted and, without a word, hurried off. Giovanni stood, for a moment on the threshold, perplexed. The sudden turmoil in the young priest's face could only be connected to the presence of young Laurenti. Those two knew each other. And was Don Paolo . . . was Don Paolo possibly *afraid* of that guy?

He walked into the office. Laurenti had remained standing, in a respectful pose.

"Make yourself comfortable. Shall I have an espresso brought up for you, or would you rather have something stronger?"

"Thank you kindly, I'm fine."

They sat down on opposite ends of a large mahogany desk.

"You asked to see me. I'm all ears."

Sebastiano took a moment to size up that man; he saw a mild-mannered but determined expression. He wore civilian clothing, sober shades of gray, a turtleneck sweater, an athletic physique. Earlier that afternoon, he'd done some research, spoken to some reliable sources. The judgements ranged from *ethical* to *inflexible*, with hints and references to an unsettling propensity for mysticism. Another pure soul in a reform church led by the purest of all popes.

A serious pain in the ass.

Even though history abounds with mystics perfectly capable of understanding more wordly languages.

In any case, he needed to get his hooks into the bishop immediately. This mess with Mariani offered an excellent pretext.

"My company provides consulting for large-scale projects and many other endeavors. In the context of the work I do, I work with one of the oldest and most respected companies in Rome, Mariani Construction . . . Mariani renovated the apartments of the former Vatican Cardinal Secretary of State. It was responsible for the recent reinforcement and consolidation of Bernini's colonnade. It worked on the rebuilding of the Papal Offices on Piazza di Spagna . . . "

Talking about the Mariani company was like talking about Roman History. And doing so in the headquarters of those who had made Rome great, for the last couple of millennia, anyway. Sebastiano started getting worked up. The setting was getting him stoked. The bishop's icy calm, as he sat there with his eyes resting levelly on the other man, toying with a cheap rollerball pen, laid down a clear challenge. Sebastiano turned back into the boy from Prati he'd once been, educated at the finest boarding schools, and for a fleeting moment he reappropriated his old identity, long since deleted by life on the street. He forgot the blood and the violence. He rose to the heights to which he'd originally been destined and which had even once belonged to him, if for ever so brief a moment. Without fear, and with great pride.

"Yesterday, a man fell victim to a cruel beating. That man is the director of the Mariani construction site for the metro station in Piazza San Giovanni, just a short walk from here. The reason for the assault is an unpaid debt. Danilo Mariani was forced to turn to loan sharks. He was unable to repay the loan, and that man was punished in his place, but believe me, that means he was punished too . . . "

"Why are you telling me this story, Dottor Laurenti?" The priest's face had become an icy mask. But deep in his eyes, a glitter revealed his extreme attention. Sebastiano decided he liked this man. He had something of Samurai's inflexible determination. We might even become friends, thought Sebastiano. Or else, excellent enemies. Here was another of Samurai's teachings: better to fight enemies who are at your level than slimy spineless invertebrates willing to indulge in all sorts of treachery.

"Mariani, Your Excellency, like many other Roman companies, is involved in work on the metro. And the work is behind schedule because the Interministerial Committee for Economic Planning, which, as you know very well, is a government agency, refuses to release the payments that it is required by law to make. Consider me, at this moment, as an emissary from the healthiest, hardest working part of Rome. If you were to offer your elevated intervention, it might prove decisive. Not only for Danilo Mariani, but for the entire city."

"My intervention?"

Now the glitter had become a gleam of authentic amusement. Something along the lines of: I know that you know, so act accordingly. Sebastiano understood that the time had come to become a street thug again.

"You know very well, Your Excellency, that the metro project dates back to 1996. The original idea was to join two basilicas that are symbolic of Christianity itself, St. Peter's and St. John's, and to do so for the Holy Year of 2000. Today, on the eve of a new jubilee, the construction of this project is an ever greater necessity . . . for us, and for you . . . To say nothing of the fact that unlocking these funds might spare the young life of Danilo Mariani from further retaliation."

Giovanni took a lengthy pause before answering. What an immense burden he had taken onto his shoulders. He looked at Sebastiano, considering him with the utmost attention. In his turn, he had asked a few questions. Reckless, ruthless, he had said to himself. The son of an honest man who'd committed suicide over his debts. And yet, Giovanni told himself, a man who knew more than a little something about the human soul, a man not entirely damaged. At times, in the young man's words—between an allusion and a veiled threat—he thought he'd been able to detect a vein of authenticity. That young man is a typical soul caught between the Angel and Satan. And unfortunately, as is so often the case, it appeared that the Great Seducer enjoyed a considerable advantage.

"And naturally, you can't reveal to me the names of those loan sharks."

Sebastiano threw his arms wide.

"Only because I care too much about your safety, Your Excellency."

"Have you considered the possibility of filing a criminal complaint with the judicial authorities?"

"I have more faith in your discernment than I do in human justice. Saving the Mariani company would mean having a great . . . friend in the city of Rome."

The two men stood face-to-face for an instant. The bishop with a wandering smile stamped on his handsome face, Sebastiano progressively becoming less and less sure of himself.

"I thank you for this visit. Truly . . . illuminating. You'll be hearing from me."

After saying farewell, Sebastiano remained in the waiting room for a few seconds. If nothing else, that meeting had swept away any potential fog. The bishop was on the other side. A worthy enemy, but an enemy nonetheless. He couldn't count on him to get the funds released. Still, Fabio Desideri would have to be paid. He sent a text message to London.

For the text message he made use of an untraceable SIM card. Even though it was a well known fact that the cops were very actively eavesdropping and surveilling and wiretapping, you wouldn't believe the number of idiots who every blessed day tumbled into their nets due to sheer excessive talkativeness. And yet, the lesson ought to be clear to one and all: never talk about business on the phone—never, with anyone! Therefore, Sebastiano owned "official" telephones and "safe" SIM cards. He obtained them thanks to Samurai's longtime friendship with Shalva, a boss in the Georgian Mafia. Even though he was a sidelined player in the bigger games, Shalva was still a person deserving of the utmost respect.

Samurai really was taking the long view: he knew when and how to strike, and when he decided to make such a move, there was no way out for the designated victim. But he used his power only sparingly, faithful to Machiavelli's teaching: practice cruelty with overwhelming force, but in one, single, conclusive dose.

Rather than kill men, it was smarter to make them your

friends. Samurai knew how to show clemency, and this knowledge had endowed him with unquestioned prestige. Sebastiano still had a great deal to learn from him.

But you can't go on forever as a disciple: sooner or later, you must become a master yourself.

As he started down the corridor that led to the street he looked around. The young faggot priest who he'd seen trailing along after the monsignor, tail wagging, had vanished now.

D on Paolo hadn't waited for him. He'd taken to his heels, in the throes of who knows what phantoms. To each his own. Monsignor Giovanni Daré indulged in a long stroll, and enjoyed the sweet-smelling evening. There is something magical about the Roman spring, and therefore, to a believer, it is divine.

A cigarette.

With a vague sense of regret for the irrevocable decision to stop smoking, he lingered on the Ponte Sant'Angelo, captivated by the play of light of an incendiary half moon that was fragmented in the black waters of the Tiber, animating shards of glittering gleams, multiplied by the reflection of the glowing streetlamps.

Rome, the only place like it. Rome, city of the damned.

He'd been assigned the duty of piloting a gigantic vessel to safe harbor. The sea was bristling with shoals and dangers, the crew he'd been summoned to command was poisoned with all sorts of ex-cons and jailbirds. He was being asked to be rigid but flexible, well aware that excessive rigor only leads to paralysis, while excessive flexibility leads to a fracturing of the stable body. From this point of view, Rome struck him as the most acute possible metaphor for human nature. Cellini's Angel had been conceived and executed by a willful, cruel artist, and yet it was, and always would be, Cellini's Angel. The countless testimonials to human genius with which Rome abounded . . . Credit for all of it, after all, belonged to sodomitic cardinals, brilliant murderers, cruel madonnas, liveried professional killers. Without murders, there would be no art, and without art, there would be no murders. Without evil, no goodness. Without goodness, no evil. In the end, everything boils down to this. The great questions of the Fathers of the Church that inexorably arise again and again, unaltered after millennia.

Rome, the only place like it. Rome, city of the damned.

One foot in front of the other, protected by the cloud of his thoughts, Giovanni found himself inexorably filled with pride at his mission. A sin of boastfulness? So be it. The church is a demanding mother. She has equal need of philosopher children and warrior children. Here and now you're a warrior, Giovanni. Nothing and no one is going to deflect you from your mission.

At Enzo's place on Via dei Vascellari, he found his usual little table and a bowl of meatballs with tomato sauce. Giovanni poured the white Castelli wine into two glasses and waved the restaurateur over to join him.

"They stuck you with a hot potato, looks like," Enzo said.

"What do you know about it?"

"It's on all the television networks, Giova'."

"Is anyone ever going to be able to keep a secret, in this city?"

"It strikes me we're not going to be seeing much of you in the months to come."

"May the Lord's will be done."

"With the Lord, I can even reason, it's your little friends that I'm worried about. And you ought to be just as worried as I am."

You can say that again, he was tempted to answer him. But he refrained. Enzo's anticlericalism was the stuff of legend. That was why, in this little family-run restaurant, Giovanni felt completely at home. He used to come dine at Enzo's as a young man. With Adriano and with Rossana. Sometimes all three of them, other times with one or the other. For so many years, now, though, he'd been coming here all by himself. He started mulling over old memories. Rossana and Adriano. Another lifetime. Another world. Endless evenings spent talking and discussing and arguing with only one objective: how to save the world from itself. They took it for granted that salvation was a commonly shared aspiration. That had been their underlying error.

"Hey, it seems to me that this evening they gave you all a night out at the monastery."

Giovanni looked up when he heard this wisecrack of Enzo's, and found Don Paolo standing in front of him. He looked chilled. A whiff of sweat had eradicated the faint flowery perfume.

"Sit down. You disappeared."

The young priest took a seat. In his hands he was holding a stiff case, covered with red fabric.

"Did you follow me?"

An affirmative nod of the head.

"Why?"

"That man . . . Sebastiano Laurenti . . . are you friends? I have to know."

"Will you eat something?"

"I'm not hungry. That man . . . "

"I'm done, too. Let's go."

He paid, leaving a generous tip.

They walked out into the night that was overrun by tourists. A small crowd of drunken girls cut in front of them. A little brunette said something in an incomprehensible language, pointing at the young priest. The girls laughed. Don Paolo, clearly startled, crossed himself. Don't overdo it, thought Giovanni to himself, His Holiness is giving serious thought to the celibacy of priests. Then he recalled the rumors he'd heard and a smile escaped him. He regretted it instantly. But after all, it's only human nature. We're just built wrong. He made a mental note to recite a rosary of repentance. Then he grabbed the young priest by the arm and dragged him down a secluded alley.

"I'm no friend of Laurenti. That was the first time I'd ever seen him. Will you please just calm down? Do you know each other?"

"Your Eminence . . . Don Giovanni . . . I . . . he is . . . he's part of that crowd . . . "

"What crowd?"

"Bad people. I've sinned, Father. I've had relations . . . "

"Listen to me, my son. If you're going to tell me about Monsignor Tempesta, save your breath. His Holiness has been very clear on this point: Who am I to judge . . . therefore, *ego te absolvo*, and let's talk about more serious matters."

"I've done awful things. Things I'm so ashamed of. I . . . "

"That's enough!" Giovanni snapped.

But then he repented of this abrupt outburst, too. Don Paolo was a broken twig. In his eyes he glimpsed the same anguish that he'd first guessed at when he was a little boy and his beloved little Sponky, an irresistible mutt, wound up under the wheels of a moped. The dog was dying, and it didn't understand why. It looked up at the helpless little boy and asked for help that couldn't be given. Why? Why?

Impulsively, Giovanni embraced the young priest. He ran a hand through his hair. Don Paolo sank into his arm; little by little the shaking subsided.

"Are you feeling better, now? You're absolved. The rest is between you and your conscience. Understood?"

The young priest nodded. And he put the red cloth case in Giovanni's hands.

"In here. It's all here. These are papers I took from Tempesta. You need to read them. Swear to me that you will.

You need to read them before you make any decisions about the jubilee."

"Took? What do you mean 'took'?"

Don Paolo turned away and lowered his eyes. Took. Pilfered. Stole, then. Ah, this is off to a good start. Giovanni opened the folder. Xeroxes of handwritten documents. Dates. Abbreviations. Numbers. Bank accounts. Deposit slips for IOR, the Institute for Religious Works, better known as the Vatican Bank. Money. The devil's excrement, nourishment for artists.

"It seems to me I'm going to have to study these," Don Giovanni commented, lightheartedly, to lift the gloom.

Don Paolo nodded.

"You'll have to give me a hand. Come to the Vicariate tomorrow morning. We can study together."

Don Paolo didn't reply. He grabbed his hand, before Giovanni could stop him, and planted an impassioned kiss on it, and then hurried off at a brisk step.

"Paolo!"

The young priest broke into a run. Giovanni shook his head. An elderly couple stood looking at him, disapprovingly. They must have witnessed the scene, and who can say what they had imagined. Giovanni walked toward them, fierce-faced.

The couple took to their heels, muttering insults.

What about the evil that we carry inside ourselves? The evil that shows us sin even where it doesn't exist? Shall we talk about that?

He returned to the Vicariate in the throes of grim reflections. His first day in charge of contracts and works for the jubilee was concluding in an extravaganza of alarm bells. Before dropping off to sleep, he read a few verses from an anthology edition of *The Geography of Lograire* and *Cables to the Ace* by the Reverend Thomas Merton. Merton had been a brilliant secular intellectual, until he converted to Catholicism after an apparition. A Jesuit, like Pope Francis, and a poet. A looming, massive figure who, from high on a hilltop, fired off powerful, sinewy, poetic homilies in the vain illusion that he might somehow save mankind from itself.

In those very same minutes, in his special regime cell as a prisoner under Article 41-bis, Samurai was studying the fourth satire from the first book of Juvenal's *Satires*. A fisherman has caught a turbot so enormous that there is no frying pan big enough to hold it. The Senate is called upon to solve the matter, and learned disquisitions ensue on whether and how to slice up the monstrous sea creature. In the end, one senator, as wise as he is a brownnoser, sets forth an opinion that ultimately prevails: let the mother of all frying pans be built, to the greater glory of the emperor. "From this day forth, o mighty Caesar, let potters, too, follow your armed legions." Samurai mentally prepared his sermon for his next meeting with his lawyer. The message would reach Sebastiano loud and clear: Caesar could not be excluded from such a generous fish. They must at all costs get a seat at the table of the jubilee.

In the darkness of Rome, Don Paolo hurled himself into the void from a parapet on the Vatican walls.

A DP CLUB IN THE CENTER OF THE CITY. NIGHT.

F rancesco De Gregori's voice carried out to the street. He was singing *La Storia siamo noi*—"We Are History." Yet another of the standards of the Italian left wing. Even though a fair number of recycled Fascists had adopted it as their own anthem.

In the narrow street crowded with tourists strolling along looking up, there was a palpable air of excitement. In an incessant toing and froing, the *friends* of the party—a neologism that had replaced the obsolete and deeply suspect *comrades*—kept emerging from and walking back into the small door at number 15 on the street, clutching in their hands slender, delicate flutes of Prosecco. A party. Yes, a party to ward off the danger of a funeral. The funeral of the old chapter office of the Italian Communist Party, now a *club*, to use the neologism. A losing proposition, no matter how you looked at it.

Either they came up with a hundred thirty thousand euros to get out from under the debt of who knows how many months of back rent. Or else the chapter, club, call it whatever you want, would shut its doors and goodnight, nurse. Game over. Let History look on. And that History, as the great Poet sang, would be us.

Climbing out of the bowels of the city center, Adriano Polimeni, former party senator, stopped in at the venerable old fry shop. At his age, fried foods were more or less virulent poison. Still, there are some poisons that cannot be resisted. And fried cod filets fit that bill. He took a seat on one of the rickety folding chairs in the street outside the shop, spread his legs wide, and bit into the crunchy, oily wondrous morsel, assuming the classic turkey position as he did so. His right arm raised to the level of his mouth with the food, his torso angled forward, his left hand carefully tugging shut his tweed jacket, to protect the cashmere sweater beneath. The oil started dripping on the ground with each bite. And Polimeni, chewing slowly, sat there eyeing the party activists as they buzzed with conversation in the street.

When had he first taken his membership card? It had been 1973. It was a membership in the Communist Youth Federation, affectionately known as the See-Why-Eff. It hadn't been easy to carry that card. In those days, only donkeys joined the young Communists. It was undoubtedly cooler to consort with the extremists. With them, there was never any shortage of adrenaline, hormones, sheer fun: a rare quality among the self-serious aspiring Communist *leadership*. Then came a succession of new names, the PCI, or Italian Communist party, the DPS, or Democratic Party of the Left, the DS, or Democrats of the Left, and the DP, or Democratic Party. The party had changed its name, shed its skin, and altered its identity. Everything had been tossed overboard. Literally everything. There was no political plastic surgery it hadn't been subjected to. But for some strange reason his time had never come.

He'd been with Berlinguer, and people had called him a *Soviet*. He'd supported the *about-face* with which, after the fall of the Berlin Wall, the adjective *Communist* had been eliminated from the party's logo. Which mean he had become a *Socialist*. He'd found himself caught up, in spite of himself, in the never-ending feud among the old-school *thoroughbreds* of the new *formation*. The *Thing*, that's what they'd called it. *La Cosa*. And maybe, in hindsight, that hadn't been so far from the truth after all. He'd made his way among alpha males, why deny it: what he was interested in, much more than the *Cosa*, had been the *cause*. He wanted to change Italy, not grab power and a position for himself. They'd appointed him party officer in charge of justice policies. One of those positions that everyone else tried to avoid. Officially, the party stood with the judges, the rule of law, and so on and so forth. And there actually were a few good judges, truth be told. But the DNA, the political DNA, that was quite another matter. If the party's leaders had had any say in the matter, they would have sent the judges, whatever political hue their robes might be, straight to Siberia. His advent in the Italian Parliament had begun as an exciting adventure but then, with the passing of time, it had turned into an extended session of torture.

Endless years: the present kept changing, and he, Adriano, continued to confront it with the categories of the past. Years of bitter reawakenings, experienced as the struggle to defend the idea, less and less widely accepted and shared, that the left was somehow *different*. Against everything and against everyone: against so-called progress, against the crisis of the parties, against his own comrades. A total failure. Bah. In any case, at age 58, he was a relative infant of a retiree. If someone had asked him to write an epitaph for his headstone, he'd have just used the title of that wonderful film by Nikita Sergeyevich Mikhalkov, *A Friend Among Foes, a Foe Among Friends*.

He crumpled up the greasy paper from the fried codfish filet, got to his feet, and decided to walk through the front door of the club. If for no other reason than that the Roman party was by now the only Indian reservation where he was still allowed to roam and graze. They had assigned him to do a boring, exhausting, and interminable survey about the state of membership recruitment and the relationship of the party with the region's populace. But they hadn't been at all pleased with his findings.

From the Nazareno, the headquarters that had replaced the venerable old building in Vie delle Botteghe Oscure—every time that he walked past the place his heart lurched a little—they'd sent the message that the idea of accepting the existence of a "healthy DP" and a "sick DP," and having identified and named the lords of the membership cards, "reeked of the twentieth century." It was clearly just further evidence of his resentments and his quest for personal visibility. Yes, that's exactly what they had said. Personal visibility. We are History? Just give me a break!

A black Mercedes pulled up in front of the club. A young woman got out. Adriano Polimeni recognized her. His first impulse was to turn and run. Chiara.

Chiara Visone.

She was beautiful, as always. The way he remembered her. No doubt about it. A statuesque body. Her features fine and regular, her lips sensual, fleshy, but not puffy. Green eyes that could drive a man crazy, lit up with a magnetic energy.

Chiara, who had given him the gift of an illusory second youth. Then she had mortally wounded him. But he couldn't go on running from her. It was all over by now.

Chiara seemed not to have noticed him there, but Adriano knew perfectly well that wasn't the case. He'd even picked up a furtive glance, and had noticed how she'd started ever so slightly. Proof of the existence of a flickering pilot light of warmth still burning in that magnificent carbon-based living organism, though it seemed to him that she was actually running on cold fusion. Or perhaps it was just her fear that Adriano, with one of his usual outbursts, might ruin the evening for her. But she had no reason to worry. The senator was in no mood for fighting.

A dozen or so activists gathered around her with a groupie-like intensity.

"What do you say, Chiara, shall we save the club?"

"Shall we refound this party?"

Chiara broke into a welcoming smile.

"Haven't you read my tweets?"

A guy with a foolish gaze held up his arm, displaying the screen of his smartphone:

@visone #activistsdon'tworry

@visone #historystartstoday

@visone #theclubismyhome

@visone #freeofdebt

@visone #ademocraticdrive

A hysterical wave of applause burst out that ensured that Sebastiano Laurenti's arrival went unnoticed. He'd just stepped out of the Audi that he'd told his driver to park, prudently, in front of the church of San Carlo ai Catinari. He'd wrapped up his light, short, narrow-waisted Prada overcoat and had continued on foot. Until he spotted her outside the club, surrounded by that knot of adoring fans.

Chiara Visone.

Enough to drive anyone crazy. And in fact, since he'd first seen her while channel surfing, he had gone a little crazy over her.

He'd wracked his brains for weeks trying to figure out a credible scenario whereby he could engineer a "chance" encounter and get into her life. Until one day a news brief had enlightened him.

Friday, March 13th, at 8 P.M., a special membership drive at the DP "La Bandiera" club to rescue the historic chapter from its burden of debt, 130,000 euros, a shortfall that threatens its future survival. The Honorable Chiara Visone will attend.

And people say that there's nothing to be gained from buying the daily newspaper, he had smiled to himself, tossing the copy of the paper in the air as if it were so much confetti.

Friday the 13th, he'd made a note on his smartphone.

Friday the 13th . . . That day and date, *porta zella*, to use the Roman phrase for bringing bad luck, only in English-speaking nations. And so, there he was. For the first time in his life, in a party headquarters. Certainly—as Samurai had taught him— you have politicians come pay calls on you, you don't go to visit them. Still, he said to himself, you could certainly make an exception for a diva. Even Samurai would have approved.

As he entered the club, Sebastiano saw Malgradi. He was standing there as a stiff as a man with a sandwich board next to a table with a jar for contributions from party activists. Just pathetic, the kind of thing you'd expect to see at the old Communist Festa dell'Unità. Behind him, a giant poster in various languages: Italian, English, French, German, Spanish, Romanian, Arabic, Chinese. The poster for La Casa di Vicky, the clinic of repentance. What voracious greed. The funding he got from the city wasn't enough for him. He even had the gall to ask for donations. As relentless as a garden slug. Still, useful. Extremely useful. And not as freaking horny as his brother, most important of all. Sufficient wisdom to have chosen Power instead of Pussy.

He saw that Malgradi was deep in conference with Visone and decided not to go over. Not right away, at least, limiting himself to a meaningful nod in the face of the surprised glance from the slobbery bastard, who'd noticed Sebastiano as he went on speaking in a low voice to the Honorable Visone.

"Well, Chiara, I just wanted to let you know that the issue of that back rent isn't a simple one. There's the problem of the hundred thirty thousand euros of unpaid rent and if we continue to count on the twenty-euros-a-head memberships of these paupers who belong to the club, we'll have time to change the party's name three more times."

"At the Nazareno they don't want to hear a word about it. They say that the club has to find its own solution. I'd even thought of trying to get a sponsor."

"A sponsor?

"Yes. Like I don't know, the oil company ENI, or the power authority, ENEL . . . "

"I've never heard of a state-run company sponsoring a political party."

"You must have missed Finmeccanica, Temistocle."

Malgradi lit up like a Christmas tree. All the things that Visone knew. Could it be that she too was chowing down at that immense state-sponsored feed trough?

"At Finmeccanica times have changed. And the personnel, too, I'd say," he ventured.

"So what if it was a compassionate private citizen who solved the problem?"

Sebastiano's voice made Visone whip around. Who the hell was this guy who'd been eavesdropping on them?

Malgradi muttered.

"Chiara, let me introduce a friend . . . "

"There's no need, Temistocle. I can introduce myself. I'm a grown-up."

Sebastiano put on the mask of the Irresistible Rogue. The swashbuckling smile of the fearless musketeer. The most successful routine in his repertoire. That was the moment he loved best in any courtship. His first daring lunge. Almost always decisive. One way or the other. Even better than the first night. Than the first kiss. Because that was the moment when the adrenaline surged up to your cerebral cortex, your stomach filled up with butterflies, and you could listen to yourself as you spoke. As if you were some other person.

"My name is Sebastiano Laurenti. I'm a financial consultant. I've never voted in my life, but I do know one rule. Trust your intuition."

Visone found the presentation sufficiently obvious to reveal itself for what it actually was. Arrogant and devoid of substance.

"People with intuition never listen in on other people's conversations. Ever," she said.

"I've read the newspapers, though."

Well, well, thought Chiara. If that guy was capable of taking a flat no on the fly without blinking, then maybe the matter needed to be delved into a little more deeply.

"And exactly what have you read in the newspapers, Signor Lauretti?"

What a fantastic bitch. She'd intentionally pronounced his last name wrong.

"That you need a million and three hundred thousand euros."

"Well you weren't reading very carefully. It's a hundred and thirty thousand euros."

"Well, you weren't listening very carefully. It's Laurenti, not Lauretti."

Yes, indeed, there was nothing wrong with this guy. And he was mighty easy on the eyes, when it came to that. She doled out a smile.

"Well, then, now that we've corrected each other, what does your intuition tell you?"

"It tells me this."

Sebastiano reached into the inside breast pocket of his overcoat and pulled out a cashier's check. One hundred thirty thousand euros.

Chiara smiled and shook her head.

"What is this, some kind of joke?"

"It's a donation. If you'll accept it, in the next few days we can settle the various tax issues. The companies that I represent are happy to contribute to the proper functioning of a healthy democracy."

Visone took the check, visibly flustered. She asked Malgradi to put it into an envelope, and then she turned to leave.

"If you'll be so kind as to excuse me, I need to get inside. I'm scheduled to speak and it's getting late."

"I'll stay to listen, if you don't mind.

Malgradi stood stiff and awkward as a smoked cod, and as soon as Visone had reached the speakers' table, he grabbled Sebastiano by the arm.

"Have you gone stupid? Here we're going to drag things out and then we're just going to dump this club . . . What the fuck do we need the historical location for? Do you really want to pay politicians' debts for them?"

Sebastiano went on looking at Visone.

"Oh, all right, now I get it . . . This is about the pussy . . . Expensive, though, don't you think . . . Anyway, look out. That one will eat you whole, entrails and all."

Visone took the floor, struggling a little to smother the applause. Sitting on either side of her were the chairman of the club, Marcello Lagramigna, the lord of (fake) membership cards for the Roman DP, and Malgradi.

She cleared her throat with a fetching little cough.

"My dear friends, thank you so much for being here tonight. So many of you, and you bring such passion. You deserve the best. You deserve the good news I bring with me this evening."

A satisfied buzz ran through the crowd. At the far end of the room, Adriano Polimeni was slowly massaging his eyelids, just shutting out the world for a moment. The show was beginning. He couldn't miss it for anything in the world. He had to drain the chalice down to the last bitter dregs. All of it. Down to the last drop.

"I'd like to begin with the remarkable results of our membership drive, which you know all about, and which I don't want to bore you with. Except to say, before revealing to you the big surprise that brings me here tonight, that we owe a debt of gratitude. So, *Gra-zie! Gra-zie! Grazie* to you and *grazie* to our friend Marcello."

Marcello Lagramigna. The name was circled in red in his report on the party. The top cacique of the mob of caciques—to use the term for a South American party boss—that the Roman party had devolved into. A guy in his early forties whose office had been blown up in Tor Bella Monaca shortly after opening for business. "Unknown parties" had been responsible for the bombing, which had come hard on the heels of the latest round of hirings in the companies now in municipal receivership. That office had been an old betting parlor controlled by a local ring of Calabrians; he'd repurposed it as "a meeting place with the citizens," and his name loomed large on the sign out front where you had to use a magnifying glass to find the DP symbol. Polimeni's mouth twisted into a grimace of disgust.

"*Grazie*, Marcello! *Grazie*, Marcello!"

The old fraud shot to his feet like Rocky Balboa. The only thing left to do now would be to grab his left wrist with his right fist high over his head. But for that matter, he didn't even need to, he could rely on the applause of the claque of cleaned-up immigrants with whom he'd stocked the front row and who were now clapping themselves silly. As fake as the audience with its canned laughter on TV talk shows. Miserable bums that "Grazie, Marcello" had enrolled by the hundreds into the party, paying fifty euros a membership.

Visone gave Lagramigna a hug and pointed him to his chair, believing that the minute of celebrity conceded to him had been sufficient.

"It hasn't been easy to bring the party to this point. We've had to battle against those who were unwilling to take a step backward. With many friends that we thank, of course, for what they did in the last century. But who have been unable or unwilling to recognize that this is our time. And that in a time of a liquid society, a party is and cannot help but be gaseous, free-form. A swarm of bees that gathers and scatters, as unpredictable as the wind."

"Gaseous." "Swarm of bees." Jesus Christ. Maybe it really was starting to become a bit much, thought Polimeni. Just then he felt a hand touch his arm. An elderly party activist in a wheelchair waved for him to lean in.

"She's got it in for you, you get that, right?"

Polimeni smiled. If you only knew, old comrade . . .

Visone was flying high.

"There are even those who've gone so far as to claim that in Rome there were, or even worse, there still are a *Good Party* and a *Bad Party*. A party open to the city and to the needs of the citizens, and then—I quote verbatim—a 'self-referential' party, 'which wheels and deals in membership cards and official salaries.' 'Inclined to participate in the cynical, cooperative management of that which exists.' 'A campaign committee, much more than a party.' Well, let me ask you, friends: How can you measure the activism and the state of health of a party? By new memberships, by members who think for themselves and only for themselves, or by the second, or third, term in a Parliament filled with aging professional politicians appointed by party secreteriats? And what does this term—'cooperative management'—even mean? 'Diversity' can't be a definitive condemnation to marginality. Winning means bring those who think differently from us over to our side. We aren't better than our adversaries. We simply have better ideas than they do."

The applause brought the house down. That didn't keep Polimeni from standing side by side with his little old man.

"That's right, Comrade Polimeni, she has it in for you. She's really pissed off. It seems to me that you'd better get out of here, before she overdoes things."

She'd already overdone things. Polimeni nodded. He started making his way toward the door, when he was stopped in his tracks by the big reveal.

"And anyway, friends, I'm not here to reopen old wounds. I'm here for a celebration. Our celebration. This evening we are struggling to collect funds to prevent the closure of this, the oldest of all our homes. *This home.* One hundred thirty thousand euros is a lot of money even for a community of women and men as generous as you are. But . . . "

Consummate actress that she was, she let her audience simmer for a few seconds.

" . . . but a man, a fellow citizen, has decided to push aside, all by himself, this mountain of debt that's crushing us. Allow me to introduce to you Dottor Sebastiano Laurenti. And let me show you the measure of his courage."

Like in some grand prize game, Visone opened the white envelope and extracted the check. While Laurenti got to his feet in the midst of a now silent crowd.

"We can only offer the generous Dottor Laurenti membership card number 1 of our new membership drive. The drive that I'm announcing here tonight and which inaugurates the new season of a party that is going to change in its approach to Rome and, therefore, to the country at large."

Yes, that was too much. The old man was right.

Polimeni left the club while the burst of applause and low roar of pounding feet that you'd expect at a soccer stadium brought the house down. As he walked out, he was bumped aside by a heavyset guy who was surprisingly and improbably well dressed. A camel-hair coat and a Borsalino fedora that crushed down his already short stature so that he looked like a dwarf.

Polimeni was so pissed off that he didn't even have the presence of mind to smile at that grotesque apparition. Neither did he notice, therefore, that the self-propelled refrigerator in camel hair was making straight for "Dottor Sebastiano Laurenti," the club's new guardian angel.

Sebastiano immediately recognized Silvio Anacleti and dragged him out into the street.

"I told you out in front of the club. Not inside."

"What's the difference?"

"The difference is that you wind up in a picture taken by some asshole and, a few months later, in the pages of some newsweekly, so that later a member of parliament or a deputy mayor will have to explain why they were there, sharing oxygen with a guy like you, who has a criminal record longer than his arm."

"Don't make such a big deal out of it. Who even reads newspapers anymore?"

"Listen, I don't have time to waste. I have a problem with Fabio Desideri."

"Fabio . . . Fabietto?""

"The very same."

"No kidding. What happened? That boy's good as gold."

"Nothing so far. But I've got a sneaking suspicion something's about to."

"Ah. So what can I do about it?"

"Take a look around. Very discreetly. Don't kick up any dust. I just want to know what he's got in mind."

"But what's the problem?"

"That's none of your fucking business."

"Okay, all right, Sebastia'. I'll look into it and get back to you."

"Good. And I'll buy you a new overcoat."

"Why, something about this one you don't like?"

"It makes you look too tall."

Sebastiano tried to make his way back into the main room of the club, but after a few steps he found himself face-to-face with Chiara. Who smiled at him.

"You certainly hang out with some interesting people . . . "

"I read somewhere that the DP is home to everyone. Or not? Shall we talk it over at our leisure? Maybe over dinner."

PRIORY OF THE KNIGHTS OF MALTA. NIGHT.

In the pitch darkness, the Giardino degli Aranci, or Orange Garden, was an extravaganza of perfumes. Chiara Visone burst out laughing. Sebastiano gestured for her to follow him.

"Are you sure, Sebastiano? If they find us in here at two in the morning, what are we going to say?"

"It's a public facility. And after all, you're a member of the Italian Parliament . . . "

Chiara laughed again.

"What a dope you are."

"Then we'll explain that we're here because, unbelievably, you don't know the worst kept secret in all of Rome."

"What secret are you talking about?"

Sebastiano took her by the hand and dragged her to the gate of the Priory of the Knights of Malta. Where he invited her to bend over and press her eye against the keyhole.

Chiara hesitated for a moment. Then she did as Sebastiano had asked her. In front of her, at the end of a visual corridor that stretched for miles, and which the wizardry of an eccentric genius had reduced to a few inches, loomed the dome of St. Peter's. A rarefied mirage of shapes and light hovering over the city. She felt Sebastiano's hands brush her hips.

"It's the only piece of architecture ever built by Piranesi. By eliminating space and distance, it creates a mystical conjunction between the state and faith. I couldn't come up with a better metaphor for Rome."

She turned around and searched for his mouth. Here she was, deeply moved, electrified in the presence of the miracle. Like millions of tourists before her, thought Sebastiano. With a blend of pride for his conquest and disappointment at the ease with which he had attained it.

They wound up back at his house. His father's house. The house he'd taken back as his own, making the loan sharks who had first taken it away from him crawl through puddles of their own blood. The Three Little Pigs, people used to call them.

"This is a wonderful place," Chiara whispered as she let her silk blouse slip off of her shoulders.

Sebastiano nodded.

And he took her.

Later on, while he was sleeping, stretched sideways atop the black sheets, both fists clenched and a furrowed brow creasing his handsome face, Chiara quietly got dressed. She wanted to avoid waking up together. She'd leave him a funny note, or maybe a sweet one, or maybe one that was both. Going to bed with Sebastiano had been nice. Was she getting herself into a relationship? Or was this just sex? Sebastiano had come looking for her, no doubt about it, and he'd come looking for her quite forcefully. This, too, was unmistakable. The check had been nothing more than a pretext. A man who knew what he wanted, and capable of identifying the winning strategy. A man who kept questionable company, at the very least: the oil drum in an overcoat he'd stopped to talk to at the door of the club reeked of organized crime a mile away. Were they in business together? And what sort of business? Sebastiano claimed to represent a group of companies. Which companies? She'd look into it. No question, Sebastiano was a well turned out individual, an elegant conversationalist with a rich array of ironic observations and witty ripostes. With an undertone of melancholy sweetness. A young member of the bourgeoisie with a good education and hints of mystery. Intriguing. And yet, at the same time, foolishly predictable. Ever since she'd first arrived in Rome, with a brand-new degree in Economics, not a single man had asked her out without inevitably pulling out the old song and dance of the Knights of Malta. A well established routine that she'd never once avoided or forestalled. She found it amusing to play her part, pretending to be moved, stirred, excited, in other words, the full panoply of the fresh-faced sentimental provincial girl, unconsciously seductive. Men, in their bottomless vanity, found that endlessly reassuring. Only once had she showed her cards. It happened when she'd read in the eyes of the man who had squired her there yet again a clear awareness of her bluff. She'd fessed up, and by confessing her deception had transformed a predictable defeat into a convenient stalemate.

Chiara Visone had a stab of pain.

Adriano Polimeni had never been just "a guy who squired her around." Adriano was Adriano. And for her, in spite of everything, still a problem. While she waited for her cab outside, she realized that she hadn't left a message of any description for Sebastiano: neither sweet nor funny.

# III.

## Monday, March 16th, 2015
### Saint's Day: St. Heribert, Archbishop of Cologne

A prison in the north, Maximum Security Wing.
Eight thirty in the morning.

Samurai raised himself up on his forearms. He caught his breath, resting there for a long while in a half bent-over position. Then he lay down on his cot. Another brief pause, and then he assumed the lotus position. Seventy-five push-ups. All things considered, an acceptable result, considering the fact that he was sixty. The cabinet ministers that keep pushing retirement age later and later are right, actually: we're living longer.

He took off the pants of his tracksuit and, now naked, washed himself acrobatically under the weak, ice-cold stream of a doll's house faucet.

Draped in a rough sheet provided by the prison administration, he remembered with longing the sensation of cool power that came with his silk kimonos. That really was the only creature comfort that he missed. Along with his tea, of course. The tea you got in here was a filthy slop.

But the exile wasn't destined to last much longer. Certainly, much less than the fifteen years and six months to which he'd been sentenced in his first trial and on appeal. And which the Supreme Court would soon reduce, if not throw out completely. A wistful hope? Not at all. Just simple common sense. Samurai knew too much, had too many friends, if that term could be used for his business clientele who continued to send him stalwart attestations of solidarity.

So many, too many, were dancing on the brink of the abyss. All of them bound to him by a cord that he couldn't allow to snap. Samurai couldn't afford to fall because if he did, he'd trigger an earthquake.

They'd have to kill him before they were rid of him. There were those who had tried, and they'd lived to regret it, bitterly. Now, as far as he could see, the horde of would-be suicides had died out.

But now they were trying to bend him.

He took in at a distracted glance the landscape that for the past three years and four months had punctuated his days. A cell ten feet by thirteen, a cot, a high window, well out of reach, plastic furniture with rounded edges, no flammable objects, all furnishings made of fire-resistant materials. A small table anchored to the floor to prevent it being used as an offensive weapon. A small sink and a toilet. Individual showers, once a week. Random visual spot checks. Sudden, thorough searches at any time of the day or night. One visit a month with his family members, in rooms specially designed and "equipped to prevent the handoff of objects." Audio recording, video recording, censorship stamps on the correspondence. Social interactions reduced to a bare minimum in a narrow courtyard, under the watchful eyes of armed correctional officers. Formal, rigid, chilly prison staff. A long, continuous silence.

Article 41-bis of the Correctional System. In emergency situations, the prisons are allowed to suspend all rules. The prisons that had been humanized by so many lovely reforms accompanied by so many lovely intentions draped in so many lovely speeches still take one giant step backward when confronted with murderers, terrorists, and Mafiosi. Restrictions that verged on sheer inhumanity. The theory behind this provision, to use the terminology of a nitpicking legal pettifogger: to prevent contacts amongst co-conspirators, bring to bear the full burden of the sentence. Underlying philosophy: undermine free will, encourage defections, induce hard-liners to turn state's witness.

With lots of miserable wretches, it had worked fine. But not with him. Samurai wasn't going to fold. Samurai was going to come back. It was only a matter of time. He'd lost a battle, but he sat firm in his saddle.

He was still the master of Rome, and he always would be.

From outside, the peephole was opened. Two frightened eyes appeared. A hesitant voice announced a visit from the lawyer. Thanks to the pressure brought to bear by the defense counsel lobby, the rigors of Article 41-bis, at least on this point, had been relaxed somewhat. You could only see your wife and children once a month, but your lawyer as often as three times a week.

"I'll be ready in a second," Samurai sang out, with a half smile.

The lawyer was waiting for him in the visiting room. When he saw him he leapt to his feet.

"At ease, counselor, at ease."

Manlio Setola was a tanned gentleman in his early fifties with a flowing mane of hair, a salt-and-pepper beard, and a relaxed, suavely sociable manner. He was a former prosecutor. For years he had run roughshod over evildoers, taking on all the most spectacular investigations as his own personal crusades. He was an expert at finding the legal solutions that made everyone happy. Especially the man in the street. And in one case in particular, in the distant past, he had even made a young Samurai happy, and as a result the older Samurai hadn't forgotten him. Setola had resigned from the magistracy just moments before being actually ejected, possibly with a sharp, swift disciplinary kick in the ass, and had transitioned into the ranks of criminal defense lawyers. Samurai had divested himself of his old legal counselors, who were far too punctilious about professional standards of legal practice, and had hired him full-time. Samurai was, practically speaking, his only client. In terms of technical proficiency, he was no fool. But

what counted most was that he couldn't really afford to dis-
obey any of Samurai's orders.

"You're in good shape, I see."

"I'm up to seventy-five push-ups. But I'm starting to notice
a certain weariness, especially with the food. The cooking here
is hard to digest."

"The Supreme Court hearing has been moved up. It's a
matter of days now. We have high hopes."

"Hope isn't enough."

"For the attempted murder charges, the situation is compromised. The evidence is too strong."

"Four years of concurrent sentences for the international
narcotics trafficking and Mafia co-conspiracy . . . four years
you've already served . . . I could demand damages for wrong-
ful detention. What about the rest?"

"So about the rest . . . "

"About the rest?"

Setola sighed.

"There's that question about the surveillance, the wiretaps
. . . they're obviously unusable. That ought to be clear to everyone."

"*Ought to be* is a conditional form. I much prefer the present tense and the indicative mood."

Setola gulped.

"It's clear."

"Now that's better. Any other news?"

"Have you heard about the jubilee?"

A broad smile appeared on Samurai's face.

"The time has come for us to do good deeds, counselor. Let
you-know-who have a full report."

ROME, TESTACCIO QUARTER. PIAZZA DELL'EMPORIO.
KREMLIN. MORNING.

For some time now, Senator, or shall we say instead, former Senator, Adriano Polimeni had gone to live in the large ocher-yellow apartment building on Piazza dell'Emporio that was jocularly known as the Kremlin because it had historically been the chosen residence of big cheeses and high muck-a-mucks of the old Italian Communist Party. Now the party had changed its name and also its spots, but many militants, whether active or in hibernation, so to speak, continued to live there. The Kremlin overlooked the Ponte Sublicio, which, in ancient times, as the Pons Sublicius, had constituted the most heavily armed access route to regal Rome. Legend has it that a heroic Roman, Publius Horatius Cocles, held back, single-handed, the entire Etruscan army, stymieing its attempts to cross the bridge until his fellow Romans could organize a counterattack. As Monsignor Giovanni Daré climbed up four flights of an airy, luminous staircase, he couldn't restrain a smile. A picture had flitted through his mind of Adriano Polimeni in the garb of an ancient Roman, an image that was by equal parts grotesque and heroic, perhaps ever so slightly pathetic. He was waving his sword over his head and bellowing revolutionary slogans at his enemies . . . well, now, let's not overdo it . . . Adriano had never been an extremist . . . let's just say he was spouting some leftist phrase or other . . . as hordes of artfully attired and coiffed young men and young ladies in stiletto heels tried to break through the lines . . . He halted for a moment on the landing to catch his breath. Concerning the finale of the story of Publius Horatius Cocles he remembered two versions. Having beaten back the enemy attack, the hero leaps into the Tiber. First version, more realistic: his armor drags him to the river bottom, drowning him. Second version, more benevolent and mystical: having shed the heavy armor by lithe and vigorous maneuvering, Horatius made his way to the opposite shore, ready to resume the fight. Monsignor Daré was still uncertain which of the two finales he wished upon his friend—a hero's death or survival, with the inevitable burden of further disappointments—when, even before he had a chance to ring the doorbell, the door swung open and Adriano Polimeni, attired in his inevitable light cashmere sweater, seized him in a vigorous and fraternal embrace.

As Polimeni offered him espresso, pastries, and mini-pizzas with red sauce—the ones from Linari in Testaccio, just like in the old days—his gaze wandered over the furnishings. Books, books, and more books. And a few items of special interest. A bronze bust of Karl Marx, cleft in twain by a yellow star . . .

"It's by Krzysztof Bednarski, a Polish sculptor."

"Very nice."

"Well, he had the Communists where he lived. The real ones, I mean to say."

Giovanni said nothing. He'd been captivated by a nude of a woman crouching over. An avalanche of memories swept him away. He remembered exactly when that canvas—midway between the metaphysical and pure abstraction—had been painted, who had painted it, and on what occasion it had been painted. He remembered every single point made in the debate that had followed its delivery by a mediocre artist who would never win a slot for himself in art history. But in Rossana's heart, he sure did, by God. And he and Adriano had talked themselves hoarse, insisting that that miserable scribble-and-smear completely failed to do honor to the mysterious beauty of that goddess, and so on and so forth. The scribble-and-smear was all that remained of her. The scribble-and-smear, and a stabbing pain that time can only muffle, but never erase.

"She was magnificent, wasn't she, Giovanni?"

"She was crazy, Adriano."

"And we were crazy about her."

"And she was crazy about the painter."

"I still see him around every so often."

"And?"

"And we nod, say hello."

"Even he wasn't capable of saving her from herself."

"Rossana couldn't be saved, Giovanni. She didn't belong in this world."

They sat side by side on a large corner sofa illuminated by the view of the Tiber. They remained there for a while, each of them immersed in his own memories. It was always that way when they saw each other. The lost love that had once divided them now brought them back together. But it was, in point of fact, a lost love. Giovanni thought that Adriano had gone into politics to make up for that loss. And Adriano was certain that Giovanni had turned to his religious faith for the same reason. They were both wrong, and they each knew they were both wrong. But that shared unspoken conviction was so wonderfully reassuring.

"You asked to see me," Polimeni said softly, breaking the enchantment, "and I hardly think it was just to sing me the praises of Pope Francis . . . "

"Ah, you secular humanists, all of you so captivated by Francis. There are times when I think he's more popular with you than he is with his own flock. But he's a great fisherman for souls. He's gradually bringing you all back to Mother Church . . . one at a time . . . all of you just like St. Paul, thunderstruck on the road to Damascus."

"Well, now, let's not exaggerate. Let's just say that for once you've chosen the right pope."

"Ratzinger was the true revolutionary. You never understood him. He was too subtle."

"Rome wouldn't have stood for two Germans, Giovanni."

"Are you referring to the mayor?"

"Look, I'm on his side. If he'd only learn to listen, though . . . anyway, you know my views. This collaboration between us can't exist. We're too different. We're all aiming for the absolute, and in the end . . . "

"Listen to you. You're a high muck-a-muck from a party that springs out of the union of Communists and priests. A little consistency, a sense of tradition."

"A high muck-a-muck. I'm just a retiree. They threw the report on the state of the party in Rome right in my face."

"What else did you expect?"

"They don't know how to listen. They're young, and arrogant, and . . . "

"When we were in our thirties we didn't know how to listen either, Adriano. And we hated old people."

"But we respected them."

"That was lip service we paid them."

Polimeni heaved a weary sigh. He was right. He was too damned right. He'd objected when what he should have been doing was studying and learning, and he'd bowed his head, like everyone, when he should risen up in protest. And now he was paying the consequences.

"All right, I get it. Let's get to the point now."

Giovanni handed him the sheets of paper and bit into a mini-pizza.

"Linari never disappoints . . . Take a look at these papers . . . "

Accounts. Abbreviations. A letter S circled repeatedly in red. Names of companies linked to the construction of the metro C line. Matching abbreviations that referred to the IOR. And it all flowed back to that S circled in red.

"Let me tell you a story, Adriano."

Giovanni told him about Don Paolo. About the anguish he felt at having failed to guess in what depths of despair that young soul had been plunged. The suicide had been duly hushed up, but Giovanni still carried that burden in his heart. It was also in part to honor his memory that there could be no shenanigans. And that's why he badly needed Adriano's help. He made passing reference to the visit paid him by Sebastiano Laurenti. He delved into the topic of corruption in the Vatican, the role played by Monsignor Tempesta, the mandate that he'd been given by the pope, the danger that this extraordinary jubilee might unleash the worst sorts of appetites. The ex-senator began to attribute clearer meaning to the abbreviations. He summoned that old and ruthless mental clarity that had led many to compare him to the most ruthless and bloodthirsty Stalinist inquisitors.

"This jubilee is going to be different from the others, Giovanni. Your pope wants it to be . . . scattered among all the cities . . . it might not even be such a big deal."

"How many pilgrims are going to come to Rome, in your opinion?"

"How many? . . . two, three million . . . "

"The pope agrees with you."

"There, you see?"

"But I had some serious estimates drawn up."

"And . . . "

"The very minimum number is thirty million. I think at least forty."

Polimeni nodded in surprise. Giovanni was a pragmatic man, no different than him. He wouldn't have ventured such a spectacular estimate if he wasn't absolutely certain of his numbers. He rummaged through the stack of papers again.

"Does the pope know about this?"

"I have carte blanche."

"These are stolen documents, and the thief is dead. What do you intend to do with them?"

"If I knew I wouldn't be here."

"What do you want from me?"

"You need to put the mayor on his guard."

"I can arrange a meeting for you."

"That wouldn't be appropriate. You need to take to the field in person."

Polimeni laughed bitterly. When Silvio Berlusconi has made his first triumphant entrance into politics, it has been famously described as taking to the field. How many of his youthful comrades, pardon me, *friends*, would have picked up on the subtle innuendo? Not many, he concluded, disconsolately, very few indeed. In any case, the objective was noble, and for the common good. The likelihood of success: who knows, the world had changed. The alliance that Giovanni was offering him ran the risk of coming off as bucking the trends of history. And yet . . . and yet, he was tempted. If for no other reason than a merely aesthetic consideration: Because to do otherwise would just mean giving up. Not again, not this time.

"All right. I'll do my part. But in the meantime, you could freeze these accounts."

"I already have," smiled Giovanni.

"Good work. Even if you wear a cassock, you haven't forgotten your old lessons," Adriano concluded. He was bound to have the last word, and he wouldn't give up that privilege, even under torture.

VIA LUDOVISI. OFFICES OF FUTURE CONSULTING. MORNING.

Sebastiano ended the call and slammed a fist down on the table. Can you believe that priest! To take advantage of the weekend to freeze the accounts had been a masterful move. But in the meantime, countermeasures were called for. If he wanted to operate on Italian soil, he was going to have to have traceable accounts. He'd see to that before the day was out. But then there was the problem of wherewithal. He sent a couple of text messages to London. He called Fabio Desideri and asked him to grant him some more time. He was even affectionate to him: You've got all the time in the world, I already told you so; and blah blah blah. He liked him less and less as time went by, but there was nothing he could do about it. At least for right now. During his lunch break, he paid a call on Primo Zero, the director of an outlying branch office of the Craftsmen's and Artisanal Manufacturers' Savings Bank, and gave him some good news.

"Starting next week I need three separate accounts to work on. Make sure you get it done fast."

"One week? Sebastia', I have the Bank of Italy oversight people breathing down my neck cause of a little thing I'm not going to bore you with."

"The remittances are perfectly documented. You have nothing to fear."

"But it'll still take a week . . . "

Sebastiano decided to put an end to his objections, and was forced to remind him of certain outstanding debts he still had with Samurai, and the corollary necessity of not making their mutual friend lose his temper. The director immediately fell into line. From the Audi that was taking him back to the office Sebastiano put in a call to Chiara Visone. She answered in a hushed voice; she was at a meeting of the commission. This was a crucial session. The matters under discussion were the new regulations governing wiretapping and telephone surveillance. There had emerged, even within the ranks of her own party, unexpected pockets of resistance. Obstacles that stood in the way of approval of a measure that a long-needed restoration of juridical civility made absolutely obligatory.

He was tempted to tell her that soon they'd see each other again, and where, and in what setting. But he decided that playing on the factor of surprise would redound to his advantage, and so he limited himself to a comradely "break a leg."

CAPITOLINE HILL. OFFICE OF MAYOR MARTIN GIARDINO. AFTERNOON.

The mayor's private study overlooked the Imperial Forums. "The finest balcony on earth!" he was invariably told by everyone who set foot here for the first time. And often when they came back a second time. Martin Giardino was especially proud of the changes he had made in the furnishings, transforming that grim and dusty institutional setting into a bright and airy drawing room.

"The home of all the Romans! This desk, which was buried under tons and tons of old files, I had it restored, at my own expense. I couldn't resist the temptation when I heard that it was once the desk of Ernesto Nathan, the great mayor of the early twentieth century, the follower of Mazzini . . . symbolic in a sense, isn't it? You Romans are so in love with symbols, and you know something? You have every right, Adriano. Every right . . . oh, and the chairs too, the sofa, these paintings . . . every cent paid out of my own pockets . . . Oh, excuse me, an urgent call."

Martin Giardino launched himself onto his iPhone. Polimeni heard him turn down a couple of different invitations with fervent conviction. Even in the middle of an intense workday, Martin Giardino found a way to show off what impeccable physical shape he was in, along with his unbreakable optimism. Polimeni found himself sinking into a bit of a bad mood. There was something about the healthy appearance of Rome's first citizen, and the fact that he instead had started his day with pastries and mini-pizzas, following it up with a generous bowlful of a homemade version of pasta alla gricia. Martin Giardino only made things worse with an ironic comment about Adriano's waistline.

"The bicycle, Adriano, the bicycle. Twelve miles a day and you'll feel like you've been reborn . . . or even six, if your . . . what is it you say in Rome? If your pump won't hold up . . . "

"You're making progress, Martin, very good. Anyway, I prefer pistons. Two pistons, or four, depending on the day."

"Because you're an incurable nostalgic for the old left wing. I find all this cultural resistance . . . inexplicable, yes, just inexplicable."

"Martin, please, the environmentalist sermon, no, have pity. I love motorcycles, and I consider your policies concerning the closure of the Imperial Forums right up there with Nero burning the city. Since you've become mayor, if you want to get from Piazza San Giovanni to Largo Argentina you need to take a day off work."

Martin Giardino broke out into sincere laughter. No doubt about it, this man had his charm. All the same, Polimeni couldn't spare him a mild dart.

"You, laughing? You really are making progress."

The mayor shook his head.

"Do you think I don't know that they call me the German . . . do you think I don't know that they do everything they can to remind that I'm not a seventh-generation Roman, that I'm an alien in our lovely city . . . a foreign body . . . all they ever do is tell me so, over and over, right here in the party, too . . . do you think that I don't know that you were the candidate, and that in the primaries . . . "

Polimeni put both hands together, as if in prayer. Ah, Martin, Martin. All the nonsense you swallow as if it were the truth. This rumor about his own failure to run for mayor was one of the most venomous fables that the up-and-coming young turks of the party had circulated as a way of discrediting

Polimeni. A genuine, colossal piece of horseshit. The problem was that Martin Giardino, suspicious and apprehensive as an ape, had swallowed it, hook, line, and sinker. And now here he was, throwing it in Adriano's face. Fine: politics has never been an arena for tender souls, but there was a long way from that to outright slander . . .

"Martin, if you choose to believe that, be my guest. But I'm here as a friend. I don't have ulterior motives and I have nothing to ask of you."

"Well then . . . "

Another urgent phone call for the mayor. A new interruption. Martin Giardino was waving his arm in large loops, apologizing for his inability to cut off a conversation that was clearly unwanted, but of some importance.

Polimeni moved discreetly into the waiting room. A couple of ushers dressed in fancy livery snapped to attention. They recognized him, the aged politico. Obsolete, but you never could tell. Better to stay on his good side. A couple of city commissioners from the old guard stuck their faces in, stared at him in astonishment, then turned to go with a hasty farewell. A couple of high officials of the city constabulary came in, deep in a bitter argument over shifts, vacation time, and retirement, the customary grist of the civil servant's mill. More council members, both majority and opposition, showed up, looked around, registered, smiled, and withdrew.

Polimeni couldn't help but notice the marked "aesthetic" difference between Martin Giardino and the flock of second-rank politicos surrounding him. A *homo novus*, or new man—in every sense of the term—in the midst of a souk. It was inevitable that the man's unprincipled, conniving, winking, disingenuous surroundings should react badly, as if in the presence of an invading barbarian. We gaze upon him with suspicion, and he perceives that feeling. He must feel a little lonely. Malgradi had offered him a shoulder to lean on. And Giardino was in desperate need of allies. Still, there was a great deal to be commended in his obstinate determination not to allow himself to be *Romanized*. And perhaps, he told himself, just maybe a whiff of something new could only prove helpful, salutary for Rome. Perhaps, with all his shortcomings, Martin Giardino really can offer some hope. And maybe, there were topics that could be discussed in those rooms where even the walls had ears. And therefore, when the mayor stuck his head in to discuss the matter, he told him that perhaps they could find a time for a less formal chat, and invited him to dinner.

And, to his great surprise, Martin Giardino accepted.

They'd all shown up. Incredibly punctual, Sebastiano noted, as he watched them batten down on the light aperitif and snack he'd had arranged at the center of the long oval table in the conference room. Shrimp toasts, crabs on a cracker, Mondragone mini-mozzarellas, gingersnaps, fruit cocktails, and Campari Orange drinks. Watching them scarf down the food as if there were no tomorrow and they didn't have serious matters to discuss in a few minutes was a spectacle at once revolting and deeply instructive. A little bit like watching one of those documentaries on the savage eating habits of lions or crocodiles. The way they wolfed food down told you everything you needed to know about their basic nature. Which surprised him every time he was brought in touch with it, even though he always thought he knew all there was to know.

Jabba had overturned the tray of shrimp toast onto the cobalt-blue file marked "Public Works Contracts." Malgradi was sucking Campari through a straw, making the sound of a sink draining or a toilet flushing. Mariani was visibly in the throes of his usual chemical hunger, and he was simultaneously chomping down on cookies and mini-mozzarellas.

"Sebastia', we can start the council meeting, what do you say?" barked Malgradi, bursting into laughter.

Of course, the "Council." The real one. The smoke-filled room where the fate of Rome was decided. Sebastiano looked around at them one more time as they finally took their seats around the table, with a sensation that was a mixture of contempt and contentment.

Malgradi, Jabba, Mariani.

Majority, Opposition, Party of Builders.

The government of Rome.

They were all there. And there could be no doubt that democracy worked more efficiently when it only involved three voices. Excuse me, five voices, if you counted Samurai, temporarily away, and he, who served as Samurai's proconsul.

"You know the agenda, right?" Sebastiano began. Malgradi took the floor.

"As you requested, I worked with Jabba over the weekend on a breakdown of the public works for the jubilee. Considering the urgency of the matter, and in contrast to the normal requirement of a pan-European bids process, the decree we're going to have the German sign calls for an order of direct assignment. The vote is rock solid. Majority and opposition in total lockstep. Also because with what it costs us to feed those piranhas on the city council . . . "

Sebastiano interrupted him.

"How much are we talking about now?"

"The foot soldiers, a thousand a month. The chairs of the committees, three grand, even four. That depends. And then there are extra fees for heavy decree orders. Anyway, like I was saying, we have a few idiots from the Five Star Movement working against us, though we're doing our best to crack that nut. Jabba, if you would, please read the list of projects."

Sebastiano stopped him again.

"Whoa. Take it easy. Who told you that the German will sign without raising objections over the procedure of extraordinary assignment of contracts?"

"Well, to make sure, I had a couple of bedsheets' worth of paper written out . . . how is it the good ones put it? *Parere pro veritate*, as they say about independent expert opinions, but that *veritate* part might not have much to do with what got written, ha ha ha . . . Yes, anyway, a nice fat expert opinion drafted on a consultancy basis by that friend who's been at the Ministry of Infrastructure for a lifetime. You know who I'm talking about, don't you? The one they call Mephistopheles . . . The one who did thirty years of legwork for ministers and members of parliament, on the right and on the left, dazzling them with DPRs, or presidential decree laws, regulations, and public works contract law, and all the other bullshit you can use for these purposes."

"I know who you're talking about."

"Well, it cost me fifty thousand, cash on the barrelhead, and fifty more when the decree order is signed. But it's a bombshell. If we assume that the German does read it, makes it to the end, and understands a few words of it, he's sure to sign it. And now, if you like, Jabba can tell you about the public works."

"I told you, don't be in such a hurry. The resources? How much can be assigned to the budget?"

Malgradi made an embarrassed face.

"Sebastiano, let's just forget the jubilee of 2000. That budget was 3.5 trillion old lire, which amounts to 1.75 billion euros."

"And now?"

"Now we're at a level of roughly a billion, including the 500 million for expansion of the transit system. So 500 million for bricks and mortar and 500 million for rail."

"I would have expected worse."

"Me too. Therefore, we have every reason to be optimistic. And now, if Jabba would care to read us the list."

Sebastiano nodded. Jabba put on his reading glasses and dusted a mountain of crumbs off the greasy sheets of paper on the table in front of him.

"All right then, we have:"

"Renovation and updating of the railway station of Vigna

Clara with completion of the railway circuit out to the Nomentana station;

"Restoration and reinforcement of the quays along the Tiber between the Ponte Milvio and the Ponte Marconi;

"The establishment of at least five new electric bus lines;

"Repaving of the street grid with pedestrian areas and partial pedestrian areas along the so-called 'pilgrimage routes' in the historical center: Via delle Botteghe Oscure, San Carlo ai Catinari, Via dei Giubbonari, Campo de' Fiori, Via del Pellegrino, Piazza Vittorio;

"Special plan for the construction of fifty public urinals;

"Renovation of the area around the Termini Station . . ."

"All right, all right, I get it . . . " Sebastiano cut him off. He spoke to a silent Mariani.

"What about you all?"

Sebastiano wasn't using the royal "you" suitable, as the man once said, only for kings and tapeworms. And anyway, that cokehead hardly deserved it. But Danilo wasn't just speaking for himself. For some mysterious reason—even though the most obvious explanation is that they didn't want anything public to do with it—the other major families of Roman builders had chosen him as the spokesman for the consortium.

Mariani ran his hands through his greasy hair and gave his oracular response.

"In spite of the crisis, we've decided to stick to the 2000 agreement. Which is the same as for the metro C line."

"About which, you'd be so kind I'm sure as to remind us of the details," Sebastiano stared at him with his serpentlike eyes.

"So, 20 percent goes to Politics, 10 percent goes to Neapolitans and Calabrians to be added to the subcontracts, 5 percent to the technical structures of the city government and the ministry, 2 percent for charity and good works, and . . . "

"And?"

"And 13 percent to Samurai . . . Yes, in other words, to Future Consulting."

"Did you say 13 percent?"

Mariani flashed the faint smile of someone who was wetting their pants.

"That's what Samurai got in 2000 and what you're already getting on the metro, so we thought . . . "

"You thought wrong. What's today's date?"

"Monday," he said, with his lower lip quavering in fear, the big baby.

"I said date. I didn't ask what day it is."

"It's the sixteenth. Today is the sixteenth."

"Right. So we'll take 16 percent."

"Of course . . . Of course."

"And do you know why we take sixteen percent, you idiot? Because without me, payment for the various construction sites is going to remain frozen. And without me, you're going to wind up in a real shithole, right?"

Malgradi and Jabba turned inquisitive gazes toward Sebastiano.

"Those are our businesses."

"Of course . . . Of course," they cried in chorus.

Mariani, drawing upon God only knows what hidden vein of courage, or perhaps of desperation, decided that the time had come to speak up.

"Excuse me, Sebastiano, but seeing that we're talking about the agreement, I wanted to inform you that this morning I was informed, and the other companies were likewise informed, that . . . well . . . that our accounts with the IOR bank were frozen, and so I was wondering how we are supposed to send . . . Yes, that is, what system we're supposed to use to . . . "

Sebastiano extinguished with a glare the flash of uneasiness he'd caught on Jabba and Malgradi's expressionless faces. And he decided that he owed them no explanation at all.

"I know. I'm seeing to it in person. This isn't our problem. In fact, forget about it. When the time comes, I'll tell you what procedures to follow. And we need to start thinking about a security plan. My sources speak of a flow of more than thirty million pilgrims to Rome. We'll have to start up security communities especially for this purpose . . . That too is an ad hoc business sector."

"Ad what?" asked Danilo.

"Go on home now. I'll explain to you tomorrow," Sebastiano said brusquely, his patience at an end.

TESTACCIO QUARTER. THE KREMLIN. EVENING.

Martin Giardino showed up at nine on the dot. Alone and without his bodyguards. In one hand the helmet of his inevitable bicycle, in the other a Jewish pizza from the old baker's shop in the Ghetto. Polimeni, who was starting to like the German much more than he had, laid out the evening's menu.

"*Carciofi alla giudia, rigatoni colla pajata . . .* " Polimeni listed the dishes he'd prepared: Fried artichokes, Jewish style, and short noodles with the intestines of an unweaned calf, Rome's classic *pajata*.

"But *pajata* is against the law," Giardino pointed out.

"Wrong. They just made it legal again. And anyway, this *pajata* comes from Bruno, my longtime butcher. From the indoor market on Via Catania. A Communist, like back in the day. I need to introduce you sometime."

"But are you sure . . . "

"There are no alternatives. Take it or leave it."

"Just a taste."

They talked about old books and old love affairs. In the relaxed atmosphere of Polimeni's home, Martin Giardino seemed like a different man. He's trying not to give in to the *homo politicus* that he can feel growing within him, Polimeni diagnosed his guest. He can tell he's in midstream, he knows that some compromises are going to be inevitable, but he wants to get out with his hands clean. He accepts without blinking an eye an invitation to dinner from a potential adversary because he ardently wishes to make him into an ally.

Martin told him about the social event he'd turned down for the evening. A group of builders, certainly interested in trying to get some of the work for the jubilee; avoid like the plague that race of goons with their overdressed, over-made-up wives. A high muck-a-muck from the old days and his cohort of Freemasons, in search of an appointment to the board of directors of one of the companies taken over by the municipal administration. Even cultural events were occasions to be approached only with the greatest caution, because you never knew who you might be helping out and who you might be harming, and to think that he's a guy who's always loved cultural events and openings and such. In these conditions, it's a short step to the brink of paranoia.

When Polimeni looked at the mayor, he was reminded of the young Lucien de Rubempré in Balzac's *Lost Illusions*. A talented young man, but incurably provincial. Lucien found a teacher and guru in the aristocratic de Marsay. Could it be that Martin Giardino had found something similar in Malgradi?

Rome knows how to be cruel, but also welcoming. That axis with the foul Malgradi needed to be severed.

It was over a malt whisky served in an antique set of metal jigger glasses—a gift from an old English Labour Party friend—that the senator spoke to him, laying all his cards on the table, about the conversation that he'd had that morning with Giovanni Daré. About the construction sites that had been shut down because of a lack of funds from the Interministerial Committee for Economic Planning, or ICEP. The maneuvering now under way to get their hands on anything that wasn't nailed down. He told him about his evening at the Democratic Party club. About that Sebastiano Laurenti who had gone to see his friend the bishop and how a few hours later he "had decided to take responsibility" for the debts of the old Communist Party chapter. He described the young man with a very particular dislike and resentment, the reasons for which eluded the mayor, who was surprised at the vehemence he showed. Realizing that he'd overdone it, Polimeni very skillfully steered the conversation to Temistocle Malgradi.

"What do you have against him? He's loyal."

"Loyal? Malgradi? Do you have any idea where that guy comes from?"

"His political history is different from ours, but that hardly seems a sufficient reason to discredit him, and after all . . . "

"Don't let him get his hands on the public works for the jubilee, Martin."

It seemed that he'd made an impression on the mayor. Maybe it had been his tone of voice, or it might have been his arguments, and certainly the particular atmosphere that had been created must have something to do with it, but he seemed willing to take the warning under serious consideration. For the first time in all the years he'd known him, Polimeni saw him looking undecided, willing to listen to advice. He tried a final lunge.

"Choose and appoint a special delegate for the public works projects of the jubilee. I don't know, a sort of city commissioner without portfolio. Exclude from the bids all those lovely companies that have been running the ghost construction sites for the metro. Order all your people to shut the doors in this Sebastiano Laurenti's face. At least until we have a clear idea what sort of interests he represents, and on whose behalf he's really acting. Break up the games. After all, that's your specialty, isn't it?"

"That might mean turning the whole party against me . . . "

"You can do it," he told him, looking him right in the eye, "you're the only one who can pull it off, Martin. Your supposed weakness with the party can become your hidden strength."

He walked him to his bicycle; they exchanged farewells like

old friends. Polimeni wasn't sleepy. The night was cold, but the adrenaline was surging in his bloodstream. He ran to catch a cab and asked to be dropped off in the center of town. His last line sounded very much like something out of an American movie. *You can make it . . . you alone . . .* But who ever said that an ex-senator getting along in years, and who was raised in the school of Togliatti, can't keep up with changing times? A few minutes later, as he was walking down Via Caetani, where thirty-seven years earlier the dead body of Aldo Moro had been found, he remembered that on that long-ago March 16th, the history of Italy had changed forever. And he, it occurred to him with a shiver, was one of the last ones around to remember it.

A little after two in the morning, the mayor called Malgradi. Temistocle extricated himself from the slightly humid embrace of the blonde he'd picked up, half an hour earlier, at a discotheque on the Via Cassia, and braced himself to get his balls busted for a while.

"Ciao Temistocle, am I bothering you?"

"Not at all, Mayor."

"I wanted to tell you that I've had an idea."

Malgradi put his hands on his balls, in the traditional gesture of warding off evil.

"Oh, really? Let's hear it."

"Yes, in short, it's an idea that I know you're going to support. Because you heard the pope's words, didn't you? You're very familiar with his battle against corruption, of course? In other words, we're no longer living in the days of that poor wretched brother of yours."

"Martin, I have to beg you not even to say his name."

"Well, okay, so the idea I've come up with, then, is to appoint an extraordinary delegate in charge of the public works for the jubilee."

Malgradi opened both eyes wide. The blonde gave him a quizzical glance. Malgradi waved for her to leave the room.

"Look, Martin, I'm stunned. I don't know if I deserve such great trust. I think that I'd certainly be a first-rate delegate, but I'd like to make sure you've carefully thought through what you're offering me here. Yes, in short, I wouldn't want my last name to expose you to . . . "

"No, sorry, Temistocle, forgive me. Maybe you've misunderstood."

"No, no, the only reason I'm saying it is that . . . "

"Temistocle, Temistocle, would you just let me speak, if you please? I wasn't thinking about you as the delegate."

Suddenly Malgradi felt his head start whirling.

"Then who . . . ?"

"I'm going to appoint Adriano Polimeni. The former senator. I imagine you know him, right?"

"You bet I do."

"And I can also imagine that you can imagine why him. Unlike you, he's not one of my own men and he isn't considered to be. Which means that no one could accuse me of Caesarism. What's more, he has a history in the party, controversial, but crystal clear and clean . . . "

"I know everything, Martin. I know it all. And now, excuse me, but I really have to let you go. Maybe we can talk about it in person. Excuse me, excuse me, excuse me."

He ended the call and let himself go to an unrepeatable curse. The blonde came over again. She tickled his earlobe with the tip of her tongue.

"Not now. In fact, do me a favor, leave me alone. Let me call you a taxi, okay?"

Now you look at this, this fucking German . . . and what am I going to tell Sebastiano?

# IV.
## TUESDAY, MARCH 17TH–WEDNESDAY, MARCH 18TH
### *Saints' Days: St. Patrick, St. Alexander of Jerusalem*

LONDON.

C hiara Visone deplaned at Heathrow a little before ten in the morning. Throughout the flight she'd worked on her iPad on the speech she was going to deliver at the next executive board meeting of the party. The question of wiretapping and surveillance was becoming thorny. It was incredible, if you stopped to think about it, but there were still people in the party who felt nostalgic for the terrible years of the Clean Hands investigation, when the nation's prosecutors had liquidated an entire political class. Errors that ought never to be repeated. But the battle would be harsh, and the outcome still looked uncertain.

Upon her arrival, she found cold, foggy weather. Waiting for her was a red Jaguar XE with a uniformed chauffeur. They took more than an hour to reach the London Baglioni Hotel. Chiara had just handed over her passport at the reception desk when she felt a hand touch her shoulder. Annoyed, she turned around and found herself face-to-face with Sebastiano. He wore a grisaille executive suit, and carried his overcoat draped over his arm. Next to him was a creature of indeterminate sex, a small, nervous thing, with blonde hair tending toward the ash white, pierced lips and a corona of earrings, ripped jeans and an oversized shapeless coat, a piece of street fashion.

"I see that you like the Baglioni, too, Chiara. A little old-fashioned, I'll admit. But I prefer it to the Kempinski, even if that place is more fashionable. All that Slavic glamor depresses me. I'm here on business. What about you? Weren't you all taken up with the commission?"

There was nothing fortuitous about that seemingly chance encounter. Chiara's presence at the meeting of the International Board of Justice and Economy had been abundantly publicized. And Sebastiano was a careful reader of the right news publications. It might be that he really did have business in London, but the real reason for that trip was her. She felt a hint of disappointment. Chiara was well aware of the allure that she radiated. She had been a much doted-upon little girl, her every whim a command, and then she'd gone on to become a young woman mythicized by others her age in her adolescence, immune to the anguish of inferiority complexes. Therefore, it stood to reason that Sebastiano had to have come for her. The usual foolish little man, wagging his tail at the sight of her regal entrance. At that moment, she found him elegant, well put together, and even handsome. After that night in the Orange Garden, he hadn't been persistent or annoying, he hadn't presumed, he'd limited himself to one courteous phone call. But now, London. Yes, decidedly disappointing. There was no reason to display any excessive warmth.

"The topic was economics and law, and they needed someone with a decent command of the English language. And that's all."

"This is Alex. Alex, this is Chiara."

"Hi, Alex."

"Hi, Chiara."

"Alex is an old friend of mine. She knows all about London. Even more than you, who, as far as I know, lived here for some time. London School of Economics, right? If your other commitments don't interfere, we could eat together tonight. What do you say, Chiara? Appointment here in the lobby at 6:30 this evening?"

"Well, it's a perfect excuse to get free of those intolerable stuffed shirts."

And with a smile, she headed off toward her room, inwardly pleased with her response, which had all things considered been lighthearted and nonchalant.

Sebastiano exchanged a glance with Alex.

"What do you think?"

"She's certainly classy, but . . . "

"But what?"

"I don't know . . . there's something cold about her."

"She's a woman with power."

"It's not just that."

"Then what is it?"

"I'll try to find out, Seby."

The sign said Real Estate Investors, Ltd., and it enjoyed a somewhat obscene pride of place on the townhouse in Belgravia, in the heart of the most prestigious, and expensive, residential district in the world. This ostentatious claim bore the unequivocal brand of property ownership. As if to say: I own, and I can therefore do as I please. I can even profane the holy sanctuary of ancient lineage with my nouveau riche arrogance. Her Majesty's subjects could turn up their aristocratic noses just as high into the air as they might care to: only a very few of the elect could afford a haven in that neighborhood where property values sailed along at forty thousand pounds sterling per square foot. Sheikhs, Indian, Chinese, Malaysian, Thai, and Pakistani businessmen, and even a few of their Brazilian counterparts, Russian Mafiosi, and movie stars, of course.

And, naturally, the Fascist comrade Pasquale Pistracchio, better known as Frodo, in homage to Tolkien's little hero, with an extra sarcastic jab at his decidedly diminutive stature. In the old days of the Idea, Frodo had earned a reputation as a solid, reliable foot soldier. Perhaps not a rocket scientist, but serious, trustworthy, and loyal. Most of all, loyal. For a certain period, he had worked alongside Samurai in the armed robbery line. Not the strategist you'd sit down and work up the details of the plan with, but certainly the guy you'd entrust with standing watch and keeping a lookout on the bank, or even driving the van, certain that you'd find him at the right place at the right time. The kind of guy you could rely upon not to betray you. That's why he'd been appointed the group's treasurer. But as soon as the interest of the state had focused on that small band of combatants that had replaced the vague concept of a *Cause* with the new, assuredly more specific and concrete concept of *Cash*, Frodo had, to put it in idiomatically Roman terms, "*dato*," or vanished in the wind. And with him, in fact, had vanished the cash.

Having arrived in London after transiting very quickly through the ranks of the IRA, the Irish Republican Army— "Genuine lunatics, Sebastia', I saw them do things that . . . let's just drop it"—Frodo had revealed an unguessed-at talent for business. Remarkably skillful at diversifying his investments, he sank roots into the fields of restaurants and catering, fashion, and especially real estate. His marriage to the wan and pallid heiress to an aristocratic dynasty in the outlying regions of the kingdom had thrown open to him the doors of the most exclusive drawing rooms of London. He remained a foreigner, no doubt, but a wealthy stranger who had married well: and that made all the difference. Once he'd established himself, he had worked tirelessly to settle matters with his old Fascist comrades, who, all too understandably, had sworn to take their revenge upon him. He had doled out modest sums of money to the families of his old comrades behind bars, he'd found jobs for those forced to flee the country, given housing to fugitives, and invested small change in businesses that were limping along. Hate had been transformed, first into mistrust, and later to a state of truce, and then peace. Everything seemed to be going well. Frodo was a happy man until one day, returning home at dawn from an orgy in a refined nightclub in Tottenham, he found his two daughters, Trish and Judy, in the company of an elegant gentleman dressed in black.

Samurai.

Samurai, with the utmost courtesy, sent the little girls to play in the other room, and asked Frodo to make him a cup of tea. Frodo started raising objections. Samurai interrupted him brusquely. He complimented him on his lovely home, his adorable little girls, his wife, whom he had greeted the night before, even kissing her hand. He praised Frodo's wise decision to get out of a losing fight in Italy and start over elsewhere. Frodo had shown talent and enterprise, and for that he deserved a just reward.

Frodo started breathing again. He coughed out a pathetic little speech about the affinities between the Teutonic spirit, which had once captivated them all, the old Fascist comrades, and the noblest fraction of the English population. He declared that the *Cause* still enjoyed many sympathizers both at court and among the aristocrats. He yammered on about a plan to found a new nationalist party. Samurai raised an eyebrow, visibly bored. Frodo brought up the solitary flight of Rudolf Hess, Hitler's heir apparent who had handed himself over to the British, confiding, mistakenly, in the tacit alliance with the Duke of Hamilton and the ex-King Edward VIII. At this point, Samurai pulled out a revolver and laid it down on a precious marble table.

"You can save that bullshit for the assholes back in Rome."

Frodo turned pale.

"You said that . . . you mentioned a reward . . . "

"The reward is that, if you'll stop spouting bullshit, you'll be allowed to live. Everything, of course, has a price."

That morning of twenty years ago, half of Frodo's assets were transferred over to Samurai, who, in his turn, entrusted to Frodo the management of his richest accounts. A profitable agreement for them both. Now that Samurai was temporarily out of play, his role had been taken over by Sebastiano. Whom Frodo, in fact—a different Frodo, erect, sober, in suit and tie—welcomed with all the honors of the house. Including a Port Ellen whisky, aged thirty-six years.

"This is stuff that costs two thousand pounds a bottle," he smiled, preening like a peacock.

Sebastiano declined. Among Samurai's many teachings, there was abstinence, as well. Frodo resigned himself to drinking alone, and he slugged back half a glass of that precious nectar at a single gulp.

"Shall we talk about business, Frodo?"

"Go right ahead, comrade."

"I'm not your comrade, and I'm going to have to ask you to do me a favor and keep your mouth shut."

Frodo nodded, with a certain exaggerated sarcasm. His attitude suggested: you may act like Samurai, but you aren't him. So calm yourself down, kiddo. Sebastiano felt the rage rising within him. It had happened before, it kept happening, with increasing frequency. The more time Samurai spent behind bars, the looser his grip became. Fabio Desideri had been a signal, Frodo was a signal. He needed to make a statement with that miserable wretch.

"In ten days I'll let you know the details of the new Italian accounts you'll be operating through, after the ones with the IOR are shut down."

"That's not a problem."

"By tonight I'm going to need five hundred thousand euros in cash. Bills in large denominations, preferably five-hundred-euro notes."

Frodo turned pale.

"Now that might turn out to be a problem, Sebastiano."

"Make sure it isn't. We'll see you at 6:30 this evening at

Roka," he said brusquely, putting an end to the conversation. Before Frodo had a chance to suggest the traditional visit to the "memorial sanctuary," the armor-plated cellar room where he kept his beloved Nazi memorabilia. Because, in the end, that idiot, like so many of Samurai's other longtime followers, really had believed in that swastika bullshit.

At Roka, at number 37 Charlotte Street, you could enjoy the world's finest Kobe beef. It was flown into London every day via Japan Airlines. Wagyu black, raised in Hyōgo Prefecture, in the ancient province of Tajima. Hand massaged and lovingly fed until its final destination as the food of the gods. A dish that ran three hundred pounds, commented Frodo, and then, turning to Alex, added:

"But of course, these are things you don't understand."

"More than anything else, I don't agree with them," she retorted, in a subdued voice.

Alex was strictly vegetarian. A total dyke whom Sebastiano used for his purposes, which did not include, of course, fucking her. There was a singular tenderness between the two of them, something Frodo found inexplicable. Frodo detested Alex and everything that perverts like her—he couldn't think of any other word to describe them—represented. That was not the way he felt about the hot babe that Sebastiano had brought with him. Chiara Visone. A piece of pussy to die for. Maybe a little skinny for his tastes, but Frodo definitely wouldn't have kicked her out of bed. His pale wife wasn't that great, in comparison. And after all, for fuck's sake, a man is a man.

Sebastiano asked Chiara how it had gone with the Board.

"Like always. The English always claim that they've invented the perfect formula to bring together justice and business. They call it 'doing business justice.'"

"And what would that be?"

"Rush the trials through and always find the stronger party to be in the right."

"Right!" Frodo exclaimed. "And get rid of judges and trade unions!"

"I hate talking about politics," Alex broke in, exchanging a knowing glance with Sebastiano.

Chiara smiled politely. In a certain sense, she actually agreed with Frodo. But this wasn't the time or place to admit it. Not for a member of parliament for a left-wing party. And after all, that Frodo was horrible. Alex and Sebastiano continued to exchange glances. What were they communicating? Something that had to do with her, Chiara?

When the sommelier came to the prestige table that dominated the dining room, Sebastiano ordered a cup of tea, a selection that was greeted by the sommelier with a bow and by Frodo with a disgusted grimace. The short, corpulent Fascist comrade devoted himself to a scrupulous examination of the wine list. Chiara bet herself that he'd choose *chille ca costa 'ecchiú*—whatever cost the most. And sure enough, Frodo ordered a bottle of the 2006 Châteauneuf-du-Pape Croix de Bois, inevitably making a point of the price.

"What about the ladies?"

"The proper accompaniment for a meal in a Japanese restaurant would be sake," Chiara observed.

The sommelier's face lit up.

"Allow me to recommend our Junmai, an authentic miracle of purity."

"Purity is everything," Frodo jumped in, "that's what I always used to hear Samu . . . "

Sebastiano shot him an angry glance that silenced him immediately. And yet, he'd warned him in advance. No Fascist talk, no allusions, and most important of all, no names. Frodo pretended to have a coughing fit. Alex chuckled. For the rest of the meal, Chiara remained vigilant. She observed, scrutinized, absorbed information. That Pasquale Pistracchio, *Sir* Pistracchio. A Fascist. A worthy comrade of the Mafioso with whom Sebastiano had chatted two evenings earlier at the exit from the party club. It irritated her to think she was being treated like an idiot. If there was anything to be understood, she was sure to figure it out sooner and clearer than anyone else.

She'd known dozens of guys like that Pistracchio, in Naples. They'd frequented her father's law office, her father's Socialist friends, her father's social evenings. They were all, officially at least, businessmen, just like that Pistracchio. They handled substantial sums of money. Every so often, one of them disappeared. Sometimes for a very long time. But they always reappeared, eventually. Interchangeable faces of a standard model that were always replaced by new specimens, different and yet identical. Chiara had learned from her father how to keep them at bay, without causing breaks in relations that could lead to unpredictable consequences, and how to make use of them when needed. She was no fool, she hadn't been born yesterday, and Sebastiano needed to get that through his head. No one becomes a member of parliament at thirty if they haven't figured out exactly how the world works. They were surrounding themselves with far too many masks. It was up to her to decide which of those masks to drop. But in that scenario, Sebastiano was still an anomalous element, impossible to classify.

Sebastiano saw he was getting a call. He excused himself and walked away from the table. Alex ordered a second bottle of sake. Sir Pistracchio had a brownish stain at the corner of his mouth.

"When I was a kid, they called me Frodo," he confided, between one bite and the next, "you know Tolkien?"

"That's a real mystery about you Italians," Alex jumped in. "Tolkien was an anarchist and a pacifist. He wrote *The Lord of the Rings* to warn against the dangers of Nazism. And you Italians think of him as being a right winger."

"Things aren't so simple," Frodo observed, grimly.

"Excuse me," said Sebastiano, returning to the table.

Chiara noticed how pale he was. For no good reason, she laid a hand on his arm. He turned to her with a luminous smile. In spite of herself, she felt a wave of warmth wash over her. *Who the hell are you, Sebastiano Laurenti?* Alex got up and said that she wanted to smoke a cigarette. She invited Chiara to join her. Chiara followed her out of the restaurant. The evening was cold, but at least it wasn't raining. Alex rolled herself a cigarette.

"We can speak English, if you prefer, Alex."

"No, I'll take advantage of the opportunity to practice my Italian."

"You speak it beautifully."

"Thank you, Chiara."

For a while they fell silent. Then Alex burst out laughing.

"If you're thinking that I go to bed with Sebastiano, just let me inform you that I'm a lesbian, and I'd be delighted to take you out for a spin. Have you ever been with another woman?"

Chiara laughed, too. For a while she'd assumed that Sebastiano and Alex shared some secret perversion. That at the end of the evening they were going to suggest some kind of threesome. And she'd wondered how she would react. She hadn't been able to conceal from herself, with a shiver, the idea that it might even be exciting. But no, Alex had been assigned another function. That singular creature was studying her. This was some kind of exam.

"Alex, let's just say that if I ever did feel like it, I'd want to be taken out for a spin by you and no one else."

And then she added: "I'm a member of parliament for a left-wing party, but in any case, my generation has a very open relationship with sex. In short, it's your own business who you want to fuck. And desires shouldn't be repressed."

Alex told her about her childhood in Scotland, the drugs and depression that had accompanied her for many long years. Chiara spoke of her own childhood in Naples, her father the notary, the hopes and the force of will that accompanied her still. Alex rolled herself another cigarette. Chiara asked her if she worked for Sebastiano.

"Let's just say that I work with him."

"What exactly is it that you do for him?"

"Lots of things. Let's say I'm his sentinel . . . "

"His sentinel."

"That's right. I'm his sentinel in London."

"And what is it that does?"

"The same thing everybody does. Business."

"What sort of business?"

"Someone might think this was an interrogation, Chiara."

"Someone else might think that you're trying to figure out what kind of a person I am."

"Why would I want to do that?"

"So you can tell him."

Alex sighed.

"Whatever happens between the two of you, Chiara, don't judge him too harshly. He's better than so many others, believe me. And he has really suffered."

"Do you mean because of what happened to his father?"

"Once you get to know him better, you'll understand that this life he lives isn't his real one. But I'm not the one who ought to be telling you that."

"I like you, Alex."

"And I like you. But don't overdo it. I'm a fragile, horny girl."

Just then, the men left the restaurant. It was early, and Frodo wanted more to drink. Alex dragged them to the café at Paddington Station. Chiara was stunned and impressed. One wing of the old building had been converted into a hotel for travelers; another wing housed a nightclub that was noisy, cheerful, and full of music, people, and life. Sebastiano went off into a corner for a new phone call. Increasingly pale. Something was going on. Chiara was eaten alive by her curiosity. When she and Alex went off together to the ladies' room, Sebastiano confronted Frodo.

"It's getting late. Give me the money."

"I don't have it, Seba. Forgive me, but I'm going to need a few days to scrape it together."

"I don't get it."

"There's not that much to get. I've invested a large sum in certain Asian funds . . . stuff with an incredible return on investment. Put in a hundred and back comes three hundred. Samurai is going to be happy about it, believe me. It's just a matter of showing some patience."

They were sitting on a circular sofa; the seats left empty by the girls separated them. Sebastiano grabbed the fork that Alex had used to lazily spear her pineapple, leaned over toward Frodo, and stabbed him hard in the crotch.

"But you're . . . "

"Shut the fuck up, or I'll rip your balls off. You have until tomorrow morning at eight."

"Fuck, man, I can't!"

"I don't give a damn whether you can or you can't. Sell your house, sell your car, rob a bank, after all, that used to be your specialty, didn't it, you little worm? I want that money by eight o'clock or you're done for. Have I made myself clear?"

Frodo nodded, drenched in sweat. Sebastiano withdrew the improvised weapon. A small drop of blood oozed down the tines. The girls came back from the bathroom.

"Pasquale is tired. You ought to understand: he just doesn't have the physique he used to. Sleep tight, my good friend."

In the lobby of the Baglioni, Sebastiano greeted Chiara with a gentle caress and headed over to the bar. He ordered a double malt whisky. Only at exceptional moments did he indulge in alcohol, and this was one of those moments. With the recalcitrant Frodo he'd been forced to resort to drastic methods. And, as always, the excitement that came with the exercise of power was a fleeting moment. It vanished quickly, and in its place an empty sense of nausea settled.

In Rome things were going badly. The appointment of Polimeni was a very bad piece of news. He was going to need to get Chiara involved, and he didn't know exactly what moves to make. Alex had sent him a short report via WhatsApp: "C. understands everything. She's a pure diamond, but go slow with her: one wrong bump, and the diamond will shatter." Alex too had sensed Chiara's overwhelming whiff of seduction. But she hadn't said exactly which diamond would shatter into a thousand pieces. Whether it would be Chiara or Sebastiano. And he still couldn't have given an exact definition of what it was that he expected from her. Complicity. Or something deeper. He was falling in love. And falling in love was an error.

He heard Chiara's voice behind him.

"I'm not sleepy. And I feel like talking."

"Here I am."

"Who are those people, Sebastiano? That Frodo . . . is a Fascist."

"He was one once, and deep inside, maybe he still is. But for the rest of the world, including me, he's just a very wealthy man."

"And you manage his business concerns."

"Just like I do for lots of other people."

"And are they all like Frodo?"

"Some are."

Chiara ordered a cardamom herbal tea. She stared at him, she scrutinized at him, as if expecting who-knows-what revelation. Chiara had guessed at Alex's mission: observe, report back. He couldn't hide from her. Sebastiano understood that something needed to be said. Something approaching the truth. Everything that could be said.

"Someday I'll invite you to my company headquarters, Chiara . . . "

The offices of Future Consulting s.r.l. on Via Ludovisi were a perfect copy of what had once been the executive headquarters of Laurenti Engineering, s.r.l. He had reproduced the bronze conference table with the rainbow onyx surface, the classic Thonet chairs, the damasked silk embellished with art nouveau motifs. He'd purchased the prints on the walls from a junkman, or antiquarian, whom he'd allowed to profiteer on his sentiments. It all gave the offices a decidedly antiquated, and yet measured, tone. The finest tribute to his late father, the engineer. An old-school conservative, a man of another era. He had created out of nothing a solid, reliable company that planned and supervised civil engineering projects. When the time had come to start giving bribes as a way of getting along, he had refused. It had been explained to him in no uncertain terms that this eccentricity of his was unacceptable: the system couldn't tolerate exceptions to the rules. Either he could bend with the times, like everyone else, or he'd be swept away. Deaf to flattery and threats, he'd continued along his straight and narrow path. He had refused to transform Laurenti Engineering into a paper mill emitting invoices for nonexistent projects, to take work assignments that entailed kickbacks of ten percent of the total value of the project, kickbacks that were paid to politicians and highly placed mandarins in the Ministry of Infrastructure or the city government. Slowly, they had built a wall of hostility around him. Until they'd finally destroyed him. *The Others*.

That's what his father called them.

*The Others*. It had been the others who'd pushed him to financial ruin and death. He'd never again seen a single job, a single contract. Not a project, not a supervision of construction. They'd all shunned him like a leper. He'd fallen into the hands of the loan sharks, setting the noose around his neck that they'd then used to strangle him.

If it had been entirely up to his own personal taste, Sebastiano would have opted for something more modern in terms of decorations. But Cucchi, Fontana, Boetti, and Paladino enjoyed pride of place in his private residence. The old family villa that had fallen into his hands after the shipwreck of the Three Little Pigs, the loan sharks who had first taken it away from him when he was just a young orphan ravaged by the blows of injustice. The company's headquarters, now that was a museum. That was a temple.

Chiara had listened, in something approaching religious silence. But her voice rang out surprisingly ironic when she told him that if the story he'd told her had any moral at all, it was that he, Sebastiano, had now officially become *The Others*. The people who know the rules of the game. Or, actually, the ones who set those rules.

"But what does it mean to become *The Others*, Seba, you still haven't explained that to me."

No, and he couldn't explain it. He certainly couldn't tell her that he'd stained his hands with blood. It had been his only option. He'd won. And that's what mattered. There were no longer *Us* and *The Others*. There was only victory and power. And the bitterness that came with all that.

"It means doing exactly what everyone else does, Chiara. Nothing more and nothing less."

"I'm going to get some sleep, Sebastiano. Tomorrow is going to be a long, hard day."

At seven thirty the following morning, a young man deposited an envelope for Mister Laurenti at the reception desk of the Hotel Baglioni. When the envelope was delivered to him, Sebastiano hefted it, without bothering to open it. The weight, roughly speaking, corresponded. Frodo had fallen into line. For the moment, anyway. When they met in the lobby—they were on the same flight—taking advantage of a momentary distraction on Chiara's part, he slipped the envelope into the young woman's elegant Vuitton travel bag. A simple precautionary measure, he told himself, to lighten his sense of shame. When they landed at Fiumicino, he realized just how advisable his foresight had been. Chiara passed unquestioned through the sliding glass doors, while he was stopped by the customs agents, and his suitcase was searched with great care. He was released a half hour later, with copious apologies, to which he responded with a polite smile and words of praise for the agents' professional rigor.

That bastard Frodo. He'd called in a tip. Otherwise, there was no explaining all this determination in the search.

Chiara was waiting for him outside the bookstore in the arrivals hall. She handed him an envelope with a defiant smile.

"Were they looking for this?"

Sebastiano didn't apologize, and he didn't fall back on his dazzling smile. Instead he looked at her, serious and sincere.

"Yesterday the mayor appointed Polimeni extraordinary delegate for the jubilee. Adriano Polimeni. You know him, don't you?"

"You sure know a lot of things about me."

"You need to go and talk to him, Chiara."

Here it was. Here was the critical point of no return. She might turn her back on him and withdraw, with great dignity, intact as a vestal virgin. She might throw a tantrum. Upbraid him for having used her. Right back to that first moment when he'd seduced her with that ridiculous novelty item of the Knights of Malta.

She could even report him to the authorities, sure, why not, Sebastiano Laurenti, the man who dabbles in strange dealings, the profiteer . . . she could . . . yes, she could . . . but London had stirred something inside her. A feeling that was still tangled, impossible to pin down. It was as if he, in the process of confiding to her certain clearly only-partial truths, were turning to her with a tacit request for help. At the same time, Sebastiano remained a challenge. The world that he represented, a world whose outlines she was only beginning to guess at, was itself a challenge. And if there was one thing Chiara Visone loved, it was challenges.

And she especially loved winning them.

"You know something, Sebastiano? I was wondering when you'd broach the topic . . . "

"Polimeni?" he asked, stunned.

"No. ICEP. I was expecting you to ask me to intervene with the government to unfreeze the funds for the metro. Isn't that why you suddenly acted so interested in me?"

Sebastiano suddenly turned serious.

"I like you, Chiara. You're like a great bird of prey lifting into flight. And it's a majestic flight, it captures the imagination. I'd never get tired of watching it, admiring it. You'll have all my support. I won't stop you. I'll be your right hand. I'll be at your side. And soon, I'll fall in love with you."

She paused for a beat. She didn't especially like the overemphasis, but she certainly found it flattering. A delicate smile appeared on her face. The contrast with the ice that remained in her gaze couldn't have clashed any more starkly.

"Please, Sebastiano, all of this rhetoric! But okay. I'll go see Polimeni. I'll do it today."

They left the airport arm in arm. A hired chauffeur was waiting for them under the large Lancia billboard. Chiara asked to be dropped off a short walk from the Montecitorio Palace, seat of the Italian parliament.

FABIO DESIDERI'S VILLA. AFTERNOON OF MARCH 18TH.

Bogdan Adir accompanied Sebastiano to the gym that Fabio Desideri had set up in the English basement of his villa on the Janiculum Hill. Fabio was running on a treadmill, wearing a gray tracksuit, with a towel around his neck.

"Come here, Sebastia', take a look at what a guy has to do to stay in shape!"

The treadmill slowed down and Fabio, with a sigh, stepped down off the belt. Sebastiano handed him the envelope, and Fabio nodded with satisfaction.

"That's great, Sebastia'. But you shouldn't have rushed all the way over here. Such a hurry . . . "

"Aren't you going to count it?"

"Are you kidding?"

In one corner of the room, which was filled with all sorts of advanced fitness machines, was a refrigerator.

"You want something to drink, Seba?"

He shook his head no. Fabio tipped his head back, draining a small bottle of dietary supplement. On the left, a small door swung open, and a young brunette, naked and wet from the shower, emerged. By no means embarrassed at the presence of the two men, she strode through the room, shot Fabio a wink, to which he replied with a half smile, and emerged from the main door.

"Geraldine," Fabio explained, "a French actress. She takes two or three saunas a day, and she likes to walk around like that. A damned pretty girl."

"Another notch on the big bad macho man's pistol?" Sebastiano asked ironically.

"Sebastia', I love you. And I respect you. But you need to learn to enjoy life, and stop thinking about nothing but money. Because, among other things, if I can speak frankly, money isn't the only thing in life."

Fabio walked over to Sebastiano with a confidential look on his face. Then he wrapped an arm around his shoulders in a parody of a fraternal embrace. Sebastiano stiffened. Fabio heaved a sigh.

"Listen to me, Seba. I want to be sincere with you. I've been feeling hemmed in for a while now."

Fabio Desideri knew how to conjure with words. The further he plunged into his plea, the greater Sebastiano's sense of uneasiness grew. The message, the real message, was about to be delivered, at last. Fabio described his life as a wealthy, successful, but slightly bored man. He argued along the lines of the concept of "vital impetus." He lingered on the importance of churning up stagnant waters. Nonsense. All of it nonsense to conceal the inevitable kicker.

"Speak clearly, Fabio."

"The jubilee. I want in."

"You?"

"Me. Why shouldn't I? I have plenty of money, good connections, my own men. The pasture is broad and green, Sebastia', one cow more or less doesn't bother anyone. Quite the contrary . . . the fatter the cow gets, the more milk it gives to you!"

"We don't need your connections."

"Of course you don't! Still, you need to give me a hand, seeing as how you're all buddy-buddy with the folks that count."

His reasoning, all things considered, made perfect sense. Fabio was a member of the circle, a person upon whom he'd been able to count, up till now. Why shouldn't he?

Because of the method, Sebastiano concluded. Because that wasn't a request, it was a false request. A demand. First I show you my muscles, and then I ask you to make a deal. Error, Fabietto, grave error.

"I'll have to talk to Samurai about it, Fabio. You know it's up to him."

Fabio once again unleashed his dazzling smile. This time, enriched with a twist of venom.

"You know, Seba, I've always wondered . . . who is Samurai, I mean, deep down? How can it be that half the world adores him and the other half shits their pants just at the sound of his name? For instance, let's take someone like you, Sebastiano. In theory, you're really the boss of Rome. In practice, though, you're—what's the term?—Samurai's proconsul. And so: I've been straight with you, now I want you to be straight with me. What is Samurai for you? A brother, a father, a friend . . . or just a boss?"

"I don't have bosses."

But he said it under his breath.

"Samurai is in prison, Sebastiano. He's serving his sentence like a man, the real man that he is. I admire him . . . "

"Samurai will get out soon."

"You think so? Here's what I say: precisely because I admire him, it's time for Samurai to step aside. He's there, and we . . . you and me . . . are here . . . "

Sebastiano felt his head spinning. A black shadow loomed over his mind. Nothing happens by chance. If this guy kept belittling Samurai in his presence, it must be because he'd sent a signal of some kind. Unconsciously, perhaps. Or perhaps deep inside, way down in the depths, they both were hoping for the same thing.

To get rid of him.

"I'll inform Samurai of your offer and I'll let you know."

Once he was alone, Fabio called Bogdan and told him to

ask Geraldine if she felt like joining him in the sauna. He stripped and, after a fast, ice-cold shower, went into the booth to start sweating. Sebastiano had reacted as per expectations, but the seeds of doubt had been sown.

Now the young man could yield territory, and Samurai could approve, or else a fight could break out. Odds, as things stood, were about even for either event. There were no certainties, except perhaps for one: from this moment on, it had become impossible to retrace his steps. And the next move had already been decided.

Geraldine entered the sauna and got comfortable between his legs.

Later, in the car, while his driver, Furio, was picking his way through crowded lunchtime traffic, Sebastiano wondered whether he might not have been too compliant. Maybe he didn't need Samurai's approval to strike back, and strike back hard. Fabio had definitely reared up on his hind legs. And he wasn't about to stop.

He remembered another one of Samurai's lessons: arrogance will destroy the arrogant, but also those who fail to recognize it in time in their enemies.

Or, as in this case, in the false friend.

But there was still a question that was tormenting him: What is it you really want, Sebastiano?

HOUSE OF JAZZ. MARCH 18TH. EVENING.

Senator Polimeni adored jazz. It had been a passion of his youth, spawned among the sleeping bags and the tent cities at Castiglione del Lago in a long-ago summer of nearly forty years ago. In the wonderful, controversial 1970s, it was fashionable among the young people to attend Umbria Jazz, a peripatetic festival, free of charge, that traveled from castles to hillsides, bringing with it some of the finest names of American jazz. Polimeni had allowed himself to be dragged along by Rossana, who was always well informed about the newest developments. But he'd immediately felt uneasy among the beards, wooden clogs, sensations, breasts, promiscuity, tattered ripped jeans, bad wine, and every imaginable psychotropic substance known to western youth. A feeling of uneasiness that had been transformed into genuine pain when Rossana, naturally beautiful and treacherous, had dumped him unceremoniously to share a two-person pup tent with a long-haired freak from Montreal. He'd indulged himself, before throwing in the towel for good, in one last vagabond evening. And that's when he had discovered jazz. It had been there, on the shores of Lake Trasimeno, in the midst of all those strangers, more interested in fleeting love affairs and improbable revolutionary utopias than in the adrenaline-charged phrasing of Archie Shepp, amidst mindless chitchat and mosquitoes, that the magic had infected him. And he would never again be free of that infection.

Now, at the end of his first day as the mayor's delegate for the jubilee, more thrilled than exhausted, he found himself in the auditorium of the Casa del Jazz, a Thirties-era villa that had been confiscated from the Mafia. The great Danilo Rea on piano was playing at being a harmonic Picasso, deconstructing and recomposing Armstrong and Monk. It was a Cubist game, brutal and deeply tender at the same time. Like life.

Excited by the cascade of notes, he abandoned himself to a gust of optimism, absolutely uncharacteristic of him, letting himself luxuriate in it for the entire duration of the concert. We can do it, we can do it, he sang to himself, wandering through the entire park along with a small throng of passionate fans. He headed for the exit, shivering in the chilly night air that already had an undertone of springtime. He'd been smart to wear his old green loden overcoat. Even though he hadn't been able to get his Kawasaki out of the garage, a symbol of a secret, and limited, pact with the overriding school of hedonism.

Then he saw her.

Chiara Visone.

Chiara in jeans, with a light blue jacket, hair pulled back. A friendly, easygoing outfit yet still vaguely professional. He walked toward her, with determination. And with equal determination, without any preamble, he informed her that if she had any matter she wished to discuss, he'd be glad to see her in his office tomorrow. Now if she'd be so good as to excuse him . . .

"Ciao, Adriano. How are you?"

The light from a streetlamp illuminated her. Polimeni dropped his eyes. That was a vision that he truly feared he'd be unable to resist. Just as he couldn't resist that faint pefume. Chiara resembled Rossana, and to a stunning degree of exactitude. That resemblance is what had first attracted him to her, back when they'd had their affair. He'd fooled himself into believing that he could find in her the great lost love of his life.

He'd soon come to realize that the physical resemblance didn't mean a damned thing. Rossana was all impetus, passion, and extremism. Chiara was a cold-blooded creature. She had placed herself strategically under that streetlamp, to offer him the most seductive part of herself. Chiara possessed an arsenal whose power was completely self-conscious and self-aware. Resigned, his hands plunged into the pockets of his loden overcoat, he stopped to hear what she had to say.

"I wanted to congratulate you on your appointment."

"Did Laurenti send you?"

"Listen, Adriano . . . "

"I saw you together, you know, at the club. How long was it before you took him to bed? Let me guess: that same night. Am I right?"

She ignored the provocation. He wanted to wound her, and he'd forgotten one of the many things he knew about her. There was no way to wound Chiara. Chiara was immune to wounds. And so he felt stupid and ineffectual. As usual, she had seized control without so much as moving a muscle.

"Forgive me, Chiara. I know why you're here. Everyone's salivating over the jubilee. But listen to me: the companies . . . forgive me the pun . . . but the companies that keep *bad company* are out of the running. There's no room for them in the jubilee. Tell your new boyfriend that's the way it is."

Chiara caressed his shoulder. A gentle tender caress, full of the old and robust tenderness of things once shared together, things that last forever. Polimeni recoiled, irritated.

"Stop playing around, Chiara, and get to the point."

"I know you better than anyone else, Adriano."

Oh, there could be no doubt about that. She knew him better than anyone else. And that meant she could tell him certain truths. And she spoke to him, from the heart, to the extent that such a thing was possible for someone like her. "The appointment has gone to your head, Adriano. This is the great comeback you've never once stopped dreaming of since the party put you out to pasture. You'll take on this new position with all the stubborn energy that has made you the unstoppable force that you are, you won't just do everything possible, you'll do more. If you were a man with faith, you'd put this on the level of miracles. If you were a man with faith, you'd aspire to sainthood. But you're not a man with faith, and so you'll make up your mind to design your jubilee, leave your mark, your imprint. And all this is perfectly right, Adriano, and I'm not here to question it. It's not a personal matter. There shouldn't be any personal matters involved in politics. You remember that? It's one of the things you taught me. You were my only teacher, my one, sole mentor. Everything I know about politics, I owe to you. And I have cherished those teachings, Adriano, I've treasured them. No personal matters. We're talking about Rome. Rome needs to get back on its feet, just as our country needs to get back on its feet. I'm afraid that your thirst for redemption, your need to win, will make you lose sight of this objective, and I'm here to ward off the worst. Forget about the club, forget about your long-ago protégé. Forget about the left. That's something else you taught me, once: Italy is a right-wing country. Its profound depths are reactionary. And I know how to make your teachings pay off, Adriano. In order to win, the left wing has got to disappear. It has to become a moderate wing. And I want to win."

"In other words, the left wing is going to have to become the right wing."

The line, thought Polimeni once it had left his lips, was meant to sound ironic, but he'd uttered it with an undertone of bitterness. The truth is that he needed to break the flow, or he'd be overwhelmed, submerged, drowned in it. An objective achieved at least in part: Chiara, if nothing else, had caught her breath. There was another quality of hers that it was hard to resist. Her rhetoric. Chiara knew how to communicate in an

instinctive manner. She could captivate a knot of hostile inter-
locutors, dominate a television talk-show set, whip up or calm
down audiences of all kinds. And that wasn't something he'd
taught her. She got that from within, it was in her DNA. When
he had been at the top of his game, in order to keep himself
from being slaughtered in the field of debate, he'd had to sub-
mit to the training of an expert in communications, and he was
still ashamed of the memory. He'd had to comply with certain
rules that he found hateful, because otherwise his "message"
wouldn't have fit into the standard thirty-second attention
span. Along the way, moreover, the message had become completely evanescent, but as far as he could tell, that didn't seem
to matter much.

And anyway, no matter how hard he tried, it hadn't worked.

"You're uttering quite a string of lovely words, Chiara, but
what does all this have to do with Sebastiano Laurenti?"

"Sebastiano Laurenti is just one more guy. A businessman,
an entrepreneur, a profiteer, a soldier of fortune, an organizer
of resources, call him what you want, Adriano. But we need
people like him. That's another thing that you taught me. Or
have you forgotten the 'sources' we drank from while the party
was in a state of crisis? The Russian rubles? All I'm asking you
is not to forget the past, our past, Adriano. How many ambitious undertakings were nurtured and made possible in part
thanks to ruthless men like Sebastiano? And how many noble
enterprises were ultimately sacrificed on the altar of moralism.
Weren't you the one who told me about Saint-Just, the great
revolutionary, and who asked me to reflect on that terrible
phrase of his: 'You can't govern in innocence'?"

"He meant something else by that . . . "

"The city is suffocating. The country is suffocating. When
you're suffocating you don't really care whether the hand that
gives you oxygen is clean or not. Milan had its Expo, Rome will
get its jubilee. Don't try to go against it, Adriano. That's all I

ask you. We'll do things properly, in full respect of the regulations, as far as that's possible. I don't want to die innocent. I want to live."

"There have to be some limits, Chiara."

"But of course there will. And I'm certainly not to going to go beyond them."

"Then what's your limit?"

Chiara locked arms with him and this time he put up no resistance.

"Rome's never had a female mayor."

"Martin Giardino is doing a fine job."

"And who says otherwise? But someday, sooner or later, Rome is going to have a female mayor."

"And in the meantime?"

"And in the meantime, the companies that keep bad company are out of the running, but the other companies are going to need oxygen to survive."

"You're asking too much, Chiara. And what's more, you're really not in any position to ask for anything at all. In whose name are you speaking here? Your own personal name? In the name of your party? In Laurenti's name?"

She hadn't remembered him being so rigid, so inflexible. Something she'd said had annoyed him. Something wrong. A detail she'd overlooked. Or maybe she'd only fooled herself into thinking that she could control him, the way she'd once done. Then, all at once, it dawned on her.

Adriano was jealous.

She felt a sudden burst of rage against him. After all, he was just an old man. A mangy old wolf, a top dog fading into the sunset, infuriated by the young male who had dethroned him. Why didn't he just step aside and bask in the last rays of the setting sun, and accept the inevitable end, with his books and his ancient myths that no one gave a damn about anymore?

She pulled away from him, with a hint of distaste.

"Don't try to get in my way, Adriano. You know the kind of things I'm capable of. You taught me yourself how to win a political fight. Don't forget that."

Polimeni watched her walk away, and he felt a stirring sense of satisfaction. Chiara's stride, once so lithe and self-confident, had been transformed into an angry stride, like a princess incapable of tolerating a refusal. He had loved her, and he had lost her. The satisfaction changed suddenly into bitterness. The perfect woman, the one he'd been chasing all his life, would have been a carefully mixed cocktail of Rossana and Chiara, and perhaps they even existed, women like that. It just turned out that Adriano Polimeni hadn't been lucky enough to meet one of them. Or else, more simply, the perfect woman doesn't exist.

But one thing he knew was that imperfect politicians do exist. Chiara had reminded him of who he was and where he'd come from. How accommodating he'd been in the past and how hypocritical he risked sounding, now that he had discovered a new rigidity. He, Polimeni, wasn't Martin Giardino, and he wasn't Father Giovanni, for that matter. He wasn't so pure. But, once all was said and done, it came down to a question of limits. Was Sebastiano Laurenti a man for all seasons, a soldier of fortune, the paragon of a typically Italian type . . . or something much worse? He still couldn't say, but one day, soon, he'd know. And when that day came, he and Chiara would resume the discussion.

In any case, it had been a bad parting of the ways. She had set forth a proposal that was, all things considered, perfectly reasonable, and he had let his intransigence overwhelm him and guide his hand. He'd reacted like a spurned lover more than as the *homo politicus* he ought to be. Yes, no point beating about the bush. He was still in love.

OSTIA. NIGHT.

On straightaways, the Ferrari 488 GTB regularly hit 185 MPH. It was nighttime, and a strong sirocco wind had sprung up, unleashing a furious clanking in the rigging of the sailboats moored at the central wharf of the port of Ostia. Fabio Desideri was really satisfied with the new masterpiece of engineering from Maranello. His latest toy had been delivered just a few hours ago. Two of his Albanians were barring access to the port area, ready to dissuade night owls tempted to go for a stroll in the wee hours. But no one was likely to show up, really. Ostia threatened to become a no-man's-land. Samurai on the one hand and the investigations on the other had laid waste to that stretch of coastline, once so flourishing and promising. Now the families were scraping by on crumbs. Rome was turning gray, and Ostia was dull and dying. It was up to him to turn on the bright lights again. And that's why, instead of a fantastic piece of pussy who really would have appreciated the experience, aboard his four-wheeled missile he was giving a ride to a trembling and sweat-drenched Danilo Mariani. The real estate developer had been shocked when Fabio's men picked him up from the nightclub at the Pigneto where he'd been negotiating with a couple of trannies for a couple of ounces of coke. Diseased-looking trannies, low-quality cocaine, but then, of course, no one was giving him credit anymore. Fabio had issued very precise instructions. Danilo really had slid to the bottom of the barrel. It was Fabio's job to bring him back to the surface. Under the proper conditions, of course.

"Okay, here we are."

With a sudden screech of brakes, the nose of the red vehicle came to a halt just six feet from the water's edge. Right in front of the Mykonos IV, 118 feet of carbon fiber hull that Fabio had taken away for a song from a Greek entrepreneur who was sinking under the burden of his debts. Gotta love that Merkel. The two men got out of the car, Fabio with his lithe step, Danilo panting and coughing.

"I still don't understand why you brought me here, Fabio."

"Do you remember the Waterfront, Dani'?"

"Of course I do! A world-class con job."

Samurai, and his ancient brigade of faggot priests, loan sharks, real estate speculators, retired Mafiosi, and bribe-hungry politicos, had decided to turn that stretch of the Tyrhennian coastline into a paradise for the rich and famous. A marina, designer shops, a casino and a mountain of artificial snow that not even the most perverse sheikh of Dubai would have dared to imagine. It had all gone to hell in a handbasket, of course.

"It just went wrong this time, Fabio."

"Bullshit. It was all backwards from the start, Dani'."

It couldn't have worked. Let me explain the right way to do things, Mister Coca. What's needed here is a commercial port, for freighters, big ships, with a container facility, to attract big Chinese and Indian money, and maybe even the Russians. Double the major routes leading to Rome. Serious business, not the homemade Disneyland that your friend Samurai had had in mind. Because you need to think big, starting with the jubilee. Ostia needs to become big like Gioia Tauro. Rome's great door to the world, swinging open on the eve of the Olympics.

"The Olympics?"

"The Olympics, Danilo. The Olympics that they're going to have to give us in 2020 or at the very most, in 2024, one or the other, we're in no hurry. And then don't forget about the new stadium for A.S. Roma. Where are they going to build it? In Tor di Valle. And exactly where is Tor di Valle? Right around the corner. Our fortune is all right here. It's just whether we want to reach out and grab it."

"What do you mean we?"

Danilo, shaking with a tremor that only a line of shit could conquer, stared at him with his stolid gaze. Fabio laid a hand on his shoulder. He really would have to explain every detail to him, every last thing to this moron. Like a little kid.

"You and me, Danilo. Just imagine this place full of people, ships, sailors, business . . . and imagine the sign outside the construction site, with great big flaming letters, reading MARIANI & DESIDERI CONSTRUCTION, INC."

"Mariani and Desideri?"

"You and me. Mariani and Desideri."

A spark of understanding was staring to make its way into the real estate developer's befuddled mind.

"Wait, you're offering me a deal?"

"Fifty-fifty. You need cash and I need a name. I've got cash, you've got a name. Tell me yes and tomorrow morning at 10 AM we can go to the notary's office and draw up the papers."

"Wait, but have you talked to Sebastiano?"

"Oh, Dani', you're forty years old and you're still running to ask permission from Papà?"

Danilo Mariani shut his eyes. He could feel the energy building up inside of him. Mariani and Desideri. The construction site. Starting over, and starting over in style, with serious scale. No more shuffling around trying to wheedle charity out of the others. Because how had Sebastiano treated him, when they'd had to negotiate? Like a beggar, even worse, like a homeless bum. So fuck him . . .

"Fabio, would you let me take this beast out for a spin?"

The other man opened the door for him with a big grin on

his face. Danilo got in and started the engine. A terrifying roar. He gathered his nerves and put it in reverse. He barely touched the accelerator. The velocity it took off at caught him off guard. He jammed on the brakes. The Ferrari fishtailed, then did a 360. In a state of panic, Danilo tried to shift gears. The roar died out in an aggressive lurch. Danilo got out with a sheepish look on his face.

"Oh well, maybe next time, Fabio. Thanks."

"So: are you in?"

"Yes, I'm in."

"Good boy. Tomorrow we'll make it official. The boys will take you home."

Fabio took off, tires screeching. From the far end of the port the SUV approached. Inside were the two tattooed Albanians. They dropped him off outside his apartment house. The more muscle-bound of the pair handed him a package.

"With Fabio's best regards. Take it easy, that's pink Bolivian. Ninety-eight percent pure."

Danilo stretched out on the sheets he hadn't changed in days.

He snorted the first line just to get himself calmed down. The second line was to regain mental clarity. The third was so he could think. And beneath the euphoria that he'd felt at Fabio's proposal, the euphoria that had driven him to accept the offer right then and there, a soft and insinuating fear began to slither. He tried to ward it off with the fourth snort, but the fear grew in size, looming into terror, and the terror soon degenerated into paranoia. The last time he'd done something of his own volition, without checking with Sebastiano, Fabio had beaten his accountant within an inch of his life. And then who had taken care of things and set them straight? Sebastiano. Sure, of course, Sebastiano treated him like shit, but then Fabio, he too had been all kind, plying him with blandishments, and then, once he'd gotten what he wanted, had dumped him on his henchman. That's not the way friends treat friends, is it? Which meant that Fabio wasn't a friend, he was a boss. And, hold on a second . . . what if it had all been a trap?

He could just imagine Sebastiano's furious, icy expression, his imperious command, the first rule, never, in any case, break this rule: I have to be informed of everything. Of everything, you understand? Nude as he was, he hurried around locking doors and windows, and then went back to the bed, clammy with sweat, clutching his Skorpion tactical crossbow, the jewel of his weapons collection. With that masterpiece in his hands, in the past, he'd slaughtered more or less everything that could fly in the skies over Rome and the surrounding areas. If they come to get me, I'll be ready. If they come in through that door, I'll run them through with one arrow after another. He was surprised to find himself shouting: "Come on, come on, you filthy bastards, I'll tear you limb from limb!" He caught a glimpse of his reflection in a mirror.

He searched for consolation by snorting a fifth line.

His heart was racing feverishly. His nose started bleeding. He grabbed his cell phone and called Sebastiano.

# V.
## Thursday, March 19th
### *Saint's Day: St. Joseph*

Locanda dei Briganti. Evening.

L ocanda dei Briganti, in the heart of Ponte Milvio. A location renowned for an imperial battle that took place so many centuries before new life was brought to the district by Federico Moccia and his love locks, which were fastened to the bridge in great numbers. The most fashionable place in all Rome, according to the Romans. Chiara Visone sighed. She was sipping a Bellini and looking around, deeply bored. Sebastiano was shaking hands with soccer players and actors from television series. Roman-style VIPs. It wasn't Sebastiano's fault, of course not, he was doing his best. The real problem was with Rome, or, really, with Naples. Her Naples. The most refined and pretentious city in the world. The city with the most elegant men on earth. Sebastiano, dressed to the nines, in a sober dark suit and a Diane De Clercq tie, certainly put on a nice show. But Naples was quite another matter. From every point of view. To Chiara's eyes, that restaurant was little more than a hybrid between a bordello in Tirana, Albania, and a loft party for *neomelodici*, the musicians of modern Naples. Little settees and red armchairs, white walls hanging with copies of Warhol prints, large hanging lamps fastened to the ceiling with rusty chains, cement-colored resin flooring, fuchsia and black curtains. An absolute horror show. But at least, according to what Sebastiano had said, trying to reassure her, no one would be selling coke, and there were no escorts cruising the dining room. A rare respite.

Her father had explained to her once and for all, when she

was a little girl, the difference between a Gentleman and a VIP. And she had understood then and there why Gentlemen were necessarily leftists and VIPs veered right. They were on Ischia at the time, on the terrace of the family villa, with a breathtaking view of the Bay of San Montano. Her father had shown her the villa of Luchino Visconti. A Gentleman, not some ordinary VIP. And where do Gentlemen go, that is, those in search of beauty, men who are animated by an aristocratic detachment and precisely as a result of their disdainful attitude are more capable than anyone else of being in tune with the moods of the lower classes? To Ischia, certainly not Capri. There you are. The Locanda dei Briganti was the extreme Capri of a city that will never discover its own authentic, profound, unattainable Ischia. Because, all the VIPs you could ask for, but Gentlemen—aside from her, since she considered herself to belong to the category—not a one. Roman-style VIPs, no doubt about it. No matter which way you look at it, in this blessed city everything comes down to belly, tits, and glitter. Noise, excess, and boorishness. At last, Sebastiano, having finished his round of greetings, came over and sat down next to her. He was making an effort to act relaxed, but Chiara could sense some anxiousness in him. And what she was going to have to tell him wouldn't improve the situation. She told him all about her meeting the night before with Polimeni. Sebastiano furrowed his brow.

"I'd hoped it would go better. But the man has changed."

"Maybe he's just jealous, Chiara."

"I thought I could . . . guide him. More or less the way you do with Alex, but . . . "

Sebastiano abruptly changed the subject.

"What did Alex tell you about me?"

"Maybe it would be quicker to ask, what *didn't* she tell me."

"Well, she's a sweet girl, no doubt about it."

"She's suffered a great deal."

"She's a real storyteller, believe me, you can't believe half of what she says. Just for starters, her father's a lord of the realm."

"But her unhappy childhood and all the rest?"

"All made up. She can go anywhere she chooses by sheer right of inheritance. That's Alex. But she likes you. Maybe next time she'll introduce you to her longtime girlfriend."

"Ah, so she has a longtime girlfriend?"

"Another aristocrat just like her."

Chiara heaved a weary sigh.

"Well, now that we've thoroughly explored the topic of Alex and her posh little friends, is it clear to you that Polimeni might become dangerous?"

"So what are you planning to do?"

"I don't know yet, Sebastiano, I don't know. I need time. I just wonder if this isn't one of those situations where what we need to do is knock over the table."

"Which means what?"

"Trigger a crisis of confidence. Bring down Giardino. But it's a risky move."

"A lot of the time the riskiest moves are the best ones, Chiara. But let me take a stab first. I've got an idea."

A man in his early forties, tall and fair-haired, appeared at their table. Sebastiano introduced him with a tight smile on his face. The unease grew more palpable, and it wasn't just because of the conversation about Polimeni. Fabio Desideri performed a perfect hand kiss. Then he grabbed a passing waiter and ordered him to make himself available to Sebastiano and Chiara.

"And tonight you're my guests here. Don't try to argue. My mind is made up."

Sebastiano let a few moments go by, then he excused himself and went off after the proprietor of the establishment. So his anxiety had something to do with that Desideri, Chiara concluded. Another figure from the indecipherable demimonde to which her association with Sebastiano was introducing her. People like Frodo and the human refrigerator at the DP club. This Desideri was wearing a Kiton suit and a Marinella tie. A would-be Neapolitan. But his manners and his look were in open contrast with an underlying vulgarity that Chiara had immediately caught a whiff of. All things considered, she preferred Sebastiano's imperfection to the fakery of that . . . what was it they said in Rome? *Coatto!* Hoodlum. A cleaned-up hoodlum. She preferred Ischia, and Sebastiano, she told herself, polishing off that Bellini.

Sebastiano followed Fabio Desideri to his office, and shut the door behind him.

"I talked to Danilo."

"So?"

"Well, frankly, Fabio, you shouldn't have made him that offer. Am I wrong or did we have an understanding that first I was going to inform Samurai?"

"*You* had that understanding. I didn't. I do what I think's best."

"Well, maybe you shouldn't. You're doing things you think are best a little too much these days."

"And you, my golden boy, aren't Samurai."

Sebastiano came back to the table, grim-faced.

"Everything all right?" asked Chiara.

"Everything's fine."

He was a bad liar. She brushed his hand with a protective gesture.

"Can I be straight with you? This place is depressing."

"Then let's get out of here."

In his eyes, Chiara glimpsed a flicker of gratitude.

Men, frankly, are elementary animals, very easy to handle.

Fabio Desideri waited for the punk kid and his icy female companion to vanish over the horizon, then he went out the tradesman's entrance, crossed a courtyard, came to a low building, and knocked on an armored door. Bogdan opened up immediately. From inside the room came the excited voices of the esteemed guests. Bogdan escorted him into a vast room where, around an oval table, Rocco and Silvio Anacleti and the emissaries of the Mafia families of the South were eating oysters, drinking champagne, and smoking. Fabio tipped his head to one side and then started rotating it in a slight stretching movement. The time had come to lay down his ace. Upon his arrival, silence fell over the room.

"I have a proposal I hope you'll find appealing," he began, with his usual sneaky half-smile.

"Let's hear it," muttered Rocco Anacleti.

"How much is Sebastiano demanding for getting you in on the jubilee? Thirteen?"

The man sitting around the table exchanged troubled glances.

"Fourteen? Fifteen?"

More silence.

"No, say it isn't so. Sixteen?"

Rocco Anacleti nodded. His grandson Silvio nodded. Everyone nodded.

"Well, you listen to me. I say that number should drop to twelve. Sixteen's not realistic. It's strictly for pimps. And I say that all of us together, all of us together, understand me clearly, in the end, we'll get to twelve. What do you think?"

All hell broke loose. Fabio Desideri lit a cigarette and made a phone call.

DANILO MARIANI'S HOME. NIGHT OF MARCH 19TH.

The girl had a bored look on her face. Maybe we should add, a vaguely disgusted look. Danilo Mariani realized that in the last hour he hadn't looked any higher than the marble line of her tits. Her magnificent tits. As fine as her ass, Lord knows, which in its utter perfection looked like something drawn by Milo Manara. He looked at the time on the iPhone sitting on the nightstand. Three in the morning. He ran a hand over his hairy belly, patting it like the head of a dog, and looked around for the cigarettes without finding them.

"What's the matter?"

"You seriously have to ask me?" she asked, getting up off the side of the bed and heading over to the vast wall of glass panes overlooking a 180-degree view of the luxuriant darkness of Piazza delle Muse. The heart of the Parioli quarter, a green terrace above northern Rome, was a spectacular symphony of distant shadows and lights. The silhouette of Monte Mario, the curve of the Tiber. Another city. The other Rome.

"If I ask you, it's because I don't know. It seems like somebody drowned your kitten. If you want to snort another line, there ought to be some more left on the table."

"Of course, that's what I need. But don't you see what a mess you are these days? With all the coke you're doing you can't even get it up anymore."

"I was tired. Today wasn't much of a day."

"Sure, you were tired. Forget about tired. You were dead. Or actually, your little buddy down there was dead."

"Fuck off. I work all day."

"Oh, you don't even know what work is. You've never tried it."

"Well, listen to the string of horseshit this whore spews out. Listen, if you don't like it here, you can beat it. You know how many sluts I can find who'll do a better job of sucking me off than you do?"

"You make me want to puke."

So what if he gave her a good hard smack, that mouthy bitch? Danilo grabbed his tactical crossbow off the nightstand. "Oh, right, good idea," she cackled, "you might be able to hit the target using that."

"You forgot your panties," he said, setting down the weapon.

"You can keep them, as a souvenir. Use them to hang yourself, maybe."

Danilo sighed, deflated.

"I love you, you know that."

He'd said it tenderly. His declaration caught her by surprise just as she'd reached the door. She stopped for a second and smiled, touched.

"You want me to call you a taxi?" he shouted from the bedroom.

"When you think you can get it up long enough to fuck me, give me a call, darling," she said, closing the apartment door behind her as she left. And she smiled.

Alone at last. Danilo jumped to his feet and walked away from the bed, naked, crossing the room and standing aghast in front of the bathroom mirror. Fuck, his pupils were the size of cherries, and his legs were rigid as a couple of boards. He'd already snorted three quarters of Fabietto's gift pack. But at least he hadn't betrayed Sebastiano. And Sebastiano would take care of Fabietto.

As she left the elegant apartment building, the girl paid no attention to two men who crossed paths with her, courteously holding the street door open for her. The taxi had already arrived. The two men watched her leave and then slowly climbed the steps leading up to Mariani's penthouse apartment. They rapped their knuckles against the door.

Danilo dragged himself to the door, without bothering to turn on the light.

"What did you forget, my love? Or did you miss me already?"

He put on a world-weary smile, pulled open the door, and the only thing he remembered was the vicious, violent punch that smashed his lip and the taste of iron as his mouth filled up with blood.

He opened his eyes again after a period of time he couldn't calculate. Probably not long, but long enough to wake up on the set of a porn film.

He was on his knees on the bed, and they'd tied him down to the four corners of that bed, wrists and ankles bound. He had something on his head that seemed like a hood, and in short order he realized that it was the black lace panties that his girlfriend had left him as a memento. Gagging his mouth was a wet towel from the bidet, knotted at the back of his head. The scene was lit up by two big floor lamps, which the two men had fetched from the living room, dragging them over next to the bed.

"Oh-oh-oh, good morning, Signorina!"

Danilo Mariani bit hard into the towel, feeling it scratch his tongue and the top of his mouth. The guy came around in front of his face. And that's when he observed the ten letters tattooed, one on each of the fingers of both hands.

F-R-I-E-N-D-L-E-S-S.

The tattooed guy reached into a sort of fanny pack and pulled out a big vibrator. Danilo Mariani passed out again.

What awakened him again was the stabbing pain of deep

lacerations and the progressive sense of suffocation of a position he couldn't remember ever having experienced before. He now lay on one side, his ankles and wrists bound together, in the reverse-arched position of *incaprettamento*, the classic Mafia execution method. And to complete the torment, a sheet tying both wrists and ankles to his throat.

The man with the stubby hands was laughing. The other guy was taking pictures. Click. Click click. He went on taking them.

His temples were throbbing frantically, his eyes were on the verge of bursting from the skyrocketing blood pressure.

They untied him just an instant before it killed him. Or at least, that's certainly what it felt like. And as he was vomiting mucus and bile onto the mattress, the two men went into the kitchen. They came back with an ice-cold bottle of champagne. They popped the cork with all the good-natured cheer of a surprise party. They drank from the bottle, wiping their mouths with a white Comme des Garçons shirt that they'd found in the clothes closet. Then they poured the rest of the champagne over the back of his neck.

"Wake up, Signorina! And don't get used to the treatment, eh," they said in farewell.

Then they headed for the door. Except the little guy seemed to change his mind. He retraced his steps. He leaned over the bed where Danilo Mariani lay, curled up in a fetal position. He leaned close to his ear.

"Fabio doesn't like it when people talk too much. Keep it in mind."

They walked silently down the apartment house staircase. They got in their car.

The powerful-looking guy lit a cigarette.

"Send those pictures and let's get the hell out of here."

# VI.
## FRIDAY, MARCH 20TH
### *Saint's Day: St. Serapion, Bishop of Thmuis*

ANACLETI VILLA. LA QUIETE CLINIC. AFTERNOON.

C ome in, come in, Sebastia', we were expecting you, and our friends came to see us too . . . "

It's just like one of those stupid jokes, thought Sebastiano, as he crossed the threshold of Villa Anacleti at La Romanina: So there's a Calabrian, a Sicilian, and a Neapolitan . . . They were all there, the Calabrian, the Sicilian, and the Neapolitan. The whole crew, no one missing. And yet, he'd given very specific instructions to the Anacletis. This was supposed to be a private conversation. Rocco, the patriarch, had instead done just as he pleased. It was a clear signal, the umpteenth one. Samurai had been too indulgent with these miserable wretches. Or perhaps it was he who'd been too lenient.

"A little raki, Sebastia'?"

"Later, later."

"Some Vecchio Amaro del Capo? A Coca-Cola?"

"I said later."

They were all sitting on a circular sofa from the Seventies, the fruit of who knows what prehistoric extortion practiced by the family. Rocco, the patriarch, at the center, next to him Silvio, the smartest grandson, not even grazed by the legal tempest that had dismantled the ancient group. Yes, too much generosity. Perri and Viglione, temporarily guests of the Italian prison system, had been replaced by a couple of retreads. Sebastiano distractedly memorized their names. Calabrian and Neapolitan is more than enough, when you're nobodies. And those two were nobodies. As for the Sicilian, well . . . A middle-aged country cutthroat, wispy white hair, and sideburns from the wrong decade. He looked like he'd walked out of a gangster B movie, the ones from the old days. The Mafia, running short on young recruits, was calling its reservists for duty.

"Well, Sebastia'?"

He took all the time he needed, doing nothing but staring at them each with a contemptuous smile. To establish the distances, emphasize the pecking order. Then he pulled out his iPhone, swiped through his pictures until he came to the torture scenes of Danilo Mariani. He enlarged the picture of the builder bound hand and foot in the self-strangulation of the *incaprettamento* and then handed the device to Rocco Anacleti.

"This is what Fabio Desideri did to one of our men. Hand it around, please, Rocco."

Rocco did as requested. Everyone looked and nodded their heads. No one seemed a bit impressed or surprised. When the iPhone was restored to him, Sebastiano went on with what he had to say.

"I have to ask myself how such a thing could have happened," he said, enunciating his words clearly and slowly, looking Rocco right in the eye. "And yet, I'm pretty sure that the instructions I issued were quite clear. You were supposed to keep an eye on Danilo. And instead . . . "

Silvio Anacleti burst out indignantly.

"Well in fact, we kept an eye, we kept a close eye, Sebastia'. And until you finally busted Fabio's balls one time too many, nothing went wrong."

Sebastiano stiffened. That was an open challenge, or if it wasn't, it was damned close.

"Explain what you mean."

"Huh, what's to explain? He asked you for something and you insulted him to his face. So he just reacted."

"And if you ask me," chimed in Rocco, who now had Silvio's back, "that dickhead Danilo asked for it."

"And you all agree?"

Sebastiano stared at the Calabrian, the Sicilian, and the Neapolitan. They kept their eyes downcast. They said nothing.

"So you think we should just let it go. Or even better, let's decide which of us will go to beg his pardon, ask Fabietto's forgiveness. You, Rocco? Or how about you, Silvio, since you've got such a nice running patter?"

The Calabrian cleared his throat.

"So what do you want, a gang war?"

"What do *you* want, for us to wake up one morning and here's some guy strutting around, lording it over us in our own backyard?"

"Sebastia', let's be clear about this: Fabio isn't just some guy. He's a guy who's growing, and fast, he's good at spinning money, and right now, the way things are . . . "

"The way things are?"

"We can use him."

"I'll decide who we can use."

"Bullshit," erupted the Sicilian.

That was the signal they'd been waiting for. The lid had come off. Excited voices as they all talked over each other, finger-pointing, beads of sweat pearling up on brows furrowed by deep creases, ponderous accents, white-hot accusations.

"Easy for you to talk, now that you're playing footsie with politicians!"

"Since Samurai's been behind bars, you've forgotten what the street is even about!"

"You want to start a war, but with what army?"

"You seem like the guy who shoulders his rifle and sets out on a charge, come on, men, follow me, and then he turns around and looks around, and he's all alone in the middle of the field!"

"If it keeps up like this, they're going to be sending UN peacekeepers to Ostia. The bulldozers are back on the beaches."

"Samurai's behind bars, and times have changed."

"War isn't good for anyone!"

"Samurai always used to say the same thing: war isn't good for anyone!"

"Let's give him the security on the construction sites, let's give him some of the cash for the jubilee, after all, what does it really matter to those asshole friends of yours, the builders? They still have to kick in the cash. Let's just sign a pact, and at least that way, we're all working, and nobody gets hurt."

"Yeah, let's make this damned pact once and for all. And let's make it the right way, good and proper," the Calabrian hissed softly, putting an end to the uproar.

They'd finally fessed up. Samurai was demanding too much. Fabio had guaranteed to bring the percentage down to twelve, and they were all in agreement. In a word, Fabietto had bought them off. And they had been much less loyal, or perhaps less naïve, than poor old Danilo. Who had paid for all their sins. And Rocco and his men were living in a fool's paradise if they thought for one second that someone like Fabio Desideri was going to settle for the crumbs from their table. Sebastiano put on the mask of the wise gang lord and smiled.

"You have a point, I hadn't considered all the different angles on this thing."

Glances of satisfaction went round the table. At last, the kid was getting his head on straight. Here he was, Samurai's unworthy heir, returning to the fold. Sebastiano understood, once again, that there was a gulf that could never be bridged between him and those people. They didn't belong to the same breed, and they never would. There would be no occasion on which they wouldn't inevitably make him pay for his roots, so different from theirs.

He only had one weapon to turn the situation around. Sheer ferocity. So ferocity was what he was going to use to play this game.

"We'll make a pact. Fabio will be forgiven. He'll join in on Danilo's construction site and the percentages will drop to twelve percent. That's what you want, right? You'll hear back from me in the next few days."

They hastened to agree. Then they drank a toast, rigorously multiethnic: raki for the gypsies, Vecchio Amaro del Capo for the Calabrian, whisky for the Neapolitan and the Sicilian. This little UN security council for cutthroats, thought Sebastiano. The meeting ended with handshakes and backslaps. Samurai would have approved. Ferocity. The maximum possible ferocity.

He told his driver to take him to La Quiete, the clinic in Grottaferrata where Danilo Mariani was licking his wounds. He found him in a dressing gown, ass in the air, a wreck, puffy with rage and thirst for vendetta.

"We're working on a deal. But we have a problem. The companies that can't be brought into the deal will have to be excluded. You're on that list."

"Me? What the fuck are you talking about?"

"You've made mistakes, Danilo, and you know it. And right now, we can't afford to make any more."

"Then what am I supposed to do?"

"All I ask is for you get yourself straight again, and to get some rest and take things easy. Think you can do that?"

"Don't worry, Sebastia'! But that piece of shit Fabio."

"I'll take care of him. You just try not to pull any more boneheaded moves."

# VII.
## MONDAY, MARCH 23RD
### *Saint's Day: St. Walter of Pontoise*

OLGIATA GOLF CLUB. MORNING.

N arcissist that he was, Setola had chosen the western eighteen. Eighteen championship holes. And he hadn't had time to choose the club from his golf bag before he started up with his gobbledygook. To Sebastiano's ear, it was little more than a succession of sounds, an indigestible and vainglorious cavalcade of phrases from English golfspeak, made up of memories from epic games that had never been played and poorly digested fragments from the specialty press.

"I don't know if I ever told you about that year at the Alps Tour in Zurich when . . . Well, Rodman had a great backswing, and I remember his face when I notched that birdie. I was sure it was going to be a bogey but instead . . . "

Sebastiano wasn't exactly in the mood for this, but he knew that this round of torture was necessary before they could get to the heart of the matter. Setola loved golf like all the nouveau riche latecomers of his ilk in Rome. And already, that alone would be enough to make Sebastiano hate that morning on the greens at Olgiata, the enclave for VIPs along the Via Cassia, just north of the city. One of those places where what counted most was going there to make sure you're seen. Most of all, though, the source of that hatred, once again, was the memory of his father. He used to play, too. He too had forced Sebastiano to play when he was a boy, and he'd dreamed of his son turning professional one day. Not one of his father's dreams had come true.

"So, Sebastiano, like I was telling you, the game goes on, and guess what I come up with?"

"What do you come up with?"

"A nice fat chip shot."

"Don't tell me."

"No, for real. The only way to attack that dogleg is to try to end it with a draw."

Setola was, of course, a terrible golfer, and the boredom and half-hearted nature of his shots was in keeping with the relentless chitchat that accompanied them. At the fifth hole, Sebastiano decided to call an end to it.

"Have you talked with Samurai about that matter with Fabio Desideri?"

"Yes."

"Well?"

Setola turned cautious, his voice dropping to little more than a whisper.

"You know that Samurai is against street wars. He always has been."

"Fabio challenged me, my friend. And he did it because Samurai's in the big hotel and Fabio thinks that I'm a weakling. I have to fight back."

Setola sensed in Sebastiano's words a dangerous quivering of rage. But as was so often the case, his narcissism kept him from halting short of the brink of disaster. He recovered his ball from the bottom of the sixth hole and, as he bent over, without bothering to look up at Sebastiano, he continued.

"He says you need to sit down at a table with Fabio and come to an agreement."

"Fabio isn't looking for any kind of agreement. Fabio just wants to eat everything up, have it all for himself. That's not hard to see."

"Well, Samurai says that . . . "

"That's enough! I've had it with this fucking Samurai!"

The fury with which Sebastiano had uttered those words froze Setola to the spot. And he immediately went all mellifluous.

"Forgive me, Sebastiano, I only meant to say . . . "

"What exactly *did* you mean to say, huh? *Samurai* says, and *Samurai* thinks, and if *Samurai* were in your shoes he'd . . . . I'm sick and fucking tired of it. I'm not Samurai. I'm Sebastiano. And, until shown otherwise, I believe that I'm the one who's out here in the streets. His money, his respect, his name all depend on me. And on me alone. I didn't lose my father to have him replaced with another father who I didn't choose and who, for that matter, didn't even have the courage to bring me into the world in the first place."

"Or to leave you an orphan, either."

Setola cursed himself at the exact instant that his last syllable reached Sebastiano with all the violence of a stabbing knife thrust. But it was too late to summon those words back. Sebastiano stared at him with an unnatural glare. He grabbed the golf club he'd been holding with both hands. He raised it over his shoulder, charging it with all the strength and fury he had in his body. With a shout, he unleashed the golf club, swinging it straight at Setola's skull, bringing the murderous implement to a halt scant inches from the lawyer's left eye.

The lawyer took a step back, pushing both arms straight out in front of him, as if trying to put some extra distance between him and Sebastian. Who shot him an evil grin. And pulled the club back over his shoulder again. This time with both arms straight, the club swinging in a rocking pendulum behind his head. This swing lurched straight out at the lawyer's left wrist. And just like the first time, it came to a halt just an inch from the target. Which was now the Rolex, Setola's pride and joy.

"At the very least, I ought to shatter your wrist. If I spare you, it's strictly out of respect for Mr. Rolex."

Setola thought he could glimpse in Sebastiano's words a

glimmer of peace that he ought to try to capitalize on. Immediately.

"Sebastiano, please forgive me. I didn't . . . didn't . . . "

"Stop whining."

"Listen, Sebastiano, Samurai says that Fabio has an army, and you don't. What do you have right now that you can call your own, aside from the power of money?"

"But money is everything. I'm surprised that Samurai could forget such a basic law of power. Money will give me the army I need."

"He told me one more thing."

"What's that?"

"Swear you won't get mad. These are his words."

"I'm not going to get mad."

"He said that if you're going to fight a war, you have to take your gloves off."

Sebastiano sank into a silence that Setola wisely avoided interrupting. That morning, he'd already been reprieved once. He accompanied what remained of that golf game with only essential waves of his head and club. Now to point the way to the next hole. Now to comment on the score.

Sebastiano was thinking. Samurai doubted his military abilities. There could be no other explanation. Prison couldn't have conditioned him to the point of falling for promises of peace from someone like Fabio Desideri. Samurai doubted he was up to the job and reserved the right to postpone the war to a more favorable moment. When he was back out on the street. But this is my war, too, Samurai. This is my war most of all.

At the last hole, Setola started fooling around, trying first one position and then another, and then the first again. He gripped the iron and loosened his grip, visibly a prisoner of a sudden anxiety that betrayed, once again, his remarkable mediocrity at that game. A sort of bewitched tarantella that so unnerved Sebastiano that he finally just grabbed the club out of Setola's hand. He twisted in a magnificent swing. The ball sailed high in a perfect curve, as if designed by a protractor. Ace.

Sebastiano handed the club back to Setola and smiled.

"You see? You just won."

Setola smiled hesitantly. He cleared his throat with an angry but brief fit of coughing.

"So, what should I tell Samurai?"

"That he should reread his copy of Nietzsche's *Collected Writings on Wagner*."

Setola stared at him, flummoxed.

PIAZZA TESTACCIO. AFTERNOON.

For an afternoon of sheer glory, you need a lot of things. Or just a few, depending on your point of view. The fact remains that in that piazza, for Martin Giardino, all those things were finally there. Aligned, like the stars. Yes, this was his day. For that matter, how many times had they whistled at him in derision, there in Testaccio, as he raced away on his bicycle during his furtive inspections of the never-ending construction site for the renovation of the old market piazza? How many times had he been chased by those howls of scorn that some guy, short and getting along in years, regularly unleashed on him every time he saw him go by, cupping his hands to make sure the sound was amplified and no one in the quarter—seriously, no one at all—could claim not to have heard it?

"Geeeerman. Hey Geeeerman. Geeeerman, make us laugh!"

And now, on a magnificent sunny afternoon, yes, the people of Testaccio were laughing. Laughing hard. The piazza was being given back to the quarter. Restored to spaces that were lost in the memories of the old people. What's more, the Fountain of the Amphoras was triumphantly back in the place it belonged, after a decades-long exile on Piazza dell'Emporio, facing the Kremlin, where it had wilted for more than half a century, transformed into a traffic median. The fountain was a symbol of the origins of Testaccio. The Monte dei Cocci, literally mountain of shards, built with the rubble of broken crockery that imperial Rome unloaded from ships at the nearby River Port.

From the stage for the speeches erected on the short side of the piazza, facing which a crowd had gathered, Giardino was observing the party, greatly pleased. Like in a gigantic mirror. He looked down at the people of Testaccio, the *testaccini*, and thought to himself. About how suddenly the wheel of his popularity had turned in just one short week. The announcement of the extraordinary jubilee and now his reconciliation with one of the "reddest" quarters in the city. He'd never felt so powerful before. He was bobbing in a state of grace that, for once, didn't reduce him to the caricature that his enemies and, even more, his friends in his own party had made of him. So this was the moment to enjoy that force and power. But it was also the moment to dare, to run a risk. He'd made up his mind. He was going to give the city his announcement that he'd chosen Adriano Polimeni as his extraordinary delegate for the jubilee.

At the foot of the stage, Temistocle Malgradi observed Giardino as he preened in his joy like a peacock. Old political slut that he was, Malgradi was hardly surprised. All the same, knowing something about life and therefore about human vanity, he was still convinced that the Polimeni matter could be resolved. He'd explained it to Sebastiano in clear and definitive terms, and he expected him to report it back to that babe he was screwing, Chiara Visone.

"I'll take care of this Polimeni."

All he needed to do was let Giardino puff up like a toad and then he himself would transform Polimeni into one of those statues up on the Janiculum Hill that were only good for pigeons to shit on. Polimeni wasn't the first and wouldn't be the last extraordinary delegate in the history of the Eternal City. And just like the first one and all those that had followed in the first one's footsteps, he wouldn't count at all—nothing is what he'd matter. He knew how to tame the German. So he climbed the few steps up to the stage and, as a giant screen played images of the restoration of the Fountain of the Amphoras for the piazza full of people, he took the mayor aside.

"What a show, Martin!"

"Yeah."

"You deserve it."

"You think?"

"Yes, absolutely."

"In fact, I think I deserve it too."

"Now you ought to cash in on it."

"That's exactly what I mean to do."

"With the city at your feet, you can do just as you please with the jubilee."

"That's right."

"The important thing is not to lose control."

"Or never have it in the first place."

What the fuck kind of line was that? Malgradi glowered.

"I don't understand, Martin, excuse me. What do you mean by saying that the important thing is never to have control in the first place?"

"A good politician doesn't sit down to draw up public works contracts. A good politician traces the general outlines. And then separates his responsibilities from the bigger picture of execution."

"Excuse me, I don't know if I agree entirely."

"There's no need for you to agree or disagree."

What the fuck had this asshole gotten into his head? Look out now, I wouldn't want the German to get the idea that he was actually the mayor.

"I really have to insist on this point, Martin. I believe that, even though Polimeni is no doubt an excellent choice, you ought to . . . "

Giardino interrupted him. The documentary about the

restoration of the fountain was over. He walked over to the microphone to address the piazza.

"My dear friends of Testaccio, just a few words before I leave you to enjoy what is yours by right . . . "

Just a few words. Sure. Giardino started talking and it felt like he was never going to stop.

A buzz of voices arose and from the opposite side of the piazza, an old woman confined to an electric wheelchair began to manifest signs of particular intolerance. She had a copy of *Il Corriere dello Sport* in her lap and she was chain-smoking like a chimney, one cigarette after another. Behind her, a woman who could easily have been taken for her sister was every bit as itchy. She kept her forearms resting on the handles of the wheelchair, as if resting up from some deep ancestral weariness.

Neither of them was just any ordinary woman. Word had it that this was the mother and the sister of Libano. The bandit who, until he wound up facedown in a pool of blood in front of the bar where the tough guys of the period gathered, had been the last king of Rome. No one knew whether those two *lumpen* matrons really were his last surviving kin, but one thing was clear about how things worked in Rome: between a mediocre reality and a venerable legend, it's always the legend that prevails.

"Can you just imagine with a clown like this one what a ruckus Libano would have kicked up? Just take a look at what we've come to. Now we're supposed to say thank you to these filthy pigs," said the old woman as she chain-smoked, in a voice they could probably hear over on Via Marmorata.

The sister couldn't believe her ears.

"What did you say his name was, that jerk who's talking right now, the mayor, whosis?"

"I don't know. The German . . . I think."

"But that's not his real name, is it?"

"Why, you think our Libano was really named Libano?"

"But when are they going to let Samurai out of jail?"

"No idea. I think they might have thrown away the key."

"Yeah, they threw it away . . . "

"But what does it matter anyway? Don't you see that around here there's not even a whiff of real, old-time *testaccini*, the people of this quarter?"

"Yeah, they're all actors, movie directors, newspapermen."

"That's right. Every one of them people who ought to erect a monument to Libano. Forget about this fountain. 'Cause without him, what kind of story would they have told?"

At last, after twenty minutes of jacking off about the restorations and the first discontented shouts from the audience: "Hey German, give it a rest!" but especially the first wisecracks: "Hey, now that we have the piazza back, give us back the Testaccio Stadium!" Giardino got to the point.

" . . . And so, my dear friends, I won't steal any more of your time. The experience of this piazza, restored today to its people, leads me to say that this city is finally ready to take back its own self-government. It has all the qualifications to do so. Enough with public works contracts assigned on an exceptional basis. Enough with claques and influence mongers."

The old woman in the wheelchair lit her umpteenth cigarette off the stub of the one before.

"What is this, some kind of a joke?"

Giardino took a well-timed pause.

"Now, I'd like to announce to you all and to the city at large that I've chosen as the single responsible official for the public works of the jubilee a man above all and any suspicion: the former senator Adriano Polimeni. A citizen of this neighborhood. One of *you*. And therefore, one of *us*! Together, we shall give due and serious consideration to the extraordinary nature of this occasion, which will turn the eyes of the world toward us. And we shall do so with the only weapon that an open and democratic city like Rome, our magnificent city, possesses: the transparency of good government and respectable people."

For the old woman, enough was finally too much.

"Get out of here, go on . . . Put this wheelchair in gear and let's get out of here."

Malgradi was furious. He was sweating like a pig. He confronted Giardino the minute he stepped down off the stage.

"Martin, why didn't you just say that you would have the last word on public works projects for the jubilee? You're making a very grave political error."

"Because that's not what I've decided to do. And, like I already told you, for once I'm not in agreement with you. And what's more, it doesn't matter whether or not you're in agreement with me."

"So what are you saying?"

"I'm saying that, from now on, if you have anything to say about the jubilee, talk to Polimeni."

Malgradi flickered a slimy smile at him, which barely concealed the underlying hatred. You're a dead man, he thought to himself. You're washed up as mayor. He walked away toward Via Galvani as he dialed Sebastiano's number.

La Casa di Vicky Clinic. Evening.

Two black men, tall, strong, strapping, and mean, were standing in the parking lot of Temistocle Malgradi's clinic. They seemed to be waiting for someone. Sebastiano brushed past them, glancing at them as he passed. Two genuine bastards, that was clear. Dealers, or more likely, pimps. From the main building came an excited buzz of voices. Sebastiano went in, nodding hello to the uniformed security guard. The man in the guard booth pointed to the little knot of people standing at the center of the atrium. Two volunteers, a young man and woman, and a young black woman who was in tears. Sebastiano went over to them and briefly questioned one of the two volunteers.

"She doesn't want to leave. She's afraid because her pimps have tracked her down, and they've let her know that if she doesn't come with them now, sooner or later they're going to catch her and then they'll cut her into tiny bits."

Sebastiano stared at the girl. Her tear-streaked, acne-ravaged face summoned up no form of pleasure he could think of. But that didn't matter to the pimps. No one is happy to give up their own capital assets.

"So you want to stay here?" he asked.

The girl nodded her head.

"Wait here five minutes."

He went back into the street. The pimps were still waiting. They were smoking cigarettes and exchanging phrases in their guttural pidgin English. Sebastiano's driver was standing next to the Audi, parked at the center of the square. He summoned him with a jerk of the head. As the drive was coming over, he thought back to one of Samurai's many lessons. In the world of crime, as in the normal world, there exists a well established pecking order, a food chain. Down at the very bottom of that order are the child molesters and the rapists. For them, no pity to be shown. Just one rung up, pimps. You can do business with them, but by their very nature they aren't trustworthy. Cannon fodder. When you teach a pimp a lesson, Samurai had explained to him, you're certainly not doing it out of a sense of mercy. It's strictly out of a sense of aesthetics.

"What is it, Sebastia'?" asked his driver.

Sebastiano pointed at the two black guys. Furio nodded and extracted his handgun. They took up a stance, face-to-face with the Nigerians. Sebastiano pointed at the gun, which Furio seemed to handle with lazy carelessness.

"The girl isn't coming with you.

"Says who?" reacted one of the men, the most arrogant one.

"Says this," Sebastiano explained, turning around to point at the gun again, "this and Samurai. You know who I'm talking about."

The Nigerians exchanged a few hurried words and, with a glare of hatred and a shrug of the shoulders, they turned and left. Furio made certain that they were gone, then headed back to the Audi, muttering something under his breath.

Sebastiano could have read his mind. Why go to all this trouble for a black whore? Samurai wouldn't have done it, it was none of their business and, above all, there was nothing to be earned from it. But then he wasn't Samurai.

He went back into the clinic. He told the girl and the volunteers that the matter had been taken care of. He strode on, ignoring the outburst of tears and astonishment, and slipped into Malgradi's office. Temistocle was frantically typing at his computer. He broke off with a broad smile.

"Ah, Sebastia', thanks for coming. I'm getting a little package ready for that asshole Martin Giardino."

"Have you talked to him, at least?"

"No, it won't do any good. He's obsessed with Polimeni. He's given him full powers. Full powers, you understand? He told me that I—you understand, even me—have to talk to Polimeni and nobody else if it's anything to do with the jubilee . . . *Madonna santissima* . . . "

"Explain what you've got in mind."

"I'm going to blow him right out of that office. Martin Giardino is done for. No more than a week and his coalition will collapse, and then he can go back to studying algebra with all those fucking Germans just like him."

"How are you going to do it?"

"I have my ways."

"And then?"

"And then we'll run a primary against him and we'll kick his ass."

"You?"

"Yeah, me. What, don't you believe it? Me and your friend Chiara Visone. You get what a ticket that would be?"

Sebastiano nodded.

"Go ahead. But make sure you don't make any missteps. This is a delicate maneuver. We only get one shot at it, and it better be a good one."

And he turned on his heel and left, giving the man no time to reply.

GALLERIA ALBERTO SORDI. NIGHT.

C hiara emerged from the front entrance of Montecitorio, home to Italy's parliament, a little after midnight. Exhausted but happy, she announced to Sebastiano, who was waiting for her outside the Galleria Alberto Sordi, busily tapping on his iPhone, that she'd managed to get a vote on the wiretapping and surveillance law onto the agenda.

"And so, specifically?" he inquired.

"Prohibition on the publication of content obtained through wiretapping and surveillance until actual indictment, nothing more than a summary in preemptive detention warrants. Narrow interpretation on the use in drafting the sentence on the part of the judge, and absolutely discarded as evidence if the wiretapping and surveillance is conducted outside of the legal guidelines. Limitations on the use of conversations overheard in other investigations. Terrorism, of course, falls outside of these restrictions, you can't expect any different."

Samurai was right. When they make their minds up, these people on the left are good at tying things up with a bow on them. Sebastiano brought her quickly up-to-date on the situation. Chiara bowed her head.

"I would have preferred a different solution, but if it's got to be done, let's do it."

She seemed sorry. Hypocrisy? Or authentic regret? There was still something that bound her to Polimeni, something so deep that it sowed in her a degree of uncertainty—she who was usually so decisive.

Later on, after sex, he caught her busily tapping away at her iPhone.

"Secret messages?"

"Public photographs. Just look."

She handed him her smartphone. Images of young people, Asian and northern European, with expensive purses, high-performance cars, against backgrounds of exclusive hotels and dreamy locations. A procession of young oafs and slutty girls, arrogantly proud of their nothingness.

"What the hell's that?"

"*Rich Kids of Instagram.* Some fashionable bullshit. Young billionaires who are determined to inform the world how rich they are, and who can afford things that ordinary mortals can't even dream of."

"And you like it?"

"I love it."

As sleep carried him off, a thought caught him off guard. It had something to do with Chiara's naïve infatuation with the gilded world of rich idiots. A harmless dream. The fact that she could indulge that whim. His dreams had all been stolen from him. He wanted them back. Was Chiara that opportunity? His one great opportunity for . . . he didn't even know how to describe the confused tangle of sentiments that for the past few days had been stirring him inwardly. Or maybe he knew all too well. And he was afraid of it.

Change. Change your life, Sebastiano.

TOR SAPIENZA. NIGHT.

The VW Golf was sailing along on the deserted beltway, heading east, and Beagle Boy was deep in a silence charged with tension. Wagner turned to look in the back seat and rummaged around in a duffel bag, from which he pulled a pair of black jeans, a dark blue sweatshirt with a large logo on the chest—"Italia"—a pair of sneakers, a khaki field jacket with the German flag stitched onto the right sleeve, a ski mask, a set of brass knuckles, and a switchblade knife. His uniform, his identity.

They left the Beltway near the Via Collatina, and that's where they started to see the lights of Tor Sapienza. Wagner turned on the stereo. *The Flight of the Valkyries* filled the car. It was this piece of music that had earned him his nickname. In the world of the kids of Casal del Marmo—a place you wouldn't send a dog, in short—at a certain point the fashion of Nazis had exploded. And there were those who took the name Kappler, others Priebke, and two brothers had chosen to share a name, one of them Kessel and the other one Ring, because the name Kesselring taken all together was too difficult to pronounce, and after all they were twins, and they always shared everything, and they didn't feel like arguing. To Luca Neto—this was Wagner's real name—that music had exploded in his ears one time when he'd hooked up with a tough little chick from the rich part of town. Softened up good and proper by a joint, the girl had let him fuck her on the good sofa in the living room, while in the background the whole time this para-parapara-para-parapara was going at full volume . . . Maybe it was just because of the memory, or else because the composer was a Kraut, anyway Wagner was the nickname that stuck to him. And Luca had grown fond of it. Because you can say what you want, that was music that lights a fire in your veins. And that's why, every time, before they went out on a job, he'd listen to it ten, or twenty times, if that was needed. To pump himself up proper.

Wagner smiled. The day he'd tossed his first Molotov cocktail at the façade of a residential apartment house for immigrants, he'd read on Wikipedia that that little subdivision had been founded in the 1920s by an anti-Fascist railway worker from Molise. Just think of that! Deep down, the kids who'd been carrying out those attacks in the quarter, what were they asking? Give the subdivision back to the Italians, right? And what else could that anti-Fascist railway worker have been thinking a hundred years ago when he'd founded his Cooperativa Tor Sapienza dell'Agro Romano? Land for his people, right? And so? Where was the problem?

Fascists, they called them. What do you mean, Fascists? Just because of a few straight-armed salutes? Just because they were disgusted by gypsies, Arabs, and negroes? Because their attacks were reminiscent of the Nazi-Fascist *squadrismo*, as the elite newscasters put it on TV, wrinkling their noses like there was a bad smell in the room, even though I bet they wouldn't be too happy about having a thieving gypsy and a mangy negro for their neighbors, wherever they lived? Why, those punks who followed him around didn't even know what Fascism was. And frankly, truth be told, he'd never even given a damn about swastikas and lictor's staffs.

He was there for more concrete reasons. Much more concrete.

Cleansing the town of *zammammeri*, as Roman slang was for foreigners, was good business; it could make you rich.

Exactly the same as giving them a place to stay. "Millions of euros you can make. More than with narcotics," was the way a guy he knew, a friend of Samurai's had explained it to him. What is it they called that fun-house ride, anyway? SPRAR, System of Protection for those Requesting Asylum and Refugees. It was super easy. The state kicked in thirty-five euros a day per *zammammero*. Which meant if you count a thousand negroes and Arabs—and that's what Rome was paying for—it meant 35,000 shekels a day. You multiply that by twelve months a year and you get more than twelve million euros. You got that, yeah? Twelve million. Which meant there was plenty for everyone.

One night, at a table at Bounty, a beer hall over near Piazza Vittorio, Samurai's friend had jotted down a few calculations on a placemat.

The high muck-a-muck in City Hall who decided where and how many *zammammeri* to allocate got fifty cents a day per skull.

The builder who threw up the apartment houses—buildings that with the crisis he couldn't sell to save his life—got 2 percent of the total annual turnover.

The Welcome Cooperatives, both left-wing and right, since both sides were always in cahoots, social cooperatives they called them—and I just have to laugh at the thought—gobbled up all the rest.

Or rather, the rest except for the part that was due to him. To Wagner. Because in order to drive the market up, you needed to create a little frothiness, didn't you? And how could you tell the state to cough up another two or three euros a day per negro? There had to be unrest. The people in the *borgatas* had to be pissed off. You had to be able to say that "the migrants"—you tell me what a fucked-up term to come up with—needed to be moved from east to west. And then from west to south. And after that, from south to north. And all the while the fee was rising. Like in Monopoly. Bare land, then one house, two houses, three houses, and hotels. By deploying one variant, in fact.

Him. Wagner and his boys.

Is there trouble in Tor Sapienza now? He'd show up. A week out of hell, the newspaper writing about it every day, women in the street screaming, the mayor making promises. Then off to some other part of town. Infernetto, maybe. And the meter's running the whole time.

Then is Infernetto played out? Wagner to the rescue! And off he goes to Tre Teste . . .

For those jobs, turnkey, no muss no fuss, he earned ten thousand euros an evening. Nice pay, no? With one more advantage. In Rome, these days, when people heard his name, they bowed and scraped. Wagner the Defender of the *Borgate*. Wagner the Son of the People.

Of course, Beagle Boy and those other runaways who followed him everywhere knew nothing about it. But business isn't for everyone. All those guys cared about was that they got to snort a line for free every so often. They did it out of boredom and anger. And if they were happy, everyone was happy.

When the VW Golf screeched to a halt on Via Morandi, the games had just begun. The street was illuminated and the air made unbreathable by the pestilential fire from a row of dumpsters in flames. Wagner lowered his ski mask, made sure his blade was securely shoved down in the back pocket of his jeans, made sure both pairs of brass knuckles were snug on his fingers, and took his position at the head of a furious mob that was bombarding with rocks and metal bars the thin line standing guard in front of a three-story apartment building.

Wagner saw a couple of young Maghrebi men trying to sneak out the back way. He shouted with all the oxygen in his lungs.

"Pieces of shit! Pieces of *shiiiiiiiiiiiiiiiiiiit*!"

He started running as hard as he could while the two miserable wretches tripped over the low fence around what must once have been a public park. Reaching the first of the two of them was a matter of seconds. He floored him and then creased his face against the ruins of a park bench.

The little negro was sobbing. He was sobbing and he stank. He reeked of sweat and fear. With his left hand Wagner twisted his neck around, so that the piece of shit could see his right fist raised high in the split second before it came crashing down.

"You need to get the hell out of here. You're not fucking welcome. Do you get that, asshole?"

He smashed down on the poor kid's jaw. Once, twice, three times. Until his knuckle-duster encountered no more resistance.

At dawn, he returned home to the two-bedroom apartment he'd renovated with his own hands in Mandrione. A good point of departure for his bright future life. He turned on his cell phone. There was a message, from an unknown sender. Wagner read it and realized that this was an appointment he couldn't miss.

# VIII.
## TUESDAY, MARCH 24TH
### *Saint's Day: St. Catherine of Sweden*

PRATI QUARTER. PUB AR MURETTO. EVENING.

Piazza Cavour. Pub Ar Muretto. At 11 PM." Sebastiano showed up twenty minutes late. Not too late, just late enough. The place was packed. Prati had become a new destination for Rome's *movida*, very different from the respectable, quiet neighborhood, inhabited by the successful bourgeoisie, fierce and solitary, where the human comedy of his adolescence had played out. A patch of the city that was historically philo-Fascist but which little by little had been converted to progressivism. That is, if we believed that categories of the sort, in the new century, even had any meaning anymore. And, perhaps precisely because of this change, Prati attracted the occasional nostalgic die-hard: like the tough-looking kids who were conferring with Wagner, an extravaganza of forearms and napes of the neck spangled with Fascist/Celtic tattoos.

Wagner leapt to his feet, in a gesture of respect. Sebastiano extended his right hand and shook Wagner's vigorously. Looking him in the eyes, he nodded for him to take a seat.

"So, you're Wagner."

"And you're Sebastiano."

Wagner did an excellent job of concealing his nervousness, Sebastiano observed. He hadn't expected him to be so young. Even though he thought he detected a shadow in his gaze that he recognized. Life must have marked him early. And good and proper.

"Beer?" asked the boy.

"I'd rather have a malt whisky."

Sebastiano knew the proper use of silence. It was normally the first, decisive test you put to people when you're talking to them for the first time—people you don't know, in other words. It had the advantage of freeing him from small talk, and it allowed him to gauge quickly and decisively the mettle of his interlocutor, to see whether he could stand up to the pressure without flying off the handle. And from what he could tell—he noted—young Wagner emerged with flying colors. While waiting for Wagner's beer and his own whisky, which thank God arrived neat in a metal glass, the kid hadn't moved a muscle. He'd planted both elbows on the table, bracing his chin on the knuckles of the hands that clenched his forearms. And he'd stayed that way without moving for what seemed like a long, long time. Anyway, long enough to make Sebastiano decide that his first impression had been correct.

"Cheers," Sebastiano said, hoisting his whisky.

"To our meeting," Wagner replied with a smile.

Then the boy turned serious and asked Sebastiano why he'd wanted to see him.

"You and your boys are making a name for yourselves, Wagner."

The young man stiffened. Then he shot Sebastiano a suspicious glance. Ferocious eyes. With a paradoxical vein of innocence. In Rome, everyone knew that Sebastiano meant Samurai. And that's why Wagner had responded to the summons so promptly. It's not every day of the week that Sebastiano Laurenti reaches out for you. Now the young man was asking himself whether he'd committed some error, stepped on the wrong feet or kicked the wrong jaws. Sebastiano enjoyed leaving him on tenterhooks for a while. Once the young man's tension had become intolerable, he gratified him with a benevolent tone of voice.

"You're all doing great. I've been keeping my eye on you

guys for some time now. I'm very pleased. And you-know-who approves, too."

Wagner slumped back in his chair. He clenched his fists and understood that the great opportunity had arrived. And he swore that he wouldn't let it slip away. Whatever the cost.

"I know how much you earn for the filthy work you do, Wagner. And I also know that you're good at making everyone believe you are something you're not. A die-hard Nazi obsessed with negroes and Arabs."

Wagner started smiling again. Sebastiano continued.

"Now I'm going to ask you to climb down off that merry-go-round, with all your boys, and climb onto another one. Mine. I want you to be in charge of security for the construction sites for the public works for the jubilee and for the metro C line. And I don't want you to ask me why or what I have to do with the metro and the jubilee. I just want you to be aware that it's going to be a very particular security service, let's say."

"Particular . . . what's that supposed to mean?"

"You're going to work for an agency that has a legal face. By which I mean . . . You'll have access to uniforms, cars, license plates, and all that bric-a-brac that any little sheriff has. The owner is the nephew of an old Sicilian friend of Samurai's and his agency is one of the largest security agencies in Rome. They're in charge of security on both sides of the Tiber. Television stations, banks, city authorities. You and your friends will be legally hired. But your real employer will be me. You and your boy will put on your Carnival costumes and at night you'll do what I tell you to do. I'll be personally in charge. In the meantime . . . "

"Wait, let me guess: You need a quick piece of work, done right."

Sebastiano approved with a quick nod of the head.

"What's this about?"

"Fabio Desideri. You know who I'm talking about, don't you?"

Wagner was surprised.

"Fabietto? But I thought he was a solid guy, what's he done wrong?"

"He's gotten a little too big for his boots. You up to it?"

Wagner paused, then smiled.

"What's the big deal? Consider it done. But can I ask you something?"

"Certainly."

"How much is my end of this job? I mean . . . *the whole* job."

"Hallelujah! I was starting to worry that you were one of those kids who trail after their masters for the glory or, even worse, for the Idea. How much were you thinking?"

Wagner didn't know what to say.

"I don't know. A . . . hundred . . . thousand?" he tossed out.

"We can do twice that with no special effort," Sebastiano replied with a laugh.

The kid's jaw dropped. Sebastiano's smile broadened even more.

"But we could even get up to two fifty. That just depends on you."

Wagner took a deep breath. He drained his mug of beer, then slammed it noisily down on the table.

"When do I start?"

"Right away, I'd say. And one more thing. Don't call me on the phone again. Do you know Slack?"

"No."

"It's a closed digital platform for communications within a team. Messages, files, email, Skype. All stuff that the Americans may be listening in on, but not the cops here at home. I'll send you my user name. That's all."

Sebastiano got up and slapped Wagner on the back.

He hoped he hadn't been wrong about that kid.

He would be needing his army.

PRESS GUILD. CAMPI DELL'ACQUA ACETOSA. LUNCHTIME.

I t hadn't been enough to supply him with a brand-new wardrobe and assure him of a paycheck on the 27th of every month. Nor had it been enough to pluck him from the ruins of the bankruptcy of his miserable radio station FM 922 as well as from the disciplinary proceedings of the Journalists' Guild. A very serious matter that the president of the Guild—a friend—had managed to transform into a farce. Samurai was right, Spartaco Liberati was an animal and he always would be an animal. A parasite, with the nerve and the gall of those who'll give their victim one last kick once they're down. But like all parasites, very useful when what you needed was someone willing to stick their hands in the shit up to the elbows.

Now Spartaco was posing as a political journalist. Temistocle Malgradi had parked him in the newsroom of the weekly newsmagazine *Il Meridiano*, where he wrote, under strict dictation, thoughtful analyses of Roman politics. If for no other reason than that his relationship with the Italian language was still such a distant and unhappy one. And that a die-hard Fascist like Spartaco should have turned into a convinced supporter of a city coalition government led by the DP was one of those details that, after a while, no one even noticed anymore.

Naturally, A.S. Roma, his longtime passion—let's just use the phrase—hadn't stopped filling his days. Thanks to the power that accrued to him as a result of the occasional ramshackle appearance on local TV and radio stations, he continued to be able to blackmail the soccer club, or at least he tried, offering in no uncertain terms a straight barter: he'd put an end to his savage campaigns against the American ownership in exchange for a regular seat among the most illustrious fans. Until, one day, from the far side of the Atlantic Ocean, the chairman of the holding company had finally put an end to the matter. "Who is this fucking Spartaco? This asshole has finally pissed me off." In other words, let's be done with this dickhead.

And in fact, it hadn't been to talk about A.S. Roma that Temistocle Malgradi had summoned him that morning to the press club of the Acqua Acetosa sports center. A delicate matter, he had told him. Spartaco was there early and he had whiled away the time by passing in review the noteworthy asses of four "fellow journalists" playing doubles on the central tennis court. Malgradi's voice had assaulted him from behind.

"No question, these journalists don't do a fucking thing all day."

Spartaco had whipped around, throwing his arms open in a hug that Malgradi had adroitly dodged.

"Do you have it in for me, my dear Mr. Mayor?"

"Maybe. And anyway, I'm not mayor yet. Maybe soon though."

Malgradi locked arms with him and dragged him far beyond the hurricane fencing around the tennis courts. The two of them strolled along the lane that led to the outdoor restaurant.

"Do you think you can concentrate for more than five minutes?"

"Now you're hurting my feelings, Mr. Mayor."

"Then let's see whether you can surprise me for once."

He opened a file folder he was carrying and pulled out a stack of photographs, printouts of web pages, and biographical dossiers, as well as a dozen or so pages of text.

"Read this."

"Now?"

"When if not now?"

Spartaco read through to the end of the dozen pages, displaying what even Malgradi perceived to be an unusual degree of uneasiness, considering the subcortical nature of the individual. Spartaco shut the file folder, stammering as he did so.

"Damn . . . "

"So you like this piece of investigative journalism?"

Spartaco put on the expression that had made him what he was. More or less the expression of a confused dog waiting for his master's command or any other sliver of enlightenment.

"Who wrote it?"

"You did."

"*I* did?"

Malgradi burst out laughing.

"Asshole, this is the piece of investigative journalism that you're going to publish in *Il Meridiano* when I give you the go-ahead."

"I just copy and paste."

"Like always."

"But is this stuff true?"

"What does that matter?"

"I don't know, just out of curiosity. Is it really true that the mayor screwed a young girl when he was a professor? And did the priest really kill himself after meeting with the new bishop . . . because this Father Giovanni doesn't strike me as all that much of a faggot . . . "

"It's all bullshit, Spartaco. For that matter, nobody gives a damn whether the stuff you publish is true. The important thing is for it to *seem* true."

"And what if they sue?"

"The article is carefully written, but you can even add a

little flavor of your own if you want. Just be careful. In any case, we'll handle legal expenses."

"You're the best."

"Don't I know it."

They reached the restaurant. Malgradi gestured for Spartaco to take a seat at the table with the sign saying "reserved."

"Just one thing . . . "

"What are you doing now, asking questions, too? What are you, some kind of journalist?"

Spartaco didn't appreciate the joke. Maybe he hadn't even understood it.

"No, what I mean is . . . with this kind of stuff, the mayor is going to have to resign and the Vatican's going to be furious. I wouldn't want to think that . . . "

"You're not paid to think. The mayor *has* to resign. And that bishop needs to get the hell out of the way."

"Sure, of course. But aren't you all buddy-buddy with the mayor?"

"Used to be. The jubilee is coming and the party has decided that the time has come to pick a new horse. On both sides of the Tiber. Fuck Giardino and fuck Daré. Now it's my turn."

"And are Sebastiano and Samurai happy with it?"

"You know what they say in Rome? *Sta matassa è fracica, no lercia.*"

"Ah."

"You know the poet Belli . . . why, what am I telling you about this for . . . anyway: the matter isn't just serious, it's deadly serious. And when the situation is deadly serious, there's only one thing to be done: I go to the mattresses . . . understood?"

"You go where?"

"What the fuck kind of Roman are you? I go full bore, I go in fighting, I destroy my enemies. You get it now?"

"Sure, but what about Samurai and Sebastiano?"

"I'm in charge of the politics."

Spartaco, who had started scanning the menu, stopped, as if dazzled by a sudden illumination. Fine that Temistocle had started to poeticize in Roman dialect, and yes, it was true that he came from Saudi Calabria. Okay, understood, poor old Spartaco didn't count for shit. Fine, understood, he was paid to do what they told him to do. And fine, it was true that taken on his own he didn't have the gray matter of a normally endowed human being, but still, the symphony was far too clear. He was willing to bet that Sebastiano and Samurai were entirely in the dark about all this. Temistocle guessed that he hadn't been too convincing, and he unfurled a smile of the kind that are false and fraternal, all the more false the more fraternal they are.

"Listen, my good friend, do you think I'd get you involved in something bigger than the two of us? A friend like you."

"Oh good lord, no, but you know what they say."

"An ounce of prevention is worth more than a pound of cure."

"Exactly."

"Which is why you're going to write this piece of investigative journalism. Preventing is better than curing. Giardino and Daré are a metastasizing tumor, and they need to be surgically removed. Now. And the decision was made at the top, at the very tippy top."

Malgradi lifted his eyes skyward. Spartaco nodded.

"If that's the way it is."

"So then, you only need to tell me what you'll have. I'm starting to feel just a little peckish."

They chowed down on raw seafood without exchanging a single word. Malgradi left hastily, dropping two hundred euros in cash on the table, while Liberati was swallowing another in a long succession of red crayfish from Mazara del Vallo.

"One last thing, Spartaco. You need to go on a diet. You're big as a barrel."

"What are you talking about, I can still fit perfectly into the jacket from when your brother made me journalist of the year."

Spartaco grabbed a last gulp of prosecco, because God gave us these good things and it's a sin to waste them, so the Good Book tells us. "The decision was made at the top . . . " Malgra', who are you trying to kid? Forget about a shark: you strike me as one of those nice fat stupid tuna fish . . .

With a sigh, he dialed one of Sebastiano's many phone numbers.

And Sebastiano, to his immense surprise, told him it was all true.

PONTE MILVIO. LOCANDA DEI BRIGANTI. NIGHT.

Everything was ready for the night's fireworks. Sebastiano had provided the list of Fabio Desideri's clubs, indicating the first four targets. Wagner had divvied up the attack squads: the twins, Kessel and Ring, would hit Alcyone, in Fiumicino; Tigna and Pustola were assigned to the Black Crow, in Parioli; Kappler and Hippo—because of his size—had Quadrilatero, in the Portuense area. He and Beagle Boy, dressed all in black, would wait aboard the Fiat Panda that Beagle Boy had hot-wired that afternoon on Via di Portonaccio. They were waiting for the last stragglers to leave the Locanda dei Briganti. The original plan had called for them to break in at night and tear the place up. They'd changed their minds after casing the place. Too many security cameras, a security code that they'd never be able to figure out in time to deactivate it, it was too risky. He'd talked to Sebastiano on Slack, and together they'd decided to fall back on four two-bit armed robberies, as a warning. The job would need to be immediate and direct. No room for error. Beagle Boy sighed.

"How long are these assholes going to take?"

"Just be patient."

"But it's a pretty chic place, don't you think, Wagner? Fabietto knows what he's up to!"

"Sure, but he pissed on the floor instead of the toilet."

"If you say so . . . "

Beagle Boy was getting nervous. He kept talking to avoid slipping into a state of paranoia.

"I hear that this place, once, years and years ago, was one of Libano's gambling dens. And Freddo, too. And then things went the way they went, and I hear that Fabio snagged it at a judicial auction, because they say that the judge was a regular client of certain young ladies and that he liked trannies too . . . a judge, just think! When it comes to morals, we're in bad shape, don't you think, brother?"

"They're leaving, let's go."

Finally, the last noisy group of diners made up their mind to leave. Wagner and Beagle Boy armed up with two Beretta 98s with the serial number filed off, lowered their ski masks, and got out of the Fiat Panda, acting nonchalant. Beagle Boy was carrying an empty backpack slung over one shoulder. When the last echo of laughter trailed after the drunken diners and silence fell over the street, they headed in.

"Put up your hands, come on! Be good, and you won't get hurt."

The cashier, a pretty young girl, turned pale. Two waitresses threw themselves on the floor, sobbing. Beagle Boy gestured to the young woman to turn over the evening's proceeds. A sizable sum of cash wound up in the backpack. But they hadn't come in there for that handful of spare change. It was the message they were there to deliver that mattered most.

"Tell Fabietto that this is just the start," Wagner spoke the words loud and clear.

Then they turned and left, moving quickly. They had almost gotten back into the Panda, when they heard shouting behind them.

"Hey, you bastards!"

Swiveling around quickly, Wagner glimpsed the outlines of two men. The smaller of the two was swinging a long metal bar, the other guy had an axe. They lunged at Beagle Boy in an instant and smashed him with the metal bar over the forearm he was holding up in an attempt to protect his face.

Wagner whipped out the Beretta and squeezed off four shots in rapid succession. Aiming at the head. Shooting to kill. The guy with the axe flew backward like a department store mannequin. The little guy with the metal bar collapsed to his knees, and then facedown on the asphalt, with both arms and the backs of his hand splayed forward. Wagner took a few quick steps toward the corpse. He observed the tattoo that marked each of the ten fingers of the hands.

F-R-I-E-N-D-L-E-S-S.

He gestured to Beagle Boy to keep his arm pressed tight in his lap and get into the car.

"I'll drive. Get in!"

In the darkness, as they were driving up the Collina Fleming, they heard the piercing sound of sirens. Beagle Boy seemed less in pain than before.

"I think we started quite a ruckus, right?"

Wagner said nothing for a while. Then he replied, even if he was really talking to himself.

"But no one was supposed to get killed."

Still, he thought, not everything in life can be predicted. Sebastiano will understand. And maybe, most important of all, Fabio will understand. Maybe a gang war really will break out. He sure wasn't afraid of one.

Still, Wagner didn't tell Beagle Boy any of that.

Fabio Desideri understood immediately where those robberies had come from. He had to admit to himself that he'd been surprised. He never would have expected such an immediate reaction, much less such a violent one. Least of all, the killings. No question, he'd underestimated Sebastiano, and now a gang war, a real one, with ambushes and corpses, was inevitable. Fabio hadn't counted on it, but now he was ready to fight it. He had plenty of men and he'd win. There were no alternatives: they were both all in, so they were going to have to come to a grand finale. A finale that he'd write himself, putting an end to the dictatorship of Samurai and his lieutenant.

But before you write the finale, you've got to write the movie. He'd bought the Anacletis and plenty of other manpower, and in spite of that, Sebastiano had been capable of hitting four of his establishments on the same night, and with perfect precision. Shouldn't this Sebastiano be a general without a sword by now? No, what had happened meant that this kid had an army to work with. But who were these soldiers and how come he'd never heard about them? Had he let something get by him? And if so, what? He ordered his men to look into it, and he also sent a wake-up call to Silvio Anacleti, while he was at it. The gypsy showed up at the villa shortly after sunset. Fabio received him in the gym, while he tried to vent his anxiety by delivering a series of punches to the heavy bag. Silvio told him that he'd been over to Future Consulting, where he'd hoped to run into Sebastiano. Instead, he'd found a crowd of young punks who were looking very determined as they hung on the words of a very young kid, with super-black, super-short hair and earrings in both lobes. People called him Wagner, and there were two possibilities: either he was imitating Samurai, or deep down, he was a faggot. Officially, he passed himself off as a Nazi, but in reality he was the two-bit boss of a two-bit gang from Casal del Marmo that liked to go out and break the *zammammeri*'s bones for so much a pound, clear out nomad camps, the kind of thing Samurai got up to, in other words. And so did Sebastiano. Fabio thanked the gypsy for the tip.

So, now there was an army, and it looked pretty ferocious, too. Yes, he'd underestimated them. But it wasn't that serious.

"Keep looking for Sebastiano, Silvio."

"They say he's out of the country."

"Well, you keep trying to find him."

"And when I've found him?"

"You arrange for a meeting."

"Are you going to make peace?"

"What I'm planning to do is my own fucking business, Silvio."

"Oh no, that's not right, Fabiè."

"We have an understanding."

"Fabio, I love you like a brother, but hold on for a minute and listen to me: you're plenty strong, but so is Sebastiano, and don't forget who he's got behind him. And so far things have gone nice and smooth with him. Then you popped up, and you made a nice little speech, but for now it's all just talk, and we haven't seen anything concrete so far . . . "

In other words, the gypsies were sitting on the fence, far from making a commitment. Sebastiano was raising his head. Samurai was looking on and laughing. And in the meantime his two boys had ended up being carried past the long line of cypress trees. They were in the boneyard, in other words. And these guys were pretty sure the fight was over. He took the gypsy's arm and his tone of voice turned silky.

"I understand, and I can't really blame you. Take care, Silviè."

# X.

SEOUL. MARCH 25.

Adriano Polimeni landed at Incheon-Seoul International Airport at 2:20 in the afternoon local time. In his head, and what mattered more, in his body, it was 6:40 in the morning. During the fifteen-hour flight, spiced up by a frantic stopover in Paris, he hadn't been spared any of the delights that modern life reserves for economy travelers: seats built for Lilliputian infants, bad-smelling travel companions, foul food, an enforced striptease at the check-in, sprints between gates. He envied the VIPs who skipped the lines and stretched their legs in business class. Like a peeping Tom, hunched up in the first row of economy, he shot hate-filled glances between the half-open curtains separating him from business class, glaring at the fat Americans guzzling wine as they were coddled by the hostesses. He'd even rejoiced at the brutal retching of a well-dressed Japanese man. A totally shitty trip.

Only one consolation: there were those who were worse off than him. Chiara Visone and the other members of the parliamentary delegation paying a courtesy visit in the entourage of a couple of undersecretaries. Actually, a business trip that, in its intentions, at least, was supposed to persuade rich Korean entrepreneurs to invest in Italy.

For reasons of public perception and in obedience to the reigning poor-mouthing of the administration, the national-political delegation was flying economy. A brutal slap at Chiara, who had spent the entire duration of the miserable flight alternating brief slumbers with indignant silences, doing nothing to conceal her steadily worsening bad mood. "They could have given us at least economy plus. At least that." Adriano and Chiara had met in the departures lounge, at Fiumicino. She had masked her surprise behind a chilly smile.

"Are you following me, Adriano?"

"Martin Giardino got the invitation from a South Korean billionaire who wants to make a donation to the city. He got a bad case of pharyngitis so he sent me in his place. That's all."

"Should I believe you?"

"It's the truth."

In the arrival hall, Adriano found an elegant young man in a dark suit waiting for him, holding up a sign on which was written "Mr. Puly-Money." They shook hands warmly, and then Adriano followed him, while Chiara and her group trailed after another young man, a little less well dressed than his greeter had been. As they left the airport parking lot, he noticed that the Italians had been packed into a sort of bus, a jitney with with a South Korean flag on the sides. And the luxury of the Lexus that had picked him up gave him another delighted shiver of revenge. His driver was named Leo, and he spoke excellent English. He told Adriano that Mr. Gu sincerely thanked both him, Adriano, and the mayor of Rome, for having accepted the invitation, and he asked whether the senator would care to be Mr. Gu's guest tomorrow night for dinner. Out of respect for his guest, Mr. Gu thought it would be best to give him some time to get over his jet lag. Adriano thanked Leo every bit as sincerely, on his own behalf and that of his mayor, and he confirmed the dinner engagement for the next day. Then he gazed out at the landscape.

On all sides he saw hills streaming past, scattered vegetation broken by urban settlements, and groves of trees that popped up unexpectedly out of nowhere. In the distance, set against a backdrop consisting of the horizon dominated by a leaden gray sky, struggling to hold at bay any and all sunbeams, he glimpsed the skyscrapers of Seoul. Population: twenty-five million. The third greatest density of skyscrapers on earth, and Asia's fourth-largest economy, after Japan, China, and India. One of the continent's tigers. The East was on the march, he thought with an edge of concern, and old Europe was on the retreat. When we were young, we dreamed of the Red Guards. What idiots.

Leo dropped him off at the InterContinental Seoul COEX, a fabulous hotel in the heart of the Korea World Trade Center, the city's business and trade district. Leo wished him a comfortable rest, and let him know that in a few hours he'd be visited by a person whose job it would be to look after him. Adriano took possession of the suite that he'd been assigned, an apartment that was actually larger than his place in Rome, and realized that luxury no longer bothered him the way it once had. He felt a vague sense of guilt, but at last his weariness took the upper hand and he collapsed into a comatose sleep. The sound of the room phone awakened him. He grabbed the receiver. On the other end of the line, a feminine voice, young and sweet.

"Forgive me if I'm bothering you, Senator Polimeni. My name is May. Mr. Gu asked me to look after you. If you'd like, I'll be waiting for you down here in the lobby."

"Thanks. Let me just take a quick shower."

May was a young woman of exquisite, canonical beauty, if you like the Far East. Petite, dark, with short lustrous hair, large almond-shaped eyes, an elegant skirt suit, a fine piece of western prêt-à-porter. She'd studied Italian at Ca' Foscari University. She adored Venice. Polimeni, who was hungry as a wolf, plunged with her out into the night of Seoul.

While the senator and little May were exiting the hotel, Sebastiano Laurenti was entering it. The two men almost brushed shoulders, without even noticing each other. Adriano was absorbed in mirroring himself in the inscrutable smile of his chaperone, and Sebastiano was typing a text to Chiara on his iPhone. He had made up his mind to follow her to Seoul on the pretext of "business," a category that was otherwise left vague. But the truth was that he wanted and needed to be with her.

May was a courteous companion, perhaps even too courteous, verging on the ceremonious. But all that courtesy and pliability, the warmth that her body transmitted to him when she took his arm, the detailed explanations about the usages and customs of her people, the constancy with which she sought out physical contact . . . All of this only emphasized the fact that she was a paid employee of Mr. Gu. A sort of high-toned escort. She must have perceived something, because in a moment of sincerity—they were touring the Samsung museum—she explained to him, seriously, that he shouldn't expect any nasty tricks from little May.

"I'm not a flower snake girl, you can feel safe with me, Adriano."

And she told him that flower snake girls are a Seoul specialty. They're not prostitutes, but they act as if they are. They get their hooks into you and they smile, they take you out to dinner—your treat, obviously—and then the evening continues at a nightclub. The girls get you to order drinks, expensive labels, and then they let you have a kiss and maybe even a little fondling. Then, just as you're starting to rev up, the flower turns into a snake. The flower snake girl starts to shriek. Help, this swine tried to rape me! Help, help! Call the police! At this point, the nightclub's bouncers, who are in on the sting, intervene, and they give our unfortunate tourist a little talk: for what you tried to do to this poor girl, it's serious jail time, here in South Korea. And you can rest assured that Korean prison isn't like the five-star hotels you're used to back where you come from. Still, though, we're reasonable people here. We're not looking for trouble, truth be told. How much cash do you have on you? Fifty thousand won ought to be enough, it's nothing for someone like you, that's fifty euros, or fifty dollars, if you prefer, when it comes to foreign currencies we're very flexible . . . Most of the time the unsuspecting unfortunate pulls out his wallet, pays, thanks them, and goes on his way. But every so often there's a fool who decides to get obstinate. I didn't do a thing, what are you talking about. She's the one who tried to pick me up, she let me touch her, too, she practically insisted. Go ahead and call the police, I don't have anything to be afraid of. The bouncers shrug and call the police, and when the officers show up, it becomes obvious that they're in on the game. Our unfortunate tourist is arrested and thrown into jail. And sometimes he gets smacked around, if not worse.

"But that's not the way I am, Adriano. Let me say it again: You're safe with me."

Because Mr. Gu is paying, Polimeni considered. He stroked her hair and said, softly:

"Listen, May: I'm old enough to be your father."

A glint of solidarity flashed in the girl's eyes. All ambiguity vanished. They had become friends.

Mr. Gu was more or less Polimeni's age, and the young woman accompanying him was more or less May's age. She was also very similar in appearance and manners. But she didn't do the same work as May. Or, perhaps, she did it on a different level, a much higher level. She was Crystal, just Crystal, a great singer, with an exceptional voice. She was his protégé. His favorite. The apple of his eye. And for his protégé, for his favorite, for the apple of his eye, Mr. Gu demanded the best.

They were sitting at a round table in a restaurant whose name Polimeni would never be able to memorize. Mr. Gu had reserved the whole place. And an eight-piece orchestra, which Mr. Gu ordered to start playing when Crystal got up and, with studied slowness, headed over to the little stage at one end of the dining room. She sang a *romanza* from Donizetti's *Lucia di Lammermoor*. Very nice. Polimeni wasn't an expert, but the young woman did seem to possess quite a voice, well trained and, at the same time, naturally powerful.

When he came back to the table, Mr. Gu's eyes were glistening with emotion. So now they got to the point. Gu, even though he spoke highly workable English, spoke in Korean, and May translated.

Mr. Gu intends to finance a concert for Miss Crystal and he'd like the event to take place in the enchanting setting of the Basilica of Maxentius, in Rome. Mr. Gu will foot all the expenses, including the orchestra and a special section of five hundred seats for select guests from the worldwide cultural élite. Mr. Gu will underwrite the travel expenses and accommodations of all the guests. Mr. Gu will be honored if the mayor of Rome and Senator Polimeni would be so good as to inaugurate the ceremonies. Mr. Gu, aside from the expenses, is willing to underwrite a sizable donation to the magnificent city of Rome, which Mr. Gu loves like a second homeland.

Mr. Gu stared at Adriano, waiting for a reply.

The senator said that he'd need to inform the mayor. May translated. Mr. Gu nodded. The senator excused himself and stepped away from the table, pulling out his cell phone. To rent the Basilica of Maxentius so his protégé could sing there! Rome, Italy: the garden of classical Europe. The playground of capricious potentates. Of all the damned things! Is this what Italy had come to? Had politics come to this? His first temptation was to tell this fat cat to go to hell and take his corrupt whims with him. But then he calmed down. In the first place, this wasn't his decision. In the second place, politics, or, if you like, administration of the state, had also come to this:

a continual pleading and panhandling to get the damned budget to balance, the dictatorship of the economy, and to hell with it if for once a generous patron of the arts popped out of the woodwork. Martin Giardino answered on the third ring.

The pharyngitis was on the mend, and his voice was still slightly hoarse. The mayor found the offer exciting, and told Adriano that he too was working on something similar.

"How much should I ask?" Polimeni inquired.

"That's up to you," Martin Giardino exhorted him. "Go with your gut. That money is blessed oxygen for us."

Polimeni came back to the table, unfurled the smile of the consummate politico, and then improvised a polite harangue about the unusual nature of the request, the fragility of and the need to protect the artistic patrimony of a city unlike any other, a city like Rome, and then, when he was done, after a well timed pause, he named his price.

"Five hundred thousand."

Mr. Gu didn't bat an eye. He got up unhurriedly, and reached out to shake hands with Polimeni. The next day one of his men would meet with the senator at his hotel to work out the details. Mr. Gu was honored to have made his acquaintance, and happy at the way the deal had worked out. Now Mr. Gu had unavoidable commitments he would need to tend to and he was regrettably obliged to leave this very pleasurable company. And so Mr. Gu and the lovely Crystal took their leave. May laid a hand on Adriano's shoulder.

"You asked for too little. Now he's convinced he can rob you blind. I'm so sorry."

MARCH 27TH.

Sebastiano and Chiara toured Seoul in the Bentley that he'd rented, complete with chauffeur, indispensable when it came to finding one's way through the baffling traffic of the great metropolis. Chiara had had it up to here with business conferences. When push came to shove, the Koreans had proved themselves to be unrivaled in the art of negotiation, and the undersecretaries were clearly not up to the job. The sole concessions of any real worth were the ones she'd obtained, with her charm and her tenacity. Something that had greatly annoyed the undersecretaries. And in fact she had found out that an urgent meeting had been called, and she hadn't been invited to it. It had occurred to her to burst into the meeting and tell them all to go to hell, but that would have been unseemly. For that matter, when all was said and done, she alone would be returning to Rome with real, concrete results to show for her trip.

"At least for a little while I'll have you all to myself, Chiara."

She read the passion in his eyes. That young man was moving fast. She was very flattered and also a little worried.

They wandered the length and the breadth of the city. Chiara was impressed by the energy that the Koreans displayed. A continuous sense of electricity, a collective activity in no way comparable to the byzantine slowness of Italy. The future, here and now. Sebastiano pointed out to her that Seoul, like Rome, was built on seven hills and that a river ran through it.

"Rome is stuck in the past. We need to learn from these people."

"Rome is eternal."

"That's just a pat phrase."

"In any case, when we get home, there'll be a fine mess to greet us."

"Let's hope it all goes well."

"Do you still have any doubts?"

"Everything could still go sideways, Sebastiano."

"That would still be positive for us."

"I don't know, I'm not so sure."

They stopped in the heart of Gangnam, the luxurious neighborhood. Sebastiano suggested a selfie in front of the Bentley. It could be a little cameo on that *Rich Kids of Instagram* she liked so much. Chiara dismissed the idea.

"Naw. A little cameo. There's one thing about me you still haven't figured out, Sebastiano: I'm not a girl for little cameos. I'm the star of the show. Or I'm not in it."

Right before Polimeni's eyes, the Bentley went sailing past. There go another couple of almond-eyed moneybags who are dreaming about the mythical west, he thought to himself. Gangnam reminded him of the mocking video that the Chinese artist, Ai Weiwei, had made. Gangnam. A perimeter of broad avenues dominated by the signs that dominate all around the world, in so many suburbs with so many broad avenues that are absolutely identical in every detail. Pra-da-Ver-sa-ce-Vuit-ton-Ar-ma-ni-Guc-ci-Car-tier. The hysterical and obsessive mantra of globalized prosperity. The hysterical and obsessive rap of the destroyers of globalized prosperity. Pra-da-Ver-sa-ce-Vuit-ton . . . He remembered the mocking pamphlet against the dictatorship of fashion labels that he'd written years ago now. It called for incendiary prospects, it showed off destructive impulses. It never saw the light of day. After reading the manuscript, Rossana had rolled up one of the pages to light a joint off it.

Adriano Polimeni, the loyal Communist who had suddenly turned into a purveyor of incendiary tracts. "This shit has nothing to do with you, Adriano." A bitter argument had followed. Adriano had done his best to defend his position by summoning to his aid the early Marx, Lafargue, Brecht, and Mayakovsky. "If you're really interested in violating some taboos," Rossana had devastated him, "why don't you take a toke off this joint. If nothing else, afterwards, the sex is fantastic." Of course, Rossana had been right. He'd never had anything against nice clothing, especially if worn by a pretty woman or a good-looking man. And increasingly, with the passage of time, aesthetics grew more and more valuable to him. For that matter, some of these couturiers had proven to be people of genuine culture. Armani and Prada had started foundations and museums. Modern patrons of the arts. Welcome, then, my brothers and sisters, fashion designers all. We need more of you. And what about Mr. Gu! If with his money he were to help us, say, fix up a preschool or a daycare center, who could argue against that? What's more: have you ever seen a Roman real estate developer invest a penny, one penny, in his own city? Sure, he'd written that horrible pamphlet to make an impression, to seem original for once. A century ago.

His cell phone rang. It's probably Martin Giardino, he assumed. It said unknown caller.

"Adriano, what were you thinking! Here you are in Seoul and you don't even tell me! I have to find out from the undersecretary that you're here in my city! Tonight you're a guest at my house, eh, I accept no excuses!"

As a young man, Marzio Galatola had been a left-wing extremist and militant. He'd studied Asian languages—Chinese, Japanese, and Korean—and written major books about Asian culture. Over time, he'd moved increasingly rightward, until one day he'd called it quits with politics and had moved to Seoul. From there, he wrote for various publications, both print and online, and pursued an uncertain number of activities of indistinct nature and purpose. He and Adriano had known each other since they were kids. Adriano suspected that Marzio was some kind of a spy, and what's more, spying for the wrong side. But he'd never broken off the friendship. Marzio was on a first-name basis with half the world. And most important of all, he was an eternal youth with an irresistible enthusiasm.

Marzio lived on the seventh floor—the penthouse—of an elegant compound on the western limits of Gangnam. Armed guards, bulletproof glass, air conditioning turned down way too cold. Marzio greeted May as if she were an old friend and asked her to take his very warmest regards to Mr. Gu. The place was teeming with *old friends*. Chiara Visone—we met once in Beijing, a really remarkable woman, Adriano, but I don't have to tell you that—the two undersecretaries—a little helpless, they'll find their way, if you want to negotiate with Asians you need a certain amount of experience, it's not like you can come here and just order people around, they'll eat you alive, and believe me, these people have got money by the bucketful—a few grim faces, sad and morose—foreign press or locals, harmless, when I can keep them from drinking too much—and Sebastiano Laurenti.

"Adriano, let me introduce Sebastiano Laurenti."

"My pleasure, Polimeni."

They shook hands a second too long. They looked each other in the eye a second too long. They told each other everything there was to tell. Then Sebastiano veered over toward a little trio of Asians and Adriano took the master of the house aside.

"What do you know about this Laurenti?"

"He's a businessman, or perhaps I should say, he looks after the business of various entrepreneurs. When I heard that he was in Seoul, I invited him over."

"How did you meet him?"

"This is the first time I've ever seen him. He's a friend of friends."

"Which friends?"

"Just *friends*, Adriano. We're grown-ups."

Polimeni quickly grabbed a glass and turned around. Chiara was standing in front of him, smiling. Actually, though, the usual ice was in her eyes.

"May, isn't it? Not bad, your girlfriend."

"And I see that you're with your usual boyfriend. Do you bring him along with you as a lapdog, or as a guard dog?"

"He's here on his own, on business. I didn't even know he was in Seoul."

"Nice. Maintain appearances. But don't let too many people see you out and about together, you never know."

In fact, among the sofas of Marzio Galatola's apartment, Chiara and Sebastiano seemed like a couple of chance acquaintances who were doing everything they could to avoid each other. Polimeni still felt ill at ease. He tossed back one glass after another, until his head started to spin.

He caught a worried glance from May: two horny stockbrokers had wedged her into a corner. Adriano walked over and took her by the arm.

"Let's go. I feel like I'm suffocating here. Take me somewhere else. Someplace you know and like."

They left without saying goodbye to anyone. Adriano caught a sarcastic glance from Chiara, but what the hell, he decided he couldn't care less. May took him to the fish market, where they ate dinner, surrounded by noisy young people and aged fishermen, motionless in their sagacity. Polimeni was captivated by the unsettling crabs and the immense sea urchins. Two friends of May's joined them. They were studying filmmaking at the university, she explained. They know about my work. They won't cause any trouble. The sake and the company soon took effect. The senator really started to like South Korea. They wound up in a karaoke bar. This was Polimeni's first time. He treated them all: forty dollars for a private room and another forty for two excellent bottles of sake. May and a young man sang a duet of "Karma Chameleon."

When it was his turn, Polimeni furiously searched for a piece by Cohen or Dylan. Nothing. He'd run out of patience. He demanded that they turn off the karaoke machine. He grabbed the microphone, accompanied by the amused glances of the young people. He closed his eyes and started singing: *la mia solitudine sei tu / la mia rabbia dentro sei solo tu . . .* The verses of the song poured out crystal clear, his voice dripped with regret and grief. A long angry lament, dedicated to Chiara. To Chiara, lost once and for all. Then, suddenly, he got a grip on himself. What had come over him? An old drunk, pathetic and ridiculous. He gave the microphone to May, muttering his apologies. But the young people said nothing, and were clearly very respectful. Then, suddenly, a wave of applause. May was struggling to choke back her tears.

"Did she hurt you very badly, Adriano?"

"Let's go somewhere else to get a drink, May."

# XI.

## THURSDAY, MARCH 26TH–FRIDAY, MARCH 27TH

PIETRALATA.

A t five in the morning, even Pietralata seemed pretty. Or maybe it really was. Even if there was nothing left of the great fields between the Via Tiburtina and the Via Nomentana—Prata Lata they once called them in Latin. And anyway, Beagle Boy had been born there, in that borgata. Therefore, he decided, it wasn't even open to discussion. The place was pretty. Period. And those suckers from Casal del Marmo can boast all they want about their town. Pietralata was a horse of a different color. Period.

He lifted the visor of his full-face helmet, grazing with his fingertips the sticker of a beagle that adorned the front of the helmet, releasing his grip on the accelerator, and allowing the oversized scooter to lean gently into the narrow tight curves of Via dei Monti di Pietralata. He'd gotten off work half an hour early at Totalpolice, the private security agency where he and his men had been hired at Sebastiano's behest, and he couldn't wait to get out of that stupid sheriff's uniform. What a fucked-up job he'd wound up doing. Anyway, it was Wagner's orders, and there was no arguing with Wagner's orders.

Five minutes and he'd be home.

He really needed to get some sleep, in part because the thought of the two men killed at the Locanda dei Briganti in Ponte Milvio continued to torment him. Lord knows, these weren't the first people he'd seen killed. And he wasn't especially worried about the mess the police might kick up about those two murders—though he'd like to see how they could ever trace it back to him. But really, things were looking bad with Fabietto. And after all, he, Beagle Boy, had never even seen this Fabietto. Yes, he was in the network, but from there to a gang war, really . . . And anyway, the gypsy's visit to Sebastiano's office had made it clear to everyone that Fabietto had eyes and ears everywhere. It wouldn't take him long to track back to him and Wagner. That wasn't a possibility. It was a certainty. Well, then we'll see who's got balls and who hasn't.

The low fuel warning light came on and he decided to make a quick stop at a self-service station, a few hundred yards further on, on the right. He felt his smartphone vibrate in the pocket of his bomber jacket. It was Wagner. He pulled up at the gas station. He turned off the motor, pulled the scooter up on its kickstand, took off his helmet.

"I'm right here, Wagner. Yes, yes, I'm on my way home . . . Don't worry, it's all right . . . Sure, sure, I'm on the lookout . . . On the alert . . . You know for yourself, I'm not the kind of guy that lets his dick get eaten up by flies. Sure . . . we'll get them tomorrow, for sure."

Beagle Boy ended the call and ran a hand through his hair. Wagner had nothing to tell him, so the meaning of the phone call must be something else. To reassure him, he thought. And to reassure himself. The way you do with real friends. And that filled him with pride. You don't wage war all by yourself, after all.

He slipped a ten-euro banknote into the automatic vending unit, picked the octane he needed, and slowly pulled out the pump.

That's when they arrived.

There were four of them on two motorcycles. They came whipping around the curve and they didn't even give him time to grab the Beretta 7.65 he had shoved down the back of his pants. The first two were on him in a flash. They wore full-face motorcycle helmets. As did the others, for that matter. A brutal violent kick to the wrist knocked the gun out of his hand. Then he felt a metal bar brought down hard on his back, right on his shoulder blades. His lungs exploded. He fell face-first onto the asphalt and spat blood, screaming with the pain, until he felt the cold pistol barrel on the back of his neck.

"With Fabio's best wishes," said a mocking voice.

And then the gunshot.

While his men were executing Beagle Boy, Fabio Desideri was slipping the moorings of his Mykonos IV and heading out to sea with his latest hookup, an Estonian babe who stood six feet tall if she was an inch. She'd expressed a desire for "a long journey by sea, so we can get lost together," and her wish was Fabio's command. Anyone else might have thought: This isn't the time for that, there's a gang war on, you can't abandon your territory, people will say that you're running away. That's how anyone else would have thought about it. But not him.

His territory was under control and strongly garrisoned, his men were taking care of that. His retaliation against Sebastiano had hit its target even though, for the moment, in terms of the death count they were still down by one. But there was plenty of time to make up for that. No, what counted now was quite another matter. At the exact instant when he had chosen his future, Fabio had also decided that he was only going to take the best from life, leaving all the rest to the miserable losers. He didn't want to live hiding out in some foul-smelling bunker, dragging out his days in the fear of the gunshot that could arrive at any second, simmer slowly in the possession of mountains of cash that he'd never have the freedom to spend. He didn't want to live the shitty life most criminals lead. Let them believe they had him on the run. He'd get over it. And then Fabio would come back to Rome at just the right moment, to deliver the final blow.

He clapped his hands, and a sailor came running.

"Champagne," he ordered.

The girl with the long blonde hair stared out at the trembling lights along the coastline with an expression of mystical rapture.

The best, Fabio. Nothing but the best.

# XII.
## FRIDAY, MARCH 27TH–SATURDAY, MARCH 28TH
### Saints' Days: St. Rupert, Bishop;
### St. Gontran, King and Confessor

NEWSROOM OF *IL MERIDIANO*. FRIDAY THE 27TH. LUNCHTIME.

Five pages. A hundred fifty lines. Perfect. Spartaco Liberati lifted his stubby, hairy fingers from the Mac keyboard and saluted his masterpiece with a resonant baritone belch that echoed like a thunderclap in the open-plan office of the newsroom. He turned around to see what impression he'd made with his belch, but he discovered there was no one else in the room. It was lunchtime and, after the hasty meeting to plan out the issue coming out next Thursday, everyone else had taken off. Work ethic, come take me, I'm yours.

He booted up Safari to check out the online odds for the A.S. Roma game on Sunday, he made a mental calculation of how much he was out already that month—five thousand euros, damn them to hell—and decided to skip it. For once, he'd be better advised to just flatter himself by reading the copy-and-paste article that he'd dragged out of that muckraker Malgradi.

*The Investigation*, they'd headline it. More modestly, a shovelful of shit, he thought, opening the layout again.

> *Shadows on the Jubilee*
> *We reveal the secret that will nail the mayor and the suicide that's making the Vatican tremble.*

ROME—You can fool all of the people some of the time, and some of the people all of the time, but you can't fool all of the people all of the time. You can live in the secrecy of a lie, but only until the truth comes knocking on your door. Because facts are like stones, heavy and durable . . .

Oh yeah, it really was a spectacular lede.

*Il Meridiano*, after weeks of work and careful verification of sources who, for understandable considerations, asked to remain unnamed for their own protection . . .

Of course, a little lunch, a file folder with a few old clippings, an hour or so copying and pasting from Malgradi's bowl of stew, and the fear is gone.

. . . is able to document that the mayor of Rome, Martin Giardino, has for years been pursued by a terrible secret. A secret that has to do with a young, English, female student, M.A., abused on a rainy night more than twenty years ago in the dorms of Oxford University, where at the time a young professor from Alto Adige was teaching . . .

He was particularly impressed with the invention of the fictional M.A.

. . . In a small house in Manchester, where she livestoday, M.A. tells *Il Meridiano*: "I'll never be able to forget him, that man, my professor. He invited me to his room with the excuse that he wanted to give me back a paper of mine that he'd corrected. But as soon as the door shut behind us . . . As soon as . . . " M.A. bursts into uncontrollable sobs. She shakes her head. "So, yes, anyway . . . "

Manchester of all places! He'd only been to Manchester once, that time that A.S. Roma under Spalletti had taken seven shellackings from the English, and he'd wondered whether it might not be wise to choose a city that was less unlucky. Still, if Malgradi said Manchester, then Manchester it would be, and in any case the script worked well enough, so on he read.

" . . . He raped me violently. As horny as a monkey . . . "

Just why Malgradi had insisted on inserting this detail of the monkey wasn't entirely clear to him. Still, no doubt about it, this detail fit in perfectly. Even though it reminded him of something. Could it perhaps have been the mess that fat French banker got himself into . . . What the fuck was his name again . . . ? Oh, right, Strauss something . . . Strauss-Kahn . . . He'd thrown himself at the housekeeper in a New York hotel and what was it she'd said? She'd actually said he'd behaved like "a horny monkey." Okay, if Malgradi's happy, everyone's happy.

The name of that Italian professor was Martin Giardino. And on that long-ago night, twenty years ago, he'd thrown away his career, which had been a promising one, with the tacit cooperation of the prestigious English university. He agreed to leave England and the world of academia. For good. Oxford would remain silent. M.A. was never made whole for her suffering. In the past twenty years, Martin Giardino had never once had the courage to ask her forgiveness. Today, this man is the mayor of Rome. This is the man of the "moral turning point." Moral, how? Him? Moral?

What a cold son of a bitch. Spartaco caught himself actually believing what he'd written and just reread. That was proof that it worked. It worked, and how.

He clicked the mouse to scroll to the next page. Here was the main dish.

Martin Giardino's unconfessable secret is not the only long shadow cast upon the jubilee. Reliable Vatican sources tell *Il Meridiano* that on the evening of last March 13th, the very same day that the Holy Year was announced, a young priest, Don Paolo Micci, took his own life by jumping off one of the high towers of the Vatican walls. The news was kept out of the press and is still shielded by top secrecy. For two excellent reasons. The first: the young priest's sexual predilections. The second: his, shall we say, less than transparent relations with Bishop Giovanni Daré, the prelate appointed by the Holy Father as the guarantor of public works for the jubilee . . .

Nothing of the sort would ever have come out in the days of Monsignor Tempesta: homosexuality in the cassock was a taboo subject, and you can believe it, considering how they were all asshole buddies. But now, instead, that the magical partnership of bygone days had been buried by Malgradi, always a slave to his dick, at least now it was possible to beat up some faggots again, which is always a good and just thing. The fireworks about homosexuality were decisive. And it pointed to the obvious next step: the conclusion of the piece.

How can we hand over the keys to the jubilee to a mayor who's a rapist, at once lascivious and a liar, and with him, a bishop subject to sexual extortion?

Spartaco's smartphone vibrated. He looked at the display. It was Malgradi.

"Yep. I'm done . . . Yes, five pages. No, no . . . I didn't add anything of my own. The usual copy and paste. I'll send it straight over by email. After all, you can talk to the editor in chief yourself. Sure, it's going into the next issue. Thursday. It's a bombshell. An authentic bombshell."

CAPITOLINE HILL. TAPROOM IN THE COUNCIL HALL.

The fact that that hack Liberati had actually done the job he'd been sent to do gave Malgradi an appetite. So he hurried down to the *buvette*, or little taproom, in the Giulio Cesare Hall. He took a small plate and piled it high with egg-and-salami tea sandwiches, grabbed a bowl of peanuts from the counter, and ordered a Campari Orange. Then he took a seat on one of the stools on the open-air veranda, where he ran right into that bitch Alice Savelli.

That's right, the little girl who'd thrown the first stone against his brother Pericle had come a long way. First of all, she'd discarded the carabiniere she'd taken to bed—too old and too down-market, that Marco Malatesta, for a bourgeois snob like her—and then she'd become a young leader in the Five Star movement, founded by Beppe Grillo. When Grillo was a comedian, he wasn't bad, and he'd then gone on to garner a substantial following and plenty of votes under a banner that might as well have just had one phrase emblazoned on it: *Fuck off!* As far as that sentiment went, Malgradi couldn't agree more. The cunning professional politicians had quickly isolated the legion of Five Star parliamentarians, who in point of fact had been neutralized in their persistent resentments. Still, if needed, mused Temistocle, they could lend a hand. As for Savelli, who'd been chosen by an online primary—now there was some bullshit that a few thousand digital party activists had participated in—she'd been elected to the city council and then appointed contingent leader. And in that position she'd become a hardline *pasionaria* whose recurring response was "No." Whatever the question, the answer is always "No."

Naturally, the surname Malgradi had made him her obsessive target. And he didn't mind that one bit because, as deputy mayor, the attacks of that young girl had given him a notable profile.

"Good afternoon, councilwoman," said Malgradi, sketching out a sarcastic bow.

"Good afternoon, but not for long, Deputy Mayor."

"Why don't you smile every now and then, Alice?"

Malgradi had always addressed her by her first name, and with the informal "*tu*," knowing that it drove her crazy.

"I was informing you of a piece of news, Deputy Mayor. But I see that it went by you."

"Now, it didn't go by me, Alice. I got it. I saw it, and I saw the umpteenth no-confidence motion that you've lodged against the mayor and the coalition government. Which means, also against yours truly. If you don't mind my saying so, it strikes me as the usual tripe."

"Wait, do you call 'the usual tripe' the housing disaster, the shame of city cops who don't even show up for work, the revolt against the welcome centers for immigrants on the outskirts of town that your mayor doesn't even know where they are, the fraud of the cloned public transportation tickets, and three, I say *three* quarters—Esquilino, Monti, San Giovanni—that have completely collapsed after the brilliant idea of closing off to traffic an archeological dig that'll be finished God only knows when and how."

"You know what I like about you, Alice? That you never get tired of the sound of your own voice."

"Instead I'm happy to know that I've always detested everything about you and your family. Just consider, I even think you're worse than your brother."

"Are you interested in insulting me or talking about politics?"

"Excuse me, but what on earth would we talk about?"

"About what you want to achieve with your motion."

"That seems obvious. The resignation of the mayor and his coalition."

"Have you studied up on the regulations, beautiful? Do you know that the mayor elected by the populace can't be ejected with a vote taken by the city council? You know, don't you, that there can only be a constructive vote of no confidence? Which means you need to have a positive majority for a prospective successor. And with you there, who the fuck is going to govern?"

"So what? Of course we know that. Ours is a political gesture."

"There you go, nice work, you see that when you apply yourself . . . and I'm thinking politically. A motion against the mayor and against the coalition government is something you'll vote for *alone*. While instead a motion against the mayor *alone* might garner surprising numbers of votes . . . "

Alice stared at the old shark. What the hell was he talking about? Why should they evaluate differently the responsibilities of the German and those of his magical circle? Malgradi foresaw the question. His tone of voice turned silky and conniving.

"To bring home a political result, my young friend."

He patiently explained to her that in the last few months a fissure had opened between the majority and the mayor. Martin Giardino was detested by a great many members of his own party. The man was capable of being arrogant and intolerable when he set himself to it. His inability to make decisions was legendary, and when he finally set his signature to a document, well, if things went well, all credit to him, but if they didn't, then he put the blame on "old-style politics."

"Therefore, you accuse the mayor of being more or less like the rest of you," Alice jumped in, treacherously.

Malgradi pretended he hadn't heard. And he went on. The straw that had broken the camel's back: appointing that old jalopy Polimeni to oversee the contracts for the jubilee.

"Seriously, no one in Rome can take another minute of the German. We least of all."

"And therefore?"

"And therefore a motion of no confidence in the mayor, and the mayor alone, is likely to pass, and anyway, even if it doesn't pass, it carries with it a sizable chunk of votes, a lot more votes than you have. It'll be a nice fat slap in the face for the German. He won't be able to ignore it. At the very least, it'll trigger a political crisis. Maybe he'll resign, or we'll block his budget, or something—we'll see. In the meantime, you'd be the stars of the show. For once, instead of standing at the window spitting down on the rest of the universe, you'd be doing the right thing. And it would be a nice big political success."

Your people. Our people. A political success. Alice heaved a sigh of annoyance. The reason she'd gone into politics had been to change things. That's why she'd abandoned the old, compromised left wing and had launched herself with such enthusiasm into the movement. And now this old bandit wanted to drag her once again into the swamp.

"Your little games are of no interest to us," she retorted contemptuously.

Malgradi laughed and tried to touch the back of Alice's neck; she recoiled in disgust.

"Grow up, girlie."

Malgradi stood up brusquely from the stool on the tap-room veranda and, turning his back to Alice, headed off toward the Giulio Cesare Hall. Then he stopped and, with well-rehearsed theatricality, came back to look at her and take one last turn onstage.

"Remember, my dear young revolutionary, that ours is a big party with a thousand different souls. And also remember that politics is the art of the unpredictable. In any case, I've made a request and I expect an answer. It seems to me that you're going to have to inform the movement. Just think if a little birdie were to whisper to your gurus that you did everything on your own, that you dismissed an opportunity without consulting your *base*. At the very least, they'd put you on trial, the way you all like to do so much, on live streaming, and then they'd kick you out of the party. So let me know, eh, sweetheart?"

FIVE STAR ADVISORY COUNCIL. FRIDAY THE 27TH. EVENING.

She hated to admit it, but the obscene Malgradi had told her things and pointed out aspects of the matter that had forced her to give it thought. The offer itself was repulsive, but the rules of the movement were imperative. Therefore, Alice informed the other council members in the party group, and then reached out, as required by statute, to the movement's online base. All the same, in the context of submitting to an electronic referendum the proposal for a new and different no-confidence motion, this time against Giardino alone, she wrote that the shift in strategy was a product of the "possible convergence of intent among DP dissidents allied with Deputy Mayor Malgradi." That's right, she had written those exact words: "DP dissidents allied with Malgradi." Because by so doing—she had told herself—if that snake in the grass had set a trap for her, he would be its first victim.

She set a deadline for online voting of 10 PM. Three thousand votes came in. The "yes" votes were eighty percent.

Alice accepted the "virtual" verdict without too much enthusiasm. Maybe Malgradi had had a point when he called that type of electoral consultation "pure bullshit." And she also tried to figure out whether behind all those "yeses" and the hashtags that expressed them there might not be hidden the DP activists who were guided by Malgradi. A pointless question, she concluded after spending a fair amount of time contemplating the lights that lit up the night over Piazza Venezia.

Before leaving the office, she turned to her secretary.

"Stefania, I know it's late, but if you don't mind very much I wonder if I can ask you to draw up the new text of the motion for a no-confidence vote against Giardino alone. We need to get the support of at least nineteen council members, and we don't have a lot of time if we're going to try to get a vote on it inside a week. Good night."

"Certainly. Good night," the young woman replied, with a smile.

In theory, a bad case of pharyngitis constituted an excellent excuse to take a break. But Martin Giardino detested taking breaks. He'd spend the last day of his convalescence coordinating everything that could be coordinated by telephone and email, and the next morning, let the world collapse, he'd still get back to the office. In the meantime, with the aid of a linden flower herbal tea, he was trying to get some sleep, distractedly channel hopping, when he ran into Chiara Visone. A big old commercial. It must have been a recording of an old interview that they'd dug out of the files. Chiara was smiling, inspired and perky, as she fielded the questions of an aging hack, one of those journalists who make it a point of honor never to put their interviewees in a corner. Especially not if they're powerful and clearly up and coming.

"Look, I have to make a confession. Youth is, for me, an absolutely required condition. A sine qua non. Just understand that anyone who was born before the World Cup in Spain is stuff from the last century. The lord only knows, it's my own problem. That's right, a problem afflicting us millennials, echo boomers, Generation Y, I don't know, you take your pick."

Martin Giardino angrily punched the "off" button. Young people against old people, the new against the ancient. He couldn't stand hearing that trite old refrain again. What's so bad about memory? What's so bad about History? Aren't you always and inevitably building on the shoulders of those who went before you? What the hell. The World Cup in Spain. Sandro Pertini. When that had happened, Martin was twenty-seven years old, the Communists were a strange land to him, and he was studying like a dog to make something of himself, he was on the verge of trying to see what would come of an adventure in Brazil. And, most important of all, that young woman hadn't even been born yet. The truth is that Chiara Visone pained Martin. The memory of their first meeting still stung. A handshake in City Hall and that ferocious wisecrack.

"You know, I thought you were younger, Mr. Mayor."

"I'm not sixty yet," he had reacted, instinctively.

"Maybe it's the beard that ages you. You should shave it."

The old. The young. Enough, for God's sake.

He finished savoring his herbal tea, lukewarm by now, and welcomed, with something approaching a sense of relief, the ring of his cell phone. There was still work to do, evidently. Thank God, there was still work to do.

"Martin Giardino here."

It was the secretary of the Left-Wing Ecology and Freedom Club of Testaccio, Enzo Rendina. A good guy who had wound up changing his mind about the German. Whether that was as a result of the piazza restored to the quarter or for some other reason, who could say. The important thing was that he had certainly changed it.

"Excuse me, Mr. Mayor, if I call you so late on your cell phone, but I just learned something a little while ago that I found stunning and upsetting, and that I thought I should tell you immediately, because it's important . . . "

"Tell me, what's it about?"

"Well, you see, it's the Five Star Movement."

"Yes, I know. They've presented a no-confidence motion against the coalition. A piece of foolishness that the chamber will vote on and reject next week, if I'm not mistaken."

"No, that's exactly the point. The Five Star base, two hours ago, voted online for the presentation of a new no-confidence motion. Individual. Against you, Mr. Mayor."

"Huh, well I don't see what that changes, to tell the truth."

"In the debate that took place online and in the proposal put out to the base by the group leader, Alice Savelli . . . "

"Charming, that young woman. A little rigid, perhaps, but . . . "

"Listen to me, Mr. Mayor. I was telling you that Savelli explained to the activists that there was a reason for the change in the motion. The individual no-confidence motion will be supported—I'm reading verbatim here—'by DP dissidents close to Malgradi.'"

"I don't believe it."

"I'm afraid you're going to have to."

"Are you sure of what you're telling me right now?"

"Mr. Mayor, I've been deep in that blog with a fake hashtag since the day it first went online."

"Why? Why would Malgradi vote in favor of a no-confidence motion against me? What political purpose could there be in such a move?"

"It seems to me that there's no mistaking the political purpose. To give you a good hard kick in the ass, and then go for a reshuffle of the coalition council, maybe drawing in the Five Star Movement and getting himself the position of mayor. Naturally, in order to do that, it would mean that your party had chosen Malgradi. So, if I may, if I were you I'd wonder not how many votes he has, but how many votes I had."

"Thanks, Enzo."

"Don't mention it, Mayor."

As Giardino hung up the phone he was in the grip of an uncontainable rage. A rage, however, that was shot through with instinctive fear. He hadn't spotted Malgradi's machinations on the horizon. He was isolated from the party and in the party. Perhaps it was true that he was pretty green when it came to the game of politics. What the voters had recognized as a virtue now looked like it might turn into his political grave.

At this point, sleep was out of the question. Wrapped in an oversized windbreaker and with a silk scarf scrupulously knotted around his neck, he grabbed his bicycle and decided to listen to his instincts.

He pedaled along the riverfront embarcadero, the Lungotevere, for an indeterminate amount of time. He rode around St. Peter's, crossed the river, cut down Via del Corso and across Piazza Venezia, veered over toward Corso Rinascimento. Until, shortly before dawn, he found himself in one of those narrow lanes that run close behind Campo de' Fiori. The regular movement of the pedaling had brought him back to himself but, if anything, had only honed his fury to a sharper cutting edge.

He leaned the bicycle against the wall right next to a small wooden street door to a three-story building with an ocher yellow plaster front. He pushed a button next to an intercom, unmarked with any name. On the fifth buzz, he heard Malgradi's sleep-slurred voice.

"Who the fuck is it?"

"It's me, Martin Giardino. Come downstairs."

There was a long silence.

"Mr. Mayor, is that really you? Are you all right? Your voice sounds so strange . . . "

"I said come downstairs."

"Why don't you come up? We can have a cup of coffee together."

"Get down here!"

The mayor's voice had veered into a falsetto. Malgradi threw on an overcoat over his pajamas and understood that the moment had come. Giardino lit into him the minute the downstairs door started swinging open.

"I'm here because I wanted to tell you in person that from

now on, I'm withdrawing all party support. You're out of the coalition government. You're no longer deputy mayor. And don't ask me why. You know why."

Malgradi stared at him with a look of sheer commiseration.

"You know, Martin, it was a mistake for me to defend you to the rest of the party. They were right. You're a self-centered, paranoid asshole. And in any case, let me give you some news. You no longer have a majority in the city council. The Five Star Movement's motion is going to pass. But not with my votes. With the party's votes. Because in this city the party is me. You're done for."

Giardino hadn't taken his eyes off Malgradi's puffy face for even a second, and he saw all the ferocity expressed by those degenerate features.

"You're the one who's discredited. And you'll wind up just like your brother," he said.

Malgradi withdrew into the doorway.

"Me, discredited? There's a ton of shit that's about to be dumped over your head. If I were you, I wouldn't be so sure of myself . . . "

Giardino looked up at the sky. Day was dawning. He finally felt a sense of profound relief. But as he got back on his bike, he found he couldn't get that last threat out of his mind.

"There's a ton of shit that's about to be dumped over your head. If I were you, I wouldn't be so sure of myself . . . "

What was about to sweep him away?

# XIII.
## MARCH 29TH
### *Saint's Day: St. Eustace of Luxeuil*

FIUMICINO, CAPITOLINE HILL, AND THE OLD APPIAN WAY.

S eventeen calls from Martin Giardino and three from party headquarters. All in the space of the past two hours. What the hell had happened? As soon as he deplaned from the Boeing, having survived yet another nightmarish flight, Adriano Polimeni powered up and immediately powered back down his cell phone in *un vidiri e svidiri*, as his beloved Camilleri would have put it, no sooner seen than ignored. He had absolutely no intention of foregoing a few hours of well-deserved rest before plunging back into the headaches of the capital. In Seoul he had done good work on the city's behalf. He was traveling with excessive, inexorable rapidity to the threshold of age sixty, and his body was calling for a truce. Not even if the Colosseum burned down was he going to change his plans.

Still, there are appointments you can't avoid.

It's fate that demands it.

That morning, for Adriano Polimeni, fate had decided to take on the semblance of an old Roman taxi driver, the kind that has it in for the world at large, and nothing's ever right in their view. Starting with politicians, and then moving on to women behind the wheel, and inevitably continuing on through the inevitable lists of unions and civil servants. These last two categories are grouped together by a contemptuous and definitive evaluation:

"All they're good for is to eat, and they don't do a thing from morning to nightfall."

There'd been a time, faithful to the party line, when he would have willingly engaged in a vigorous exchange with that representative of the bitter mood of the populace. He would have launched into even the harshest of debates and in the end, there were no two ways about it, his dialectical mastery would have prevailed, and the taxi driver would have been brought back into the fold of respect for constitutional values, and so on and so forth. The educational role of the party, they called it back at leadership school. And it wasn't even his exhaustion that had kept him from standing up to the stream of clichés that the fascistoid taxi driver kept spewing. No. It was his awareness that the "educational role" was based on a set of values which time—and let's go ahead and call it History—had mercilessly deleted. What was it he was supposed to defend? Who? History can be a pitiless mocker, no doubt about it: and the mockery is twice as cruel if you're someone who has based his life on the concept of "historical materialism."

Then the taxi driver said those words, and Polimeni heard the first alarm bell go off.

"Excuse me, what did you just say?"

"I said: with all this mess going down in City Hall . . . "

"What do you mean by 'mess?'"

"So now it looks like the DP wants to get rid of the German."

"The DP?"

"The DP, Dotto', that's right. I can't figure out heads nor tails of it myself, I mean what? first you put him up as mayor and now you give him a kick in the ass right out the door? But anyway, it looks like that's what's going on."

Adriano Polimeni gave a reluctant farewell to his bathtub and his bed, turned his cell phone back on, and called Martin Giardino.

"Adriano, at last! You have no idea."

"I'm on my way."

The mayor's voice evoked the imagery of a shipwrecked mariner on a sinking dinghy, bailing frantically as sharks circle.

"There's been a change in plans," he told the cabbie, "take me to the Capitoline Hill."

The man snickered. He'd recognized his passenger, a well-known face from TV, or at least well-known and on TV until recently. And with malevolent delight, he resumed his litany against the notorious appetites of the parliamentarians.

Martin Giardino was pacing nervously around his office. Even though it was Sunday, the mayor had not given up his defense of the trenchworks and the garrison. He gave Adriano a hug and gestured for him to sit down. He just couldn't sit still.

"I've disconnected the telephones. Since this morning they haven't stopped ringing. I've got the newspapers after me, everyone's assuming I'm going to resign."

"What do they say at the Nazareno?"

"Pardon my French, but they say it's none of their fucking concern."

Polimeni halted the river of words with a brusque gesture and made a couple of quick phone calls. His contacts at the party's national headquarters, the ones who had reached out to him that morning, confirmed. Officially, the party considered the question to be an internal matter, quibbles among Romans, and strictly local. A rising deputy secretary had released an ambiguous statement: "Giardino shouldn't worry, he should just go on governing Rome, if he's capable."

"The party of Pontius Pilate," the mayor commented.

Polimeni threw his arms wide.

"Have you heard from Visone? What does she say?"

Martin Giardino lunged at the desk that had once belonged to Ernesto Nathan, rummaged through a pile of papers, pulled out a sheaf, and handed it to him.

"She came to see me a couple of hours ago. And she gave me this."

Adriano Polimeni read the byline. Spartaco Liberati. Then he read the body text.

"The dirt machine is working at full function, Martin."

"Not a single word, not one word, of what's written in that article corresponds to the truth. You have to believe me!"

"There's no need for you to have a pharyngitis relapse, Martin. If a piece of news is reported by this Liberati, then that automatically means it's a fake. Does Chiara believe in this hogwash?"

"Does she believe it? She's behind all of this. She and that . . . with Malgradi. Do you know what Chiara said to me? She said that if I resign, then this . . . oh, excuse my French, but there are times when you need to say it . . . this piece of shit won't be published. She gave me a few days to think it over. An ultimatum, you understand? To me. From Visone!"

"Try to calm down. Have you already made a decision?"

"Yes . . . no . . . oh God, Adriano, I don't know what to do. I could hold out, face the no-confidence vote, go down fighting, and I could resign with a public accusation against them, and then run for election with a list of trusted candidates. We could fight this battle together, Adriano, you and I . . . "

Tender his resignation, and then take them all on, like a solitary hero, firm in the saddle, with lance in rest. It was in keeping with the character. Martin Giardino – Don Quixote and his Sancho Panza – Polimeni. This was not the way.

"That's complete idiocy, Martin."

"You think? I believe, though, that Rome . . . "

"If you're about to say that 'Rome loves me' or 'Rome will understand,' save your breath," Polimeni interrupted him.

Martin Giardino stared at him in desolation.

"So now you too, Adriano . . .

"Why don't you throw in, 'my son,'" Polimeni mocked him

sarcastically. "I'm not Brutus and you're not Caesar, so stop feeling sorry for yourself and listen to me. I'm on your side. But don't count on Rome. There's no city on earth as fickle and slippery as this one. Here the great loves and the undying hatreds last as long as it takes to drink an espresso, Martin. In this city, kings, popes, dictators, and emperors have been hoisted high and knocked low in the time it took the breeze to veer. This is a city that kindles a new passion every minute and extinguishes a thousand others just as fast. Rome recognizes you as long as it's looking up at you from below. Once you step down from that pedestal, then you're just one more among thousands, and the cry is 'Next!'"

"Then you think there's no hope?"

"Who ever said that? Just listen to me. Take two days off, three if you need it. You just got over a case of pharyngitis, right? Well, let's just say that you had a relapse. Have a press release prepared: the mayor returned to the job still convalescent, but he had an unexpected relapse. If it comes to that, your face is scary to look at."

"I feel fine."

"Get lost. In complete isolation. Turn off all your devices. Disconnect. Speak to no one. Get that fucking bicycle of yours out and go wandering. Explore the backwoods."

"And in the meantime?"

"And in the meantime, I'm going to go get some sleep. At a certain age, when you don't have the physique of a bike racer, sleep is a precious resource. Believe me, I'll come up with something."

All the same, in spite of all his best resolutions, Adriano Polimeni didn't get a wink of sleep. He had just arrived home when Father Giovanni appeared at his front door.

"The ways of the Lord are infinite, Adriano."

"You known what I say, Giovanni? Pray to Him with all the

ardor in your body, Your Lord. Because down here, everything is going sideways."

Padre Giovanni chuckled.

"Yes, I got an advance peek at that hack article by that . . . that hack journalist Spartaco Liberati. And I can tell you that this morning the Holy Father delivered some swift kicks in the ass to two gentlemen who had come in to see him, demanding my head on a pike."

"Are you willing to put that in writing? The pope gave several swift kicks in the ass to . . . "

"It was a manner of speech."

"Giova', I have no time to spare. I'm tired, in fact, I'm wrecked. And I don't know which way to turn."

Giovanni filled two glasses with whisky and handed one to the senator.

"You know what they say, give drink to the thirsty."

"What is this? A liturgical update? Unless I'm much mistaken, in the Gospel they were talking about water, not whisky."

"The Gospel should be interpreted in light of the circumstances, Adriano. Drink, it'll do you good."

Adriano obeyed. A wave of warmth washed over him. Sometimes, alcohol really can be a blessed thing. Giovanni turned suddenly serious.

"Truly. The ways of the Lord are infinite. So listen to me now. After I froze those well-known IOR accounts, I said to myself that there could be no doubt that the people we don't want underfoot were bound to open other accounts in other banks somewhere."

"Obviously. In order to perform financial operations in Italy, you need to make reference to domestic bank accounts."

"Obviously, as you say. But it also occurred to me that those very same gentlemen might have run into a momentary crisis of liquidity."

"Huh."

"Yes, indeed. Now, they might have been crafty enough to diversify, but also foolish enough to bring it all together under one roof, in a single bank. Ours, in fact. And therefore . . . "

"And therefore?"

"And therefore I spread the word among all the other brothers I know who keep an eye on the one thing sinners care most about, their wallets. If you hear a certain name, I told them, if you notice anything funny, anything at all, even the most trifling detail, report back to me. I'll be able to make good use of it."

"So what happened?"

So what happened. As chance would have it, or perhaps he should say, the Lord in His infinite mercy, Giovanni explained, had seen to it that the commander of the customs police at Fiumicino Airport was related to a member of the confraternity, a priest from the Ciociaria, absolutely devoted . . .

" . . . to the way of justice, to the way of the light, I don't know if I make myself clear, Adriano."

"Clear as glass, clear as day."

"Take a look at this official report."

Giovanni handed him a skimpy Xerox punctuated with all sorts of inked office stamps. Adriano Polimeni read it and reread it. "As the result of an anonymous tip, Sebastiano Laurenti, businessman, whose identity is more fully documented below, is suspected of the attempted smuggling of a massive quantity of cash without proper documentation . . . "

Laurenti. Polimeni suddenly regained his mental clarity. That text in dense bureaucratic language was invaluable. Laurenti. Well, well, well.

"But what it says here is that the investigation came up empty-handed."

"He must have found some other way of getting the swag into the country."

"The swag . . . do you hear the way you're talking, Your Excellency?"

"Let's not worry about the form. The young man had hit a shortage of ready cash and he went to shake a tin cup in London."

"It would be nice to know who he appealed to for charity."

"The ways of the Lord are infinite."

"Don't tell me you know that, too? The note here talks about an anonymous tip."

"True. But the anonymous tipster used a SIM card."

"And how would you happen to know such a thing?"

"The ways . . . "

"All right. I give up. When I'm ready to recite the rosary, I'll give you a whistle, and you come hit me in the head once and for all. A single hard blow with the sledgehammer, don't make me have to remind you. It's more humane."

"The SIM card turns out to have been registered in the name of a real estate holding company. I had a few checks run."

"Again, because the ways of the Lord are infinite and they fail to take into account the privacy regulations of telecommunications companies, I'm going to guess."

"The company belongs to an Italian. His name is Pasquale Pistracchio. Does that mean anything to you?"

"Nothing at all."

"Well, you do at least use the Internet?"

"Like everyone."

"'Googlize' that name, and then you can tell me what you think. I have to go to work. Take care, Adriano."

"Googlize" . . . Of all the damned things, Your Eminence.

Alone in his home now, the senator went straight to his computer. He typed in "Pasquale Pistracchio". There appeared a porcine face in black-and-white, surrounded by Nazi symbols. The biography was a rich one. A right-wing, neo-Fascist

terrorist . . . accused of armed robberies to finance the party
. . . he fled to England . . . he married extremely well . . .
acquitted of all the lesser charges . . . not extradited for the old
charges of criminal conspiracy and association . . . prosperous
economic standing, a solid position in the field of real estate . . .

But why had Pistracchio or one of his men lodged a complaint against Sebastiano Laurenti? What link was there
between this old Fascist comrade and someone who gives a
check for one hundred thirty thousand euros to a DP club?

He remembered an old contact he had in the Carabinieri
Corps. A straight shooter, an honest officer. That there were
such people, and lots of them, was something that he'd come
to appreciate when he was a successful politician and he'd
finally learned to get rid of so many of his old prejudices. His
name was Marco Malatesta and he was widely renowned as a
pain in the ass. In spite of that fact, he'd advanced his career.
Either because when it came time to issue promotions, someone had taken their eye off the ball, or perhaps because democracy was even spreading in the Carabinieri Corps. He called
him by way of the switchboard at Central Command.

"Dear Malatesta, I'm going to skip the preliminaries even if
we haven't talked in forever."

"That, my dear senator, is why I've always liked you."

"I'm doing a historical research project into the subversive
right wing."

"I'll pretend I believe you. Who are you interested in?"

"Pistracchio."

A brief pause.

"All right, I'll take full responsibility for the things I'm
about to tell you. Listen, and listen carefully . . . "

When that conversation was over, Polimeni emerged with a
rush of adrenaline in his veins. Now the picture was clear,

crystalline in its spare simplicity. And now he had a weapon he could wield. He judged it the better part of wisdom not to inform Martin Giardino. This match would need to be fought with fencing foils. And he was the one with the light touch to do it. He thought of calling Chiara, then chose not to. As Mr. Gu might have put it, that was a meeting to be scheduled for better conditions. And he had a crushing need for rest. Still, he fell into a lull of compulsive channel surfing. Alice Savelli was delivering thunderous invective against the corrupt coalition government and its hapless mayor.

"We don't know what to do with Malgradi's votes and the votes of his crew, because we're continuing on our path without compromises. But we can't keep anyone from voting for our agenda."

There were lots of others just like her in that Five Star movement. She was a good young woman: could it be that she really had no idea she'd become a tool of the Big Bad Wolf? He was almost tempted to pick up the phone and call her, but decided not to. Alice's movement was still in the revolutionary phase. The last thing revolutionaries want is sage advice, and they're certainly not interested in listening to old, obsolete relics of the last century. That was a dynamic that Adriano Polimeni knew very well. He too had experienced his youthful seasons of political passion. Seasons that had ended all too soon, sadly.

And then, at last, he dropped off to sleep.

Wagner was waiting outside of the pub in Prati where they had met the first time. Sebastiano pulled up in his black Audi and waved for him to get in. The young man was beside himself. His eyes were bloodshot. His hands were tossed by a constant tremor. Sebastiano told his chauffeur to head for La Romanina.

"How long have I been away? Three days?"

"I had to shoot those two guys, Sebastia'. There was no other way."

"If I'd been in your shoes, I would have done the same thing. I don't blame you at all."

"Give me permission and I'll find the bastard and cut him down the middle. With my own hands. Beagle Boy was a brother to me."

Sebastiano shook his head.

"I know what you're feeling. I know it very well. More than you could ever imagine. But this is war, Luca. And if we want to win this war, we need to fight it intelligently. And intelligence demands thought. Thought. Not instinct."

At the Anacleti family villa there was no time for chitchat. Rocco, the patriarch, was sitting in a large armchair upholstered in red satin. He looked as if he'd been embalmed. And he kept staring at young Wagner, sensing something in the features and gaze of that young man that reminded him of Samurai.

"We're here to find out what you mean to do. No beating around the bush, this time. Either with us. Or else with Fabio," said Sebastiano.

Silvio, as he always did when he was trying to avoid confrontation, first lowered his gaze and then looked over to the patriarch for reassurance.

Rocco's voice arrived stentorian like a verdict from on high.

"We aren't budging, Sebastiano. We're staying here. As motionless as my arms and my weary legs."

Sebastiano dissolved into a smile dripping with sarcasm. First he stared at Silvio, then at Rocco.

"You know what the term is in chess? *Zugzwang.* Obligation to move. You are obliged to make a move. Because this war is going to end with just one winner. And that winner is going to be me. And when that day comes, it's going to be better for you if you made a choice. The right choice."

He got up from the table, gestured for Wagner to follow him, and without saying farewell, left the villa. Once they were in the car, they sat for a while in silence. Then he pulled out his cell phone. The man picked up on the third ring.

"Ciao, Bogdan, it's me. I imagine you know why I'm getting in touch."

He remained silent, listening for a brief while, then said: "I understand. Let me know when he comes back."

Sebastiano tossed his phone onto the back seat.

Fabio Desideri had gone on the run.

# XIV.
## MARCH 30TH. GARBATELLA
### *Saint's Day: St. Zosimus, Bishop*

She hadn't told him yes or no, but in the end she'd gone over to see him. She'd kept him dangling on a thread of uncertainty because she wanted to make sure that Adriano got it into his head that, if there'd ever been anything between them, that time was now over once and for all. And yet, she'd decided to go the very moment she'd heard his voice. A fine paradox. When the driver dropped her off in front of the Teatro Palladium, and she saw him come walking toward her—in his famous and inevitable green loden overcoat, along with a slender umbrella that was absolutely incongruous on that clear, mild evening—a wave of tenderness washed over her. Adriano, Adriano. So predictable and, deep down, so reassuring. It was he who had first acquainted her with that special corner of Rome, Garbatella, and he'd also explained to her that the unusual nickname of the quarter came, according to legend, from the memory of an innkeeper whose manners were particularly courteous and fine—*modi garbati*. Especially with his clients of the male sex. All the same, when he locked arms with her and thanked her for agreeing to come, the scorpion that lived deep inside her made itself heard: "What is this, some kind of pilgrimage to the locations of our lost love?"

Polimeni left that provocation unanswered.

"This is the red heart of Rome. And you, until proven otherwise, are a parliamentarian of the DP."

"Ah, there can be no doubt about that," she laughed, "but you and I belong to two different left wings. You're one of those leftists who love to lose, one of the masochists. I, however, like to win. And that doesn't strike me as a minor distinction."

"We'll talk about that later. Can we manage to indulge in a proper dinner?"

"Do you need to recover from the exertions of the young May?"

"At a certain age, those recoveries take a lot longer."


The place was called Il Ristoro degli Angeli, and minding the front door was a hostess with green hair who gave Adriano Polimeni an excited hug.

"Don't let those damned priests get too much to eat, Adrià, we're counting on you."

"If only they were the problem, Betta."

They sat down at a more or less secluded table: the place wasn't huge, but the aromas wafting out of the kitchen would have awakened a dead man.

Betta eagerly described the day's specialties. Adriano chose steamed squash blossoms with a ricotta filling and *tagliolini al cacio e pepe*, and decided to wait on desert. Chiara, who could count on her own formidable metabolism, still went along with his order, adding a dish of anchovies.

"Now, if you want to get to the point . . . "

"There's plenty of time, we'll get to it."

Adriano amused himself by keeping her on tenterhooks for the rest of the meal. Only once, between the dishes of *tagliolini* and the dessert, did he poke her slightly on the subject of Danilo Mariani.

"Do you know what I discovered, Chiara, while working on the applications for jubilee contracts and the Builders' Party? That Danilo Mariani is the heir to one of the oldest dynasties of Roman builders. The Mariani Family. They've been doing business since the Breach of Porta Pia, during the Risorgimento. Which is when one of his forefathers, a longtime vestryman of His Holiness, had the admirable hunch of joining the Società Generale Immobiliare, the General Company of Real Estate, then the largest Italian real estate and construction company. A consortium established by the Piedmontese liberators and the most devious and sly citizens among those liberated. Priests leading the charge, of course. Officially, the pope was sitting in indignant exile in St. Peter's, protesting bitterly against the illegal expropriations of church lands. But his trusted emissaries were establishing alliances with the enemy in the meantime, buying back at discount prices all the land that the new Italian state had stolen from them. Ancient history, the history of all times. Shall I tell you one good story to stand in for them all? Danilo Mariani's ancestor was one of the chief masterminds behind the Ludovisi quarter, which was built at the cost of the cementing over of an ancient park."

Danilo Mariani, the Ludovisi quarter where Sebastiano had his offices. It was clear, this was a prologue. Chiara played along, if for no other reason than to deny him any advantage. It was clear that Adriano had some surprise in store for her. As long as he didn't drag it all out too long. But, when he finally stood up to go to the cash register, Chiara realized that two hours had flown by.

A young woman dressed in the garb of a Roman peasant, with a melodious voice, improvised a few ditties on political topics. The usual masochistic left-wing material, okay, but still, amusing. Chiara sensed a dangerous lowering of her defenses. The thing was that she still greatly enjoyed time with Adriano. The thought filled her with an immediate feeling of uneasiness. She decided to reach out for her inner scorpion. She swore that she wasn't going to give him any more than ten minutes. And she immediately called her driver, asking him to wait for her outside the Palladium.

Adriano, in the meantime, was saying hello to Betta.

"A new sweetheart, Adria'?"

"An old sweetheart, I'm afraid."

"Ah. But you know, I recognized her. She's the one from the party, the one who wants to fix the mayor's little red wagon."

"I'm working on it."

"Now you're talking. Tell her to back the hell off. The German may have his shortcomings, but he's still the best card in the deck. After you, it goes without saying."

"It goes without saying, darling. Would you bring us a couple of grappas, please?"

Adriano went back to the table. Chiara stood up, regaining a chilly tone of voice.

"The driver is waiting for me."

Adriano sat down, calmly, and invited her to do the same. Chiara heaved a weary sigh. The hostess with the green hair brought the grappas. Adriano clinked the two small glasses and stared at Chiara.

"Sebastiano Laurenti is the right-hand man of Samurai, the criminal. You must have heard his name before, I suppose. He acts as his front and he's his designated successor. The money he moves is Samurai's money, the contacts he manages are Samurai's contacts. In other words, you're the business partner of a known Mafioso, and you're sharing his bed, Chiara."

A very long silence ensued. Polimeni smiled and raised his glass high.

"Excellent grappa, don't you think?"

And he sat there, enjoying her ashen expression.

Later, in the desert of her home in Prati, as her cell phone rang insistently, and indecision tormented her, she was reminded of what Adriano had said to her. She had pointed out to him that there was no proof of ties between Sebastiano and that bandit behind bars, Samurai.

"That's what my contact told me, Chiara. And you know what I said to him? Politics isn't a criminal trial. And sometimes that can be an advantage."

Sure, an advantage. Because if those libels came out against the mayor and Giovanni Daré, a minute later every blog in Rome and Italy, every website purveying unfettered political news from Bolzano to Palermo, would be telling the story of an aging Nazi who'd converted to the criminal creed, certain money hidden in London, and a young man who works professionally as a front for that bandit, as well as the details of his relationship with an attractive young party starlet.

"Starlet strikes me as offensive, Adriano."

"I apologize, but I was just trying to imagine *how* this story might be told. And you know, Chiara, once rumors start circulating, it doesn't take long to start an investigation, and the deeper you dig, the harder it becomes to say *what* won't come out into the light of day."

She also thought back to the involuntary wave of anger, how she'd been unable to control herself, and how without a doubt, a few of the diners, and possibly the hostess herself, had heard her say clearly, in an irritated tone: "Are you trying to blackmail me, Adriano?"

She remembered, more than any other detail, his smile, a blend of patience and irony, the way he rested his hand on her forearm, his quiet tone.

"President Pertini, the one who was applauding for the Italian National Team when you were being born, used to say, 'To deal with a brigand, get a brigand and a half.' When someone's overdoing it, you have to bring them back in line with reality."

"And what would be the reason, Adriano?"

"Chiara, the future belongs to you. But that future has to be free of compromises, or eventually they'll make you pay for it. You need to break free of old ties. Sebastiano is controlled by

Samurai, and so is Malgradi. This is the old, dirty Rome that's come to shake a tin cup, and it's got you in its crosshairs as a new point of reference. But you should not accept those rules of the game. You have a chance to break free of them. Do it. Don't think twice, don't hesitate for a second. This hand belongs to Martin Giardino, let him play it out. Offer him your support. You've got many more years ahead of you than all the rest of us. The next hand is going to be yours to play. Not this one. Or else you'll be crushed by that same dirt machine that you've started up."

"I haven't started up any dirt machines at all."

"Chiara, don't pretend to be a naïve fool, because you aren't one. Compromised companies aren't going to work. And Sebastiano is going to have to vanish."

Adriano had handed her over to the driver without adding another word. Adriano was offering her a way out. Adriano was still fond of her.

Adriano had decided that she could still be redeemed.

Had Adriano been right?

Her cell phone kept ringing. It was Sebastiano. She turned off the device with a decisive gesture.

She'd been going to bed with a Mafioso. The fact itself didn't bother her in the slightest: yes, she'd been going to bed with a Mafioso and felt strongly attracted to him.

The real point was another.

That relationship was threatening to become inconvenient. And she couldn't afford that.

The real point was that Adriano Polimeni had taught her a lesson.

# XV.
## April 1st
### *Saint's Day: St. Venantius and Fellow Martyrs*


City Hall of Rome the Capital. Giulio Cesare Hall.

When Alice Savelli took the floor to discuss the individual no-confidence motion against the mayor, in the Giulio Cesare Hall, the historic chamber of the Capitoline assembly, silence fell over the room. All chatter and gossiping ceased, and even the most indefatigable tweeters set aside their omnipresent smartphones, getting comfortable to take in the drama's finale. Temistocle Malgradi put on a show of lordly indifference. Defenestrated as deputy mayor, he had gone back to a peripheral seat at the margins of the council's hemicycle, seated between a has-been of the old majority and a young lioness of the new right. Being relegated to one side didn't offend him, quite the opposite. His dirty work would be done for him by those deranged freebooters of the Five Star movement. He, if anything, could come in and sweep up the spoils once the dust had settled. A political masterpiece, is what he had pulled off. Real power, for that matter, is devoid of action and dense with thought. To name just one example, Temistocle hadn't even put his name to the motion: always leave yourself a way out, no matter the situation.

Temistocle was doodling, distractedly, on a scrap of paper, every so often shooting indifferent glances at the statue of Julius Caesar, an original Roman piece dating back to the first century, which stood, between stuccoes and frescoes, watching grimly over the the day-to-day efforts of the crew of politicos high atop the Capitoline Hill. Julius Caesar: a big boss, a power monger, no two ways about it, but he'd put his trust in the wrong people. An error that he, Malgradi, was never going to make.

And so he went on doodling, this time sketching a baked kid lamb on its bed of potatoes. That lamb had the bearded face of Martin Giardino. The much-loved delicacy of the coming Easter dinner. Alice Savelli switched on her microphone and cleared her throat. But before she could begin to speak, a councilman sitting to her left interrupted her. Gioioso, one of the DP members who had underwritten the no-confidence motion.

"I request the floor for an urgent communication, Mr. Speaker."

The speaker of the assembly—an old fox who, damn his eyes, had refused to take part in the game because they'd failed to strike a deal over a couple of hires at the zoo—glanced over at the mayor. Martin Giardino gestured to proceed.

Temistocle winked an eye at Jabba, who was rubbing his hands. The dance was beginning: but first, a little floor show.

Temistocle turned toward the audience in the room and gestured to Settechiappe. The guy, who owed his nickname to his reputation as a serial winner at the horse track, had connections in the *borgatas* and the favelas, and for a thousand euros he was capable of assembling at least a thousand miserable wretches willing to show up on command. For the occasion of this surprise party for Martin Giardino, Temistocle had shelled out 1,500 euros (drawn from the funds in support of rape victims, of course), in order to ensure that there was a suitable claque on call at the event.

Settechiappe nodded, in a sign of understanding, and let go with a savage yell.

"German, go home! You've busted our balls!"

It was the agreed-upon signal. The crowd let loose. Shouts, whistles, sarcastic handclapping, feet pounding the ancient floor that was paved with marble from Ostia, wisecracks,

Bronx cheers, even party blowers left over from last Carnival, with their harsh, strident sounds.

The speaker called in vain for the chamber to come to order, demanding that the ushers intervene. Malgradi stood up and spoke in a heartfelt tone to the hecklers.

"Please, gentlemen, please! Let the session proceed in an orderly manner! Cease this ruckus!"

This too was part of the performance. Malgradi the wise, who placates the indignant populace. The shouting died down all at once. Settechiappe exhaled a last, unconvinced, "Fascists!" and let himself be dragged away by the ushers. The horde of hired immigrants and jobless men swarmed out of the chamber in an orderly line. After all, they'd done an honest day's work for an honest day's pay.

Councilman Gioioso was able to take the floor.

"I intend to withdraw my support for the no-confidence motion presented by Councilwoman Savelli."

Temistocle jumped up onto his chair. I intend to withdraw . . . what the hell was happening? He glanced over at Jabba. The stunned expression on his pallbearer face convinced him that the profiteer knew less than he did. Gioioso cleared his throat and finished his statement.

"As a result of an in-depth reflection on political issues, I have come to the conclusion that I must reaffirm my confidence in our mayor, who is doing an exemplary job and who deserves, in this delicate moment, a heartfelt renewal of our support, for the good of our beloved city."

A sarcastic buzz greeted the pompous declaration. Jabba took his head in both hands.

Two more council members withdrew their support.

Malgradi reacted. The situation had suddenly changed. Someone was trying to fix him good. But they would fail at the effort. It took a lot bigger balls than any of them had to screw someone like him. There was only thing to be done.

He asked for the floor again.

"Mister Speaker, I had a great many doubts about this motion, to which in fact I did not adhere, but I am a man of my party. In the face of a clear division between the DP and the coalition council, and the mayor's reluctance to take adequate measures to deal with the problem, I expressed to several of my friends my belief that the time had come for a clarification of ideas. But I never believed that the best way forward would be that of falling into line behind the members of the Five Star movement. Now it seems to me that wisdom is prevailing. An alarm bell has been rung, and the mayor I hope has heard. At this point, I believe, the clarification of ideas will be possible, and the motion has no more reason to move foreward."

From the desks on the right a mocking ripple of applause arose. Only Jabba seemed to understand the meaning of the about-face, and he nodded sagely to show he'd grasped it.

Alice Savelli cursed herself for not having gone with her first impulse. She should have told Malgradi to go to hell, avoided allowing herself to be contaminated. Turning to the Internet had amounted to political suicide. She felt polluted, dirty. And she too knew there was only one thing to do.

"Mister Mayor, the group that I represent withdraws its individual no-confidence motion against you. I believe that you are a very bad mayor, but in this chamber, this morning, things are happening that I don't like one bit, and that have nothing to do with you. I believe that this city would only benefit if you were to stand down. But not today and, above all, not like this."

From the right, catcalls, laughter, mockery. The speaker called for quiet. Temistocle stalked out of the hall, ignoring with great dignity the sneers that his former Fascist comrades were sending his way.

In the antechamber he found Settechiappe.

"We kicked up a nice fat mess, didn't we, Temi'?"

He repressed his impetuous desire to kick him down the hall. He wouldn't even have been able to do it, anyway. He felt weak. He could feel a worrisome sharp pain in his left forearm. The last thing he needed right now was a heart attack. Shitface turncoats, traitors, scumbags . . .

He dismissed Settechiappe with a vague wave of the hand, and he swallowed a couple of pills for his blood pressure. He sat down on a bench to get his strength back and so witnessed, helplessly, the procession of council members as they filed out of the chamber, one by one. They all walked past him, without giving him so much as a glance. And if anyone inadvertently chanced to look at him, they immediately looked away, as if suddenly filled with shame.

Someone locked the doors to the room. The drug began to have its beneficial effects. Slowly, Malgradi recovered and got to his feet, hobbling out of the Palazzo Senatorio—the Senatorial Palace. He was greeted by a sickly sun. He'd fended off the blow, but a blow it had been, and a devastating one. He got on his iPhone and made the first of a long succession of calls.

MUSIC PARK AUDITORIUM. NIGHT.

T his was a terrible situation. If looked at carefully, the
simplest move was just to go with Fabio Desideri. The
bastard was on the run. Wagner's boys were keeping an
eye on the clubs and restaurants and Sebastiano was in constant contact with Bogdan. He'd ordered a truce. There was no
point in wasting energy. Sooner or later Fabio had to come
back to Rome. And when he did, they'd nail him. The
Anacletis were at a loss. Fabio had made promises and then
gone on the run. Silvio had phoned him that afternoon. There
was a return to Canossa in the air.

The problem, the real problem, was the politics.

Chiara Visone had screwed him.

Sebastiano spoke with Malgradi and spoke with Spartaco
Liberati. The article against Martin Giardino and Father
Giovanni would not be published. The editor in chief had
blocked it. The editor in chief had done more than that. He
had fired Spartaco. With a generous severance package that
Spartaco had accepted without blinking.

"Better than a kick in the teeth, no, Sebastia'? What else
was I supposed to do?"

Sebastiano had come to learn that *Il Meridiano* was to benefit from a special round of funding from a consortium linked
to the League of Cooperatives.

There were no two ways about it. Chiara Visone had
screwed him all up and down the line.

Sebastiano unleashed Wagner and his boys. They ascertained

that Chiara was going to attend the preview of a documentary about the Resistance, at the Music Park Auditorium. A little before midnight, Chiara saw him walking toward her down one of the paths of the structure designed by Renzo Piano.

"You could have informed me of your decision," were the first words that he spoke to her.

Instinctively, Chiara wrapped the leather jacket that she wore over the long black skirt a little closer to her. Her first reaction, when she saw him, had been one of fear. After all, he was a Mafioso. But Sebastiano had a mild expression on his face, along with the smile that she had always found so irresistible. Chiara understood that he would never hurt her. She relaxed.

"You could have informed me that I was going to bed with a Mafioso," she retorted, in the same tone of voice.

"Mafioso? What on earth are you talking about it?"

"Cut it out, Sebastiano. I spoke with Polimeni. He told me everything about you and Samurai."

So she'd heard about it. But not from him.

That had been his mistake.

There had been no impassioned confession. There had been no anguished soul stripped bare. There had been no heartfelt sincerity. Polimeni had got there first. And Chiara no longer trusted him.

"I was going to tell you all about it."

"When?"

"When the time was right."

"Well, now it's too late. I don't think we have a lot left to say to each other. As far as I'm concerned, our affair ends here."

Sebastiano drew close to her. She recoiled suddenly. So she was afraid of him now. For a moment, for a brief moment, Sebastiano was tempted to open his heart to her. Confide to her the agony that had dug, and dug, and dug into him over the past few days.

Chiara, I've done horrible things, but it was nothing but the revolt of a slave. I have obligations, but in time I'm pretty sure I can get out of them. I only have one dream: to take back my own life. I'm not a bandit. And I'm going to be able to prove that. To you and to everyone. There has to be another way. There has to be a way to break the chains.

That's what he would have liked to say to her. Finish off that one last deal, wait for Samurai to get out of prison, and then . . . go away, start a new life.

I love you. Let's leave all this behind us. It's just you and me, a boy and a girl. Help me to get out of this messed-up life of mine. Help me.

But it was too late. He'd missed his chance. And Chiara . . . Chiara wouldn't follow him. Chiara would never follow anyone. Only herself.

And so he recovered from the fleeting moment and confronted her, decisively.

"Chiara, we have an agreement."

"No agreement, Sebastiano. I don't make deals with the Mafia. No questionable companies are going to work for the jubilee. And your name is at the top of the list."

"It's not as simple as that, believe me."

He stared at her for a long time, in total silence.

You think you can govern Rome without me? Without us? Then you're kidding yourself, sweetheart. The time when politics was capable of laying down the law is over. Are you planning to exclude me? Let me tell you how that will go, my poor foolish Signorina "I'll Do the Deciding." You get rid of me and Rome will grind to a halt. You won't be able to lift a finger, in this blessed city. Every construction site will stop working, and you'll have to deploy troops to guard them. But however many men you put in the field, we'll always have one more man than you do. And do you want to know why? Because this world, and this city, is full of desperate men. People ready to sell out their mother for ten euros. And we have plenty of money, mountains of cash, Chiara. Unlike you, you who have to keep careful track of the budget, follow the rules, tiptoe around restrictions and argue legal quibbles. You want to exclude me? The Roma camps will burn. The outskirts of town will explode. The buses will stop running. The metro will grind to a halt. The taxi drivers will occupy the streets and traffic will back up. The city patrol cops will look the other way. Apartments will be looted. The ultras on the stadium curves will go wild.

"This means war, Chiara. A war where no prisoners will be taken."

"Are you challenging me, Sebastiano? There's nothing I like better than a challenge. Let's see how it goes."

He watched her walk away, and did nothing to stop her. She climbed into her government-issued car. She didn't turn around. War, devastation, extermination. It was Samurai speaking through him.

## XVI.

### APRIL 2ND–9TH

*Saints' Days: St. Francis of Paola, the Fire Handler,
Good Friday, St. Isidore the Laborer, Easter Sunday,
Easter Monday, St. John the Baptist de la Salle,
Saint Amantius of Como, St. Maximus the Confessor*

INFERNETTO. APRIL 2ND. AFTERNOON.

They met at the usual place, the hovel in Infernetto, an illegal building, completely not up to code, a room with a sink, a bidet, a chair, a sofa, and a swayback bed. Scopino rented it out as a sex parlor to a ring of Nigerian whores, he worked out his union negotiations there, he used the back to store spare parts for the compactor trash trucks and street sweepers that he would steal from the waste management authority and then sell back to the waste management authority at twice market price. A clever guy, Scopino. It was Samurai who had put that obese fifty-year-old with the buzzard breath in charge of AMA—the city-owned waste management authority. Him, a couple of his brothers, and most important of all, a small army of cousins. It was a daisy chain of a family that, all on its own, controlled all the union representatives. More or less all of the acronyms. A family that only spoke one language.

Sebastiano took great care not to shake the filthy hand that was held out to him, and he handed Scopino a stack of five-hundred-euro banknotes wrapped in a black garbage bag.

"Don't go to the trouble, you might get a headache. It's fifty thousand," Sebastiano told him.

The guy grinned, baring an arc of rotten teeth.

"That's a nice chunk of cash. What do you need?"

"You need to bury Rome in its own shit."

"That can be done. You just need to tell me how much shit you need."

"All of it. For a whole week I don't want to see a single truck collecting trash inside the beltway. People should have to wear surgical masks when they leave home, and slalom around the rats. And on Easter Sunday, I want the pilgrims in St. Peter's Square to have to wear galoshes."

"Got it. We'll give them a nice fat strike."

"It's none of my business what you do. I just want results."

"You'll see, I'll make you happy. There'll be so much garbage that if they want to leave home, they'll have to call in the army with bulldozers. When do I start?"

"Tonight."

"That might be a problem."

"The word 'problem' doesn't exist."

"It was just a figure of speech."

"That's better."

Sebastiano pulled a map out of his jacket pocket, with all the districts, or Municipi, of Rome, and opened it in front of Scopino. He started circling them in sequence.

"You'll start from here," he said, pointing at the VIII district, Ostiense, "and then continue with the X, Castel Fusano, Acilia, Ostia, the XI and the XII, Gianicolense and Portuense, and then you'll cut north, Aurelio, Trionfale, Prati, Della Vittoria. Then, you'll complete the circle by heading back south, with the III district, Montesacro, the IV, Tiburtino and Pietralata, San Basilio, the II district, Nomentano, and then . . . "

"And then," grunted Scopino, "we finish up with Parioli, Pianciano, Trieste, Salario, and that fucking historical center."

"Exactly.

"Nice. It looks like a game of Risk."

Sebastiano stared at him with commiseration. He folded the map back up and put it away in his jacket pocket. Then he got back in the car and rolled down the window.

"This isn't a game, Scopino. Remember that. I don't want

to see a fucking single garbage truck, or a single fucking trash-man out in the streets."

He put the car in reverse and in a cloud of dust left behind the castle and the ogre inside it. He looked at the clock on the dashboard. He still had a couple of hours.

S tecca was waiting for him at a car wash on the Via
Prenestina, in the shadow of the highway overpass, not
far from the offices and bus parking yard of the ATAC
transit authority where, officially, he worked in the accounting
offices. But where he was actually a full-time union representative. Stecca played the same role at ATAC, the city-owened
public transit company, that Scopino played at AMA, the
waste management authority. And if it hadn't been for his wiry
physique, his hangman's build, you would have said he was yet
another one of the trashman's many cousins. An identical
anthropological type, a member of the same genus of parasites. The kind that you'll stumble across wherever there's so
much as a single euro of public cash to ransack. A good-for-
nothing who would therefore stop at nothing. He too had
been carefully recruited by Samurai, plucked from the thousands of his fellow employees, back in the good old days,
when Jabba hired staff for the city-owned authority by the
hundreds. With the adding machine of consensus and the percentages of returns on investment flowing back to the city
government in the form of slush funds. After all, who really
gave a damn about that ramshackle old company that lost
hundreds of millions of euros a year? They had even found a
lovely name for that merry-go-round, borrowing it from the
English. The spoils system.

With Stecca, too, Sebastiano skipped the conventional
chitchat. He'd decided to spend something extra to strand the

city in a world of shit. A hundred thousand. If for no other reason than that the mouths to be fed in that authority full of piranhas were too many to count. With a greasy smile, the guy grabbed the little cinder block of cash wrapped in packing paper and rubber bands. And he made sure that he'd heard him clearly.

"A week of wildcat strikes, right?"

"That's right. From tomorrow until April 9th. Easter Sunday and Easter Monday included."

"That's going to be a mess."

"Otherwise I wouldn't be here."

"How'm I supposed to do it?"

"However you see fit. Picket lines outside the parking areas. Sabotage the vehicles. Maybe even occupy something up on the Capitoline Hill. I want to see Rome collapse."

"That's not a problem. There's always some bullshit to protest about. Maybe we can invent that this thing with the German about putting badges and even more crew on the buses to check tickets, call it anti-union."

"You take care of it. You're the labor organizer."

"By the way, I wanted to tell you something about the new hires. Seeing that the Communists are in charge now, I was thinking of going thirty-seventy. After all, it doesn't much matter, since Settechiappe picks them all. Malgradi's friend, you know him, right?"

"Leave Malgradi out of this."

"Why? Okay, he's not deputy mayor anymore, but the party in Rome . . . "

Sebastiano lost his patience.

"Do your job and forget about politics, that's not your subject."

Stecca gesticulated apologetically and tried suggesting an aperitif in a wine bar at the Pigneto. Sebastiano dismissed him.

"Start tonight."

PUB AR MURETTO. PRATI QUARTER. APRIL 2ND. EVENING.

Sebastiano arrived in Prati late in the evening. He found him inside the pub. The same place they'd first met. Because, seeing how things had gone, superstition recommended not playing around with the kabbalah of locations. He was hungry, and he ordered a steak, rare, and a side of grilled vegetables.

"You going to have something to eat, Luca?"

"Later. Right now let's talk about work."

Sebastiano set out the plan. First of all, they were going to need to mobilize a hundred or so ultra kids from the soccer stadium curves, as well as the hitters under the Anacletis.

"But weren't the gypsies out of the running?"

"And now they're coming back, one by one."

Wagner nodded, satisfied with the explanation. Sebastiano continued.

"We'll start with the welcome centers for immigrants and for the homeless. Between tomorrow and the next day, they won't be able to make so much as a cappuccino. Tonight, burn everything that can catch fire. Then move on to the gypsy camps. The Anacletis will have to take care of that. And when, in two or three days, the mountains of garbage in the streets reach a height of a yard, a yard and a half, well we'll set fire to them too. Billowing clouds of dioxin. We're going to need to sow panic in the historic center."

Sebastiano gestured for the waiter to clear the table. He slowly drank a glass of mineral water, wiped his lips, and went on.

"Then we move on to the construction sites."

"I've got an idea, Sebastia'. We can start at Vigna Clara, there's an abandoned station there that they say they want to get running again for the jubilee . . . we'll go out and we'll flatten it. What do you say?"

"It strikes me as an excellent idea. I thought of something else, too, Wagner."

"Let's hear."

"A trigger for the revolt. Somebody's going to wonder why Rome is starting to crawl with gangs of nut jobs, right?"

"Sure, bound to."

"Well, I think I've figured out the right rabbit that all the other hounds can chase. Newspapers, politicians, the more the merrier."

"Which would be?"

"There's a girl I know. Wide-awake and ravenous about money. I told her that if she makes up a story tonight about how two negroes roughed her up at Tor Sapienza, then we can start our campaign of filth from there. And then, like I told you, in a single night we can take out all the welcome centers. A vendetta. It's going to have to look like a vendetta waged by Rome and her people. The spontaneous revolt of a city that just can't take any more."

Wagner was impressed. That Sebastiano was a worthy successor to Samurai. And he, Wagner: would he ever be up to his level?

"Don't disappoint me, Wagner."

Wagner raised both hands to his chest as if he were swearing an oath.

"Trust me, Sebastia'. This time, no bullshit. What about that other thing, the thing about the bastard?"

"Leave two men circulating through the clubs and keeping an eye on his house; after all, if he comes back, Bogdan will take care of informing me. Put all the other men out on the streets. We start in two hours. I'll take care of the girl. You'll find her in tears and with her pants pulled down on a park bench in Tor Sapienza."

Sebastiano slowly massaged his face and took a look at his watch. It was eleven.

"I'm suddenly feeling a yen for sweets. I think I'll have a tiramisú."

"And I'm going to get a calzone," said Wagner.

CAPITOLINE HILL. THE MAYOR'S OFFICE. TUESDAY APRIL 8TH.
MORNING.

Rome was burning. Martin Giardino was burning.
The burning sensation was driving him crazy. His eyes, at this point, were a frightful painter's palette of broken capillaries. And there were no eyedrops capable of alleviating his torment. The mayor slowly ran a tissue over his eyelids, wiping away an oozing mess of tears and mucus. In the last four days, he hadn't got more than three hours' sleep a night; more than that, though, the city's air was dense with a pestilential, stinging soot. Soot from the bonfires of garbage that, over the past twenty-four hours, had begun to catch in the city center as well. Easter celebrations had seemed like the Feast of the Apocalypse.

More than once, in his moments of greatest malaise, he'd decided that perhaps Malgradi was right. No one could redeem Rome and it might have been better to just take a step back. Which, in any case, might become inevitable at this point. No mayor on earth would have been able to put up with the burden of that catastrophe for more than a few days. To save the city, they were going to have to send for a special commissioner.

Standing there, looking out from his balcony above the Forum, Giardino was yanked out of his hypnotic thoughts by Polimeni's voice. He'd even forgotten that he'd ever tried to get in touch with him and, for that matter, that office of his—by now an open port flooded with a frantic stream of council members, city commissioners, officers from the army, the police force, the Carabinieri corps, and emergency management executives—was starting to look like a raft crawling with shipwrecked sailors.

"Ciao, Martin."

The mayor said nothing. He just started silently crying. Polimeni put his arms around him.

"You need to try to get some sleep."

"I just can't. It's a nightmare. An absolute nightmare. You know yourself that we can't go on for much longer like this. Another day, maybe two? At least tell me why. I just want to know why."

Polimeni shook his head.

"There's something that doesn't add up in all this for me either. There are inexplicable coincidences. Rome isn't London and it's not Los Angeles either. A revolt this size needs a sophisticated mastermind, and especially one with a steady hand. And no matter how hard I try, I can't bring myself to imagine anyone capable of riding this city with such a firm grip that they can force an apocalypse of this scope upon it. To say nothing of the unions. I talked to the national head offices and they told me that they're as upset and baffled as I am. Never before have they failed so utterly to get a few hotheads in the city-controlled authorities to fall in line."

"Well then?"

By now Giardino's voice was nothing but a keening lament.

"That means the bad guys are kicking up all this trouble to get their hands back on the city. And we . . . "

"We?" the mayor interrupted, anxiously.

"We'll hold out. This can't last much longer, Martin. Because one of two things has to happen. Either someone will pull out of this inferno, starting with the labor unions of AMA and ATAC. Or else whoever took the leash off these animals, soon, very soon, before there's nothing left to collect, will establish a price for putting the muzzle back on them."

"What price?"

Polimeni took a very deep breath.

"If l knew that, then I'd be able to tell you who's behind this, too. Unfortunately, the bad news is that we're not going to be doing the negotiating."

The mayor's direct line rang. Giardino grabbed the receiver. Chiara Visone's voice betrayed, even within its crystalline tone, the weight of anxiety.

"Ciao, Martin, any news?"

"What news should there be?"

"The unions. AMA and ATAC. What answer did they give to your most recent offers?"

"No go. They don't seem interested in a new hiring package, nor in a renegotiation of work shifts and overtime. They're a blank wall."

"Incredible."

"Tell me about it. You have any ideas?"

"Maybe. But it won't do any good to talk about it on the phone. Maybe I'll come by later on."

Chiara Visone ended the call and slumped back in her ergonomic chair in her office at the Chamber of Deputies. Piazza del Parlamento had a lunar appearance, garrisoned as it was by hundreds of policemen in riot gear, as well as army troop trucks.

She pulled out her smartphone, ran through the directory, and made yet another call to Sebastiano. For six days he'd been ignoring her texts and for six days the only voice on his line was that of his voicemail. She couldn't think, she didn't want to think the thought that, nonetheless, had been steadily making way in her head until it had become a certainty.

"Vodafone, the user is not available, please leave a message . . . " She ended the call.

Yes. That's right. Sebastiano was behind all this.

But how far was he willing to push it? And above all, how could he be stopped? The party demanded a solution. Either things got back to normal or else it might mean her head. She went to the ANSA news site. She'd been doing it compulsively, every since Rome first caught fire. On the banner crawl of the latest news she saw an item that froze her to her seat.

Fatal Accident in the City. Well-Known Italian Businessman Is Killed in London.

She read on, as a grim presentiment crept over her.

In a terrible car crash in London, Pasquale Pistracchio . . . an Italian businessman . . . was killed today. He was well known for his history with the extreme right wing in the capital . . . he is survived by a wife and two daughters . . .

Frodo. Dead in a "terrible car crash."

The trip to London.

The envelope with the cash.

The unsuccessful search of Sebastiano's bags, and the way he'd used her as an unsuspecting courier.

The search.

Frodo. How did the customs officers know . . .

Frodo!

She thumbed through her directory until she found Alex's number. She called her. The young woman answered on the fourth ring. Her tone of voice was cold, unfriendly. Chiara ventured a question. There was no answer.

"Seba is very angry with you, darling."

"Tell him I'm desperately trying to get in touch with him. I absolutely must talk to him. Immediately."

The call ended.

Frodo. Now she understood just how far Sebastiano was willing to go.

And she was scared.

S etola saw Samurai enter the visiting room, and he realized that it hadn't been a bad idea to board a train. Actually, though, with the usual uneasiness that always accompanied him on those trips, he wondered if he hadn't acted too late. And, as always, he avoided giving an answer that probably would just have terrified him.

Samurai carefully settled into the chair on the other side of the table and stared at the lawyer as his mouth twisted into a grimace of disgust.

"There's an insufferable odor in here. Did you jump into a sewer before coming in, counselor?"

Setola flushed red.

"I come from Rome . . . The air has been unbreathable for days . . . You know what's go . . . "

"I know very well what's going on in Rome. Everyone's talking about it. Which is one reason why it would have been helpful to see you a few days earlier. Or am I mistaken?"

"I never thought that the person you know would push things this far . . . "

"You always make the mistake of thinking too much, counselor. I pay you in order to avoid having more problems than I currently do. In fact, I pay you to solve problems and, if possible, prevent new ones from cropping up. Don't force me to try to come up with other solutions."

Now the lawyer was at a loss for words.

"No, you see . . . Of course not. In fact, if you authorize me to do so, this evening, the minute I get back to Rome, I could talk to the person . . . "

"He should have been talked to before."

"I reported your exact words to him, but he . . . "

Samurai clenched his fists.

"He, he, he . . . Stop talking about him. First a war, and we didn't win it. And now the apocalypse. Rome is burning. Who can all this possibly help?"

"You know better than I do that it isn't simple . . . Especially when a young person feels the weight of having to . . . well . . . manage and perhaps finally imagine himself independent . . . "

"Independent of whom? Anyone who's truly out of their skull needs to be stopped, counselor. By any means possible, if necessary."

"Well, you ought to consider that in my situation . . . "

"Shut up. Let me think."

Setola had never seen him like this. Samurai's eyes had narrowed to two slits. The muscles on his neck were strained in an effort not justified by the resting position. He shivered. He'd only ever seen anything like it in Namibia. But that was a cheetah about to finish off a kudu antelope.

Samurai closed his eyes.

Independent.

Sebastiano wanted to be independent.

He might have been excessively harsh on Setola, but he didn't give a damn. No, the real problem was Sebastiano. Independent. It was bound to happen sooner or later. And it really irked him that he was unable to be out in the field to play this game to its conclusion. Sebastiano had disobeyed. And yet . . . those who are on the ground, in the field, have a clearer view, are better able to appreciate the reality. That traitor Frodo had been neutralized, and his assets had been secured. And now, Rome was burning. Whereas he, Samurai, would have bent like a reed in a strong wind, waiting for the storm to end, Sebastiano had instead taken his inspiration from the old Roman saying, *si vis pacem, para bellum.* If what you seek is peace, prepare for war. Instead of riding out the tempest, he had unleashed it.

However much Samurai hated to admit it, it might even have been the most successful strategy. Samurai *Cunctator*—to use the Latin term for delayer or procrastinator that was synonymous with the great general Fabius, who invented guerrilla warfare in the Second Carthaginian War and defeated Hannibal's superior forces—humiliated by his younger lieutenant's impatience. Humiliated, yes, but it was the general who stalled for time who beat Hannibal in the end. The thought of Fabio Desideri's mutiny tormented him. His time behind bars had created a power vacuum. And that young man—he remembered him as a little bit of a lightweight, but vicious, so deeply vicious—was trying to fill the vacuum. Nature, it's well known, abhors a vacuum. Had Sebastiano been right to hit back immediately? Now Fabio Desideri was on the run. But just scaring someone away isn't the same as victory. Victory is when you can show off your enemy's corpse. Not when your enemy is safe and sound and in hiding. But that wasn't all. Sebastiano had acted exactly as he, Samurai, would have done if he'd been his age. That thought sent a stab of pain into his heart. And an uncontrollable spasm into his neck muscles.

Was that, then, the real point?

Old age?

Samurai slowly got up from his seat, putting all his weight on his forearms.

"The next time I see you here, Rome had better resemble the Garden of Eden and you had better smell as sweet as a flowering garden. Hurry up and get back home, and get yourself a shower."

Setola said farewell, unable to get the image of the kudu antelope out of his head.

C hiara Visone had stayed at Montecitorio until late and, when she left, she remembered she hadn't had a bite to eat since that morning. The sweetish, nauseating odor that was greasing the whole city eradicated all one's senses. Nor did the drop in temperature in the evening hours offer any respite from the stench that wafted off the mountains of charred garbage, as well as from the other, still unburnt garbage, intact and piled high, waiting to be collected by special teams of the army and the civil protection service.

The thought of Sebastiano was obsessive and—even though she couldn't bring herself to admit it deep down—it was evident that she had gotten herself into this catastrophe through an excess of confidence. And yet Adriano had always warned her. Never be too sure of yourself.

There's no need to humiliate the defeated.

Sure. There's no need to humiliate the defeated. Right. Exactly. Okay. But hindsight is of no particular use, is it? After all, dumping Sebastiano had just been the logical next step in a game that, at that particular moment, allowed no other solutions. And now? Just how far would Sebastiano push things? How useful could it be to him to drag Rome down into the abyss?

She tried to shake off those questions without an answer, heading for the Pantheon and imagining that a gelato with whipped cream at Giolitti's would give her some relief. Suddenly, there he was, right in front of her. Leaning on a wall. As if he'd been waiting for her.

For a moment she hesitated. Uncertain whether to attack him or ignore him, keep on walking as if he wasn't there. She turned around to make sure no one was looking. Then she put on her defiant face.

"I thought you were dead." She addressed him in the formal voice.

"Just a little problem with my smartphone battery. It happens. And anyway, didn't we used to use the informal, or am I mistaken?"

"Things change."

"I'd say from now on we go back to using it."

"You, sir, don't decide that."

Sebastiano stared at her, his smile dripping with sarcasm.

"Ha, ha, ha . . . Then you really haven't learned a thing."

Chiara hated finding herself with her back to the wall.

"Do we necessarily have to talk here in the street?"

"It strikes me as the best place, and after all, we don't have a lot to say."

"We could start with Frodo," she said, provocatively, in a burst of offended pride.

Sebastiano put on a crestfallen expression.

"A true misfortune. Luckily, poor Frodo had left clear instructions in case of an untimely death."

"Did you do it?"

"It was a regrettable accident, like I told you. But we don't have much time, Chiara. And we need to consider the *how.*"

"The *how*?"

"Yes, the '*how do we get out of this now.*' That's why you've been trying to get in touch with me for days now, right? Well, listen to me. You've seen what we're capable of. Or maybe I should say, what *I'm* capable of. Rome belongs to me. So there's nothing to negotiate about. We're going to do what *I* say. I'll step aside and for a while you won't see me around. Mariani will take a long vacation and the Consortium of

Builders for the Rome Metro and the Rome Jubilee will get a nice, clean new face. Which, of course, I'm going to choose, with the benediction of that gentleman who you never gave me a chance to tell you about but who, as you can see, is still very influential in this fine city."

"And in exchange?"

"You're intelligent, Chiara. Why would you ask me such a banal question?"

Visone lowered her eyes, pressing thumb and forefinger of her right hand against her temples.

When she looked up again, he was no longer standing in front of her.

She only had a chance to catch the sound of his voice as he vanished into the darkness of the narrow alleys around Via dei Prefetti.

"Tomorrow the forecasts call for sunshine and a light breeze, Chiara. And something tells me that Rome will open up just like the sky. Sweet dreams."

# XVII.
## April 10th
### *Saint's Day: Magdalene of Canossa, Virgin*

Piazza delle Muse.

It was past 11:30, but Sebastiano knew the biorhythms of that piece of human wreckage. He leaned hard on the intercom button, twice, then stood back to look up at the elegant apartment house on Piazza delle Muse. There was no answer, so he took the stairs, climbed up to the penthouse, and, without even bothering to knock, kicked the door, hard. Once, twice, three times. Until Danilo Mariani opened it with what was meant to be a curse but sounded much more like a death rattle.

A gust of foul breath washed over Sebastiano, reeking of alcohol and rancid sweat. His eyes followed Danilo as, naked, he dragged himself into the bedroom. He stood hesitantly in the doorway for a few seconds. Then he made his mind up to go in. The apartment was dark. The air was stagnant and stale. Leftover food and vodka bottles were scattered across the carpet at the foot of a sofa spotted with unsettling stains. Sebastiano threw open the big French door in the bedroom and the light illuminated Danilo curled up on the king-sized bed. He was clutching the edge of the sheet in a fist clamped between his thighs, while the other hand covered his eyes.

"I told you to get cleaned up," he sighed, "and instead you . . . "

Mariani turned his head on the pillow and, with a superhuman effort, managed to focus on Sebastiano's face.

"I . . . "

Sebastiano didn't let him utter a word. He grabbed him

angrily by the hair, dragged him into the bathroom, and shoved his head into the tub, under a spray of ice-cold water. Until he heard him cry out and come back to life. Only then did he yank him to his feet. He shoved him forcefully with his back against the wall. Danilo had a look of terror in his eyes.

Sebastiano stared at him with utter contempt.

"There was just one thing you were supposed to do: get back in shape. And instead, you do nothing. And yet you know that all this mess started the day you asked Fabietto for that miserable loan."

Mariani started crying.

"Cut it out!" Sebastiano shouted into his face. "Because I don't feel sorry for you. You just make me sorry I haven't already killed you. I'm going to give you one last chance, Danilo."

A last chance. To Danilo's ears, those words sounded like a sudden flash of light in the darkness of that fury unlike anything he'd ever seen.

"So . . . ?" he muttered.

"So now you're going to dress like a civilized human being, you're going to drink two quarts of water, which will help you to piss out the mountain of coke you've snorted, and you're coming with me to the bank."

Mariani, incredibly, found the strength to smile.

"There's nothing to laugh about. We aren't going for a ride in the park and I'm not about to give you any charity."

"What do you mean?"

"That you're out of the game."

"I don't understand. What does that mean?"

"That you're no longer a reputable candidate. For the Capitoline Hill, for Rome, and, especially, for me. Mariani Construction no longer exists."

Danilo was seized with a sudden cramp in the pit of his stomach.

"What do you mean, it no longer exists? What about the jubilee? What about the metro C line?"

"You're going to dissolve the company tomorrow. You're folding it. The Mariani dynasty ends with you, on the 11th day of April in the year of our lord 2015. For the past century and a half your family has been chewing the flesh off Rome. Unfortunately, all they left you was a little gristle. And you don't even have the teeth to chomp on that. You're also going to resign as the head of the Builders' Consortium. You're out of every last construction site and every public works project in Rome. You will be replaced by a clean new face."

"Who?"

"That's none of your business."

Danilo tried to play the part of the tenderhearted employer.

"But the workers' families, don't you care about them?"

"Clever Mr. Real Estate Developer. You're a pathetic asshole. Whoever takes your place is going to rehire all your workers, take over all your offices, and substitute for you in the public works contracts."

"I don't . . . "

"You 'don't' what? I'm not asking you if you're willing to do something. I'm explaining to you what you're going to do. Tomorrow. Or actually, make that now."

"But if I . . . "

"Danilo, listen to me. I don't want this to be the last time I speak to you while you're still alive. Is that clear?"

Mariani took his face in both hands. Then Sebastiano finished him off.

"You gave me no choice. Having come to this point, you are a necessary sacrifice. In your bank, you'll find an account with a substantial sum that I'll continue to replenish periodically. Let's just say that you're going to take a long vacation."

"And you've probably already chosen where."

"I see you're starting to learn. Yes, I've already chosen.

You'll leave Rome. You'll have a nice long stay on the shores of
a pristine Swiss lake. Clean air, lots of silence, and most important of all, one of the finest narcotics detox and rehab centers
in Europe. You'll get a regular course of transfusions until you
have the blood of a newborn and your brain has regained min-
imal levels of functionality. You'll stop eating crap and drinking worse. And you'll see, maybe you'll even be able to get a
hard-on."

"How long will I be away?"

"We'll see."

Danilo got dressed like a robot, more or less like a con-
demned man preparing for his execution. And once he'd tied
a knot in his tie, he nodded to Sebastiano: he was ready.

Sebastiano nodded. And only then did Mariani find the
strength to open his mouth again.

"It would have been better if you'd just killed me."

Heading toward the door, he stopped. He turned back to
look at his bedroom, staring at the tactical crossbow leaning in
a corner.

At the bank, things went smooth as silk. Primo Zero, the
messenger boy who was also the director of the branch office
of the Craftsmen's and Artisanal Manufacturers' Savings Bank,
had done things right. Mariani gave them his signature and
simultaneously obtained the details of the Ticino-based fiduci-
ary who, from that day forward, would serve as both bridge
and screen for the progressive transfer of his funds from Rome
to a bank in Lugano. An electronic front, invisible and, into the
bargain, more than reasonably priced: one percent of the sums
transferred.

Zero was unable to refrain from offering his dose of slimy
courtesy.

"You won't have to worry about a thing, Dottor Mariani. As
I like to say to my best clients, such as Dottor Laurenti, my

motto is: 'From the tree to the finished piece of furniture,' every detail attended to. And if I may be allowed to say it, lucky you, starting a new life."

Sebastiano dismissed him with a gesture of annoyance. He took Danilo back to Piazza delle Muse.

"You have a plane leaving for Milan in two hours. There you'll be greeted by a car that will take you to your destination. This evening I'll check personally to make sure that you've arrived in Switzerland. This time, there won't be a second chance."

Danilo nodded. He dragged himself back toward his apartment and, turning around in the front doorway, he said a final farewell to Sebastiano.

"See you soon, Seba."

"I don't think so."

Malgradi typed the article in less than half an hour, and then he checked it with Sebastiano who, at first, was deeply skeptical. The mayor was never going to bite. Temistocle couldn't seriously think that he could resolve the mess that he'd stirred up. Malgradi reassured him. He wasn't working for the short term, he was thinking about the future. It's obvious that as far as the jubilee was concerned, he had lost that battle. Today. But "today" and "tomorrow," he had explained to Samurai's right-hand man, are relative concepts, in politics. An expert like him wouldn't have gone to all the trouble of enlisting a new platoon of hitters and bruisers. The contacts he possessed, a food chain that reached way, way up, to the very top, my dear Seba, certainly hadn't been interrupted. If anything, temporarily suspended. At the right moment, they would come back to life, and they'd be very useful indeed. Sebastiano gave his approval, provided that his name was kept out of it. Malgradi reassured him: perish the thought.

Malgradi got to work on Visone. He delivered a little sermon, clear and simple: you're holding the reins now, my dear, but my experience may be invaluable to you. I'll act in the shadows, but I'll always be at your side. Visone made it clear to him that she didn't give a damn about his protestations of undying loyalty, and that in any case she didn't set any store by them. All the same, she added in somewhat sibylline terms, you never ought to humiliate the defeated, and she therefore agreed. Provided that *her* name be kept out of it. Malgradi reassured her as well—this wouldn't last long, his pariah status—and he asked her the favor of arranging to get Spartaco Liberati his job back. I'd be grateful to you, he explained to her, and you'll be able to use him. One hour later, Spartaco Liberati, in a brand-new banana-yellow suit, with a cyclamen-colored shirt and a white tie emblazoned with a saxophonist, was standing in front of him. Malgradi was expecting at least a thank you. Spartaco sat down and informed him that he'd been given his old job back thanks to Chiara Visone's intervention, and that from this day forward his only allegiance would be to her. Malgradi bitterly chewed that one over, and rudely thrust the article at him.

# XVIII.
## April 13th
### *Saint's Day: Pope St. Martin I*

*Il Meridiano*
Independent Newsweekly

## WITH MARTIN GIARDINO, I GOT EVERYTHING WRONG. AND I'M READY TO APOLOGIZE.

*For the First Time Since the No-Confidence Motion in the City Assembly on the Capitoline Hill, the Former Deputy Mayor Temistocle Malgradi Confesses.*

by Spartaco Liberati

Since the party dumped him, Temistocle Malgradi has been devoting himself body and soul to La Casa di Vicky, the charitable institution that Rome's former deputy mayor runs and finances, and which works to get the down and out up and back on their feet. Before welcoming me into his office, Malgradi kept me in the waiting room for a long time. But this wasn't a case of a disgraced politico reveling in petty arrogance, far from it. The mystery of the lengthy wait was cleared up when Malgradi appeared at his office door. With him was a young Rom woman in tears. Malgradi comforted her, whispering words of encouragement, and then entrusted her to a young volunteer, a girl in denim overalls. When I was finally ushered into his unadorned office, he told me that poor Olimpia (The girl's name is not disguised here. She was born in Rome to globe-trotting Bosnian parents.) had suffered a horrible and traumatic rape, and she has not yet overcome the consequences of that experience, both physical and psychological.

"And it wasn't her own people, no indeed, my good Liberati. They were Italians, people just like you and me. Which tells us all we need to know about the racist prejudices that still infect our fair city. What would have happened if it had been the other way around, if a Rom had raped an Italian girl? And, let me add, little older than a child. You saw her, didn't you? I can just imagine the headlines in the papers, the aggressive campaigns from the right . . . ah, don't get me started. This city of ours."

He looks weary, Temistocle Malgradi, but his gaze is noble, as befits someone who has decided to consecrate his life to the common good. And even though at first he tries to deny it, Rome is and remains his chief interest. His obsession, you might even say.

"Rome is about to undertake the extraordinary experience of the jubilee, and I hardly need to tell you how clearly I identify with the noble works of Our Most Holy Father. And I feel sure that, under the wise guidance of the former senator Polimeni and especially of our mayor Martin Giardino, our city will be able to show itself at its finest, thus avoiding any recurrence of the tawdry episodes of corruption and profiteering that have, unfortunately, marked such great occasions in the past. The Jubilee of Mercy will be a triumph of legality and rectitude, I can assure you of that."

Even if Malgradi appears very sincere, and his words sound convincing, I can't keep from asking a question. For that matter, the publication for which I have the honor to write isn't one of those that lies down and lets itself be used as a doormat by the mighty and the powerful.

"You've just praised Martin Giardino, Dottor Malgradi.

And yet, a few days ago you supported a motion demanding his resignation. How do you explain that?"

Malgradi throws both arms wide, and heaves a sigh.

"What can I tell you? My intention was to serve as a prod and a stimulus. I thought it was time to exhort the mayor to have a firmer grip and assume full control of the situation, and perhaps to show greater trust in his colleagues."

"So you never actually planned to demand Martin Giardino's resignation?"

"Are you kidding? I voted for him in the primaries, I was always at his side in all the most challenging moments!"

"Allow me to insist, that motion . . . "

"Let me stop you right there. There was never a motion in my name. Go check for yourself. If anyone is starting rumors about my support or even my role in such a thing, I'll reply in a court of law with an ample array of evidence and sworn witnesses."

"Alice Savelli, the spokesperson for the Five Star Movement, says that . . . "

"I've already had opportunities to talk, both in private and publicly, with Councilwoman Savelli. What I was telling you earlier applies to her as well. My lawyers are ready to take full legal action against anyone who ventures to claim that I put my name to the motion against Martin Giardino."

"So then, you have nothing to blame yourself for?"

Temistocle Malgradi, at this point, lets a sad smile play over his face. Sad and self-aware. "I was wrong about Martin Giardino, and I mean to apologize to him. Let me take advantage of this opportunity to do so publicly. I should have appealed to him in a more open fashion. Martin is a very intelligent person, he would have understood that I was simply a spokesman for a widespread politic malaise, and this darned misunderstanding would never have arisen."

"The malaise you're talking about, it's resolved now?"

"Completely. During the terrible days around Easter, the mayor showed the world that he knew how to keep things firmly on track. He proved himself to be a great statesman. Rome should be as proud of Martin Giardino as I am."

Adriano Polimeni finished scanning the article and handed the paper to the mayor. That stuff really was enough to make you throw up.

But he didn't like one bit what he could read in the eyes of Martin Giardino: complacency, flattered pride. And, he thought, with a stirring of anger, the usual, intolerable vanity.

"Look out, Martin. He's just hunting around for a path back to viability."

"Of course, certainly, but still . . . "

"But still, nothing. That man is a snake in the grass. You won't be able to rest assured that you've neutralized him until you've crushed his head underfoot."

"Don't be silly, I'd never fall for such a pathetic attempt to cozy up, Adriano. Clearly you don't know me."

When he was alone, the mayor luxuriated in the pleasure of his triumph. Malgradi publicly apologizing to him. If that wasn't a triumph . . . Malgradi humiliated, Malgradi calling him a "great statesman." No question, the phrase might be just a shade arch, that he had to admit, but since one should, as the saying about open arms to a defeated foe would have it—"for a fleeing enemy, build golden bridges"—he dialed Temistocle's phone number.

Malgradi let the phone ring and ring before answering. He'd been expecting the call since the minute that the news services, early that morning, had started excerpting pieces of the interview. When he finally did answer, he began with a restrained, sober: "Good morning, Martin, thanks for calling."

"If you think that all it takes is an interview to make me forget the mess you kicked up, you couldn't be more wrong."

"I only wanted to apologize to you, Mr. Mayor."

"You could have picked up the phone."

"You wouldn't have answered my call. And anyway, it needed to be a political apology, not just a private one."

"Well, I appreciated it."

"Thank you."

"But if you think that's enough to get you your job back . . . "

"That was never my intention, Martin. I really only ever wanted to apologize. And I'll say it again: I was wrong, and I'm paying for it. All I wanted to tell you was that you can count on me and my colleagues. Whenever you need us. From now on, ask, and it shall be given."

"We'll see."

"You won't be disappointed, Martin."

The conversation came to an abrupt end. The mayor had done his part. And yet Malgradi could practically glimpse, physically, the gleam in Martin Giardino's eye; he certainly heard his pride-filled sigh; he could imagine him clenching his fists and maybe even improvising a happy little dance step around the famous desk that had once belonged to Mayor Ernesto Nathan. The games were on again. It was just a matter of time. And patience. That was why he had taken care not to send his regards to Polimeni. In the future, those regards might be looked back upon as a sinister omen.

# XIX.
## APRIL 15TH
### *Saint's Day: St. Theodore the Martyr*

VIALE MAZZINI.

The pact that he'd negotiated with Chiara Visone had no margins for ambiguity. And all that was lacking to make it final and formal was the stroke of a pen. Which Sebastiano applied to the document in the offices on Viale Mazzini of the notary Somma—an old friend of Samurai's—thereby liquidating his company, Future Consulting s.r.l. The company would thereby be officially deleted from the registry of the Italian Chamber of Commerce. Practically speaking, the company would simply change its name once the waters had calmed down a little. It wouldn't even move from its current offices on Via Ludovisi. He just needed to take a break. A break whose duration was a dependent variable, bound up with too many conditions—not least of which the fate of Samurai—to be able to venture even a rough prediction. At least, not right then and there. In the meantime, the new armada of builders with clean faces would do whatever he had instructed them. The churn of business would continue with no significant interruptions.

Everything else had worked like a charm.

Sebastiano had miraculously freed Rome from its siege. The collection of garbage had resumed, the buses were making their rounds again, the fires in the outlying areas had been extinguished, the national state of emergency had been declared over, to the immense satisfaction of the Prime Minister's office in Palazzo Chigi, the security forces had been summoned back to their barracks, and the circus sideshow of newspaper and television reporters from all over the world had folded their tents and stolen away, unable to provide answers to the only questions that mattered: Why had it happened? And why had the gates of Hell swung shut again, just as suddenly and inexplicably as they had swung open in the first place?

For that matter, only he and Chiara shared that secret. And neither of the two of them had any interest in sharing it with anyone else. Martin Giardino had accepted the sudden return to peace and quiet with the amazement of someone with a terminal illness who had awakened one morning to discover they were cured. Now he was somehow convinced that his "political resistance" and the few concessions he'd made to the AMA and ATAC trade unions had finally ground the revolt to a halt. Adriano Polimeni, pragmatically, was ready to put an end to his "crusade for the rule of law." A new group of companies would handle the contracts for the public works projects connected with the jubilee.

As for Fabio Desideri, Bogdan had let Sebastiano know that the boss had announced in a couple of emails his imminent return to Rome. With the city all cleaned up, Wagner's boys were all at Sebastiano's service, and he knew that he could count on the Anacleti clan, as well. That meant that this game, too, was about to be tied up with a bow.

And after that, they'd see . . .

Sebastiano headed off to the Prati quarter. It was a bright morning, full of magnificent sunshine, and he decided to give in to his sense of melancholy by strolling down the wide tree-lined sidewalks toward Piazza Bainsizza, and from there toward Viale Carso, Via Chinotto, and the waterfront embarcadero, the Lungotevere. The streets of his younger life.

He decided, then and there, that as far as he was concerned, he'd come to the end of the line. He had plenty of money. The time had come to leave. Get free. Abandon everything about Samurai, even his shadow. He'd settle matters with Fabio

Desideri: his sense of fairness and gratitude demanded that of him, but then . . . Start over. Anywhere else. Nothing could keep him from doing it. He decided to leave Rome.

He looked at his watch. It was time. Chiara was waiting for him in a little bar on Via Oslavia.

It was still light out, just like that evening at the DP club. A lifetime ago. He felt calm, distant, and remote. She was sitting at an outdoor table, and at the center of the table were two ice-cold glasses of nonalcoholic fruit aperitifs.

"Ciao," he said to her.

"Ciao. I ordered for you. I hope I got it right, if I still remember your preferences."

He recognized in her smile that blend of seductiveness and ferocity that he had once found so deeply troubling and attractive. A lifetime ago. He sat down at the table and handed her a copy of the official documentation of the liquidation of Future Consulting.

"Here you are. I've officially *downed tools*. You're looking at a very young retiree. A guy with a great future behind him."

Chiara smiled again.

Sebastiano went on.

"There, now you have what you asked for, Chiara. Or, if you'd rather stay on a formal footing, you have what you asked for, Honorable Visone. Future Consulting no longer exists, Mariani has taken a very long vacation, and he'll no longer work as a builder in this city, Malgradi is a piece of political wreckage. The triumph of the rule of law, as even Polimeni might put it, right?"

Visone nodded.

"And in this new context of the rule of law, the public works contracts can finally be issued. Right?"

"Right."

Chiara's voice cut sharply.

"It's a pact that's in everyone's favor, Sebastiano. But all it is is a pact. With no ancillary implications. Whatsoever. I'd like that to be crystal clear."

There was nothing more to be said. Sebastiano stood up without having touched his aperitif. He extended his hand to Chiara, who took it in a cautious, dubious grip, a manifestation of ostentatious disinterest that, this time, did nothing to wound him.

"I'm afraid I have to go, sorry. But it seems to me that we've said all we needed to say."

"Good evening, Dottor Laurenti."

As he was heading back to the Audi, he realized that he'd made the right decision. Leave town.

Then came Bogdan's phone call.

The bastard had returned to Rome.

Wagner and his boys would pass themselves off as financial police, in an unmarked car. The proprietor of a gun store in the Salario district to whom he regularly gave gifts of cocaine had taken care of the bib vests and the official police paddle. A clever guy Wagner had met during one of those clownish shoot-out games that were raking in money these days, called "Airsoft." Where you pretend to fight a war, and you shoot 6 mm plastic pellets because you don't have the balls to do it with real guns and real bullets. Anyway, right, one of those guys who knows not to ask fucked up questions, like "What do you need these things for? What are you planning to do with them?" One of those guys who always have everything. Who never say, "Oh, that's not going to be easy," or, even worse, "That'll take a while." Especially since they didn't have time to spare, they needed to put an end to this chapter. Game over. There had been some discussion about the car, a midnight-blue BMW 3 Series sedan, stolen and fenced of course, and with a collaged license plate, that is, one that had been put together with pieces of other stolen plates. He'd had to sit through the reasoning, if that's the word one would use, of that scientist Kessel.

"I don't know, I've always only seen the financial police in those squad cars with the yellow stripes down the side. I've never seen them in plain clothes."

Wagner had been forced to claim full authority to make things clear.

"Because you're a penniless thug. A street bandit. That's why. Someone like you, the financial cops with green berets might bust you for a stick of hash, at the very most. You have to raise your sights. When you hit a higher level, the uniform disappears, *raus*, and they start putting on a jacket and tie. And they travel in unmarked cars. Got it?"

"Got it, Wagner, and don't get mad."

But Wagner was mad, really mad. Because he didn't like this plan, not one little bit. They were supposed to pick up Fabietto at the port of Ostia and, before that dickhead realized that they weren't heading for a Financial Police barracks at all, he would find himself in the hut out at Coccia di Morto that had once belonged to Number Eight, the late and lamented two-bit boss of the armada of Ostia, God rest his soul. Samurai had taken him out of circulation when he'd gotten too big for his britches. Just like Fabietto. Only they weren't being sent to do a complete job on Fabietto, no. The order was to scare him good, once and for all. Maybe by working him over proper and leaving him some nice big souvenirs, scars on his face, or under his feet, or on his knees. In other words, until it was clear to him that the time had come to settle down and behave. And what's most important, to clear out. And that's when Wagner had dug his heels in. And he'd done everything he could to make it clear to Sebastiano that this wouldn't work. Aside from the fact that he had a personal grudge against the bastard, on account of Beagle Boy, a brother, more than a brother, what kind of a ridiculous clown act was this kidnapping? Just two bullets and off you go, the problem is scratched off the list, once and for all. But there was no way around it. And in the end, Wagner had shrugged and gone along. After all, Sebastiano was paying, and generously, so he could do more or less as he saw fit.

Wagner had inspected the building with his boys. It looked like no one had set foot in that hovel since Number Eight had given up his soul to his Creator. It was a shanty made of raw concrete and corrugated tin in the middle of an abandoned field. When the twins walked in, they commented admiringly on the furnishings. A swayback armchair, a tripod for video cameras, a set of batteries hooked up to jumper cables. Baseball bats, pliers, metal bars of different lengths and thicknesses, a fireplace poker. Even an oxyacetylene torch.

"What's all this?" Ring had asked.

"It looks like an ISIS torture chamber, damn it," his brother had pointed out.

"Since you guys are Nazis, you ought to like it," Wagner had put a brusque end to the chitchat. And then, drawing on his imagination, he'd stunned them with bloodthirsty accounts of all the things Number Eight had been capable of getting up to in there when he had to deal with anyone who got in his way. At least until his path brought him face-to-face with someone more lethal than him.

It was Sebastiano who had taken care of the piece of paper to wave under Fabietto's nose. That was a job that demanded expert hands. Certainly not *their* hands. At last, everything was ready. They only needed to saddle up and go collect that miserable piece of shit. On April 17th. A Friday. A very unlucky day in Italy, the equivalent of Friday the 13th elsewhere. And to hell with superstition. After all, it was always on a Friday that Fabietto climbed aboard that floating steam iron he kept tied up alongside the wharf in Ostia.

Wagner and the twins swung through the gate bar of the port a little after ten. They wore the dark blue bib vests, with the big letters, in phosphorescent white, spelling out "Financial Police." Their BMW hardly even had to slow down when the bored security guard saw them. He immediately snapped to attention, nodded, and raised the bar when he saw the official paddle being waved out the car window. They purred along at walking speed until they reached the wharf where the big boats were tied up. Even from there, they could already see the deck of the *Mykonos IV*. They slowly emerged from the car and clicked off the safeties of their Beretta 92 pistols, slipping them behind their belts at the small of their backs. Then they strolled toward the yacht.

On the wharf, Bogdan was washing the stern of the boat with a hose, spraying away the dull stains of salt and brine. He exchanged a glance with the three young men and then, with a nod of approval, he turned off the faucet, piled the rubber hose in a tangled heap, and then headed off in the opposite direction from the way that Wagner and the twins had come.

They had Fabietto all to themselves.

"I'll do the talking," Wagner had instructed them in a low voice, since he was the only member of the crew capable of speaking a decent, proper Italian.

"Dottor Desideri? Dottor Desideri?"

The voice that came from the stern cockpit woke him up once and for all from the state of torpor in which he'd been mulling over the images from the night before. Before taking her to Fiumicino to catch her plane, he had insisted on taking Miss Colombia for a tour of the cabin of the *Mykonos IV*. He handled plenty of pussy, but he couldn't remember anything like it in a long time. They should have made her Miss Universe, not just Miss Colombia. A statuesque body. Dazzling white teeth. A belly as flat as a surfboard. And then, one orgasm after another. Even if she was just faking it, that was some job of acting.

"Coming!" he muttered, grabbing a sweater he threw on over his bare torso, and then pulled on a pair of heavy cotton trousers.

At the sight of those official bib vests on the deck of his boat, he kept his cool. If anything, he wondered what the hell had become of Bogdan and why he hadn't told those three cops to wait on the wharf. He put on a winning and hospitable smile, invited them to sit down, and asked whether they'd care for an espresso.

"We aren't here on a courtesy visit," Wagner said, stiffening.

Strange, thought Fabietto. He'd practically grown up with the financial police busting his chops. But he'd never seen one who looked like this.

"Normally, an officer identifies himself. With whom do I have the pleasure of speaking?" he asked.

"Lieutenant Mauro Arnese, tax task force. And that's the reason we're here," Wagner replied, and laid down the file he was carrying.

Fabietto opened the file and started reading the papers attentively. A confiscation warrant referencing tax evasion for the fiscal year of 2013.

"Wow," he said with a smile, never looking up from the papers, "you've picked up speed. You're already auditing tax revenues for 2013?"

"The country has changed," Wagner pointed out, starting to enjoy himself.

"It may well have changed, but it's still just as sloppy and incompetent as ever. You see, Lieutenant, I don't find in these papers any precise reference to the boat, aside from the name and the registration number, nor, what's more important, any reference to its owner."

"You're the owner," said Wagner, stiffening.

"That's not exactly right. This boat is owned by a company. I'm just renting it from that company. As a matter of fact, only for certain times of the year. If you like, I ought to have in my possession not only the boat's registration papers, but also the lease I have with that company. Therefore, if you will, let me insist on making that coffee for you, and then you can head back to the barracks to check more carefully the terms in which these documents are framed."

Wagner, who until that moment had kept both hands at his sides, instinctively moved his right hand behind his back. A movement that didn't escape Fabietto's notice. His visitors were certainly not financial police.

"You see, Lieutenant, I don't wish to seem arrogant, but I don't see what else we have to say to each other. Nor, frankly, what legitimate right you have to remain on this boat."

Kessel aimed his Beretta at Fabietto.

"Asshole, put your shoes on and come with us to the barracks."

Convenient.

"All right," Fabietto smiled. "Albeit with a less than perfect Italian, you, sir, have made your point. I'll put on my shoes, as you suggest, and I'll come along willingly."

Wagner nodded.

"Now we're talking," he said. Even if it was clear by now even to him that the masquerade had fallen through. An intuition that ought to have led him to do what, instead, he failed to do. And he certainly paid the price for ignoring it.

All alone, Fabietto trotted down the steps that led to the cabin, and quickly found a cubbyhole where he'd stashed his Comet, a marine flare gun that took shotgun shell flares. He quickly loaded a shell, and popped two more into his pocket. Then he put on his shoes and, his arm held straight before him with the locked and loaded flare gun, slowly began to retrace his steps, toward the stern cockpit.

"I'm coming up . . . " he said.

"Take your time, take your time. We're in no rush," Kessel laughed rudely.

And that was the last time in what remained of his life that his mouth had anything like a natural expression.

The shell fired from Fabietto's flare gun hit him square in the center of his jaw, taking with it a part of his face.

The scream and the stench of scorched flesh filled the space just seconds after Wagner fired a series of shots down into the staircase, and then ran up onto the gangway that connected the boat to the wharf. Ring, gun in hand, bent over his brother, who was huddled over in a pool of blood. His weapon was trembling in his hand. Tears were blurring his vision.

"You bastard! You bastard!" he shouted. Then, in his turn, he started shooting at Fabietto. An instant before the second shell hit him in the right shoulder, knocking the pistol into the water. He felt a lancing pain and, instinctively, reached up with his left hand, trying to claw out of his flesh that incandescent projectile. Now the palm of his hand was sizzling as the burn sank deep into that flesh as well, and on the wharf Wagner's shouting voice reminded him that there only remained one thing to do.

"Run, fuck it! Run! *Ruuuuuuuuun!*"

Fabietto slowly reemerged into the stern cockpit, holding a towel to stop the bleeding from the bullet hole in his forearm. The bullet had gone through, shattering the bone on its way. He saw Bogdan come running, then he glimpsed the silhouettes of the officers from the harbor police as they boarded and bent over Kessel's lifeless body. He had enough strength left in him to articulate a few words.

"There were three of them. They were trying to kidnap me."

Then he lost consciousness.

# XXI.
## APRIL 19TH
### *Saint's Day: St. Gerold of Cologne, Martyr*

PRISON IN NORTHERN ITALY.

S amurai emerged from the full lotus position and grabbed his copy of *Crime and Punishment* from the shelf on the wall over his cot. He was allowed to possess books, provided they had received prior authorization: Can you imagine any lawmaker of the European Community immune to humanitarian scruples? And culture, after all, it's a well-known fact that culture is always a good thing.

Samurai had drawn up a list. An older junior officer, something of a lifer, with brilliantined hair, had forwarded it on, somewhat disconcerted. Nietzsche, Mommsen's *History of Rome*, St. Augustine's *Confessions*, and Shakespeare's tragedies.

"Samura', what are you trying to do, get a college degree?"

"You know what they say: it's never too late."

A month later, they had delivered the first volumes. All of them scrupulously examined and all stamped, page by page. Only one request had been rejected, because it was deemed inappropriate: a collection of Carabinieri jokes.

Yet another confirmation of how there is no remedy to human stupidity: it had been precisely in order to gain that rejection that Samurai had included a request for that slim volume. Not so he could read it: but so he could offer the censor an opportunity to exercise his petty power and feel the corresponding rush of pleasure.

He didn't know where he was going, and hadn't even given it a thought. He knew one thing only: "All this has to

end today, in one go, right now." He wouldn't go home otherwise, because *he didn't want to live like this.*

He needed to meditate. Setola, in his last visit, had reported
good news and terrible news. Rome had returned to normal,
but Fabietto Desideri had survived a . . . what had Setola called
it? An attempted meeting of the minds. What a vivid imagination, the old pettifogger had. The law on wiretapping had been
definitively watered down by the scruples of the last survivors
of Italy's period of extreme legal crackdown. Chiara Visone, in
other words, had failed. For the upcoming hearing before the
Supreme Court, then, there was no hope but to rely on the
lawyer. But there was something even more unsettling than the
prospect of ongoing time behind bars. Something that had to
do with Sebastiano. The young man, according to Setola, had
become elusive, as if corroded by some internal conflict. At
first, Samurai had attributed the fury with which he'd defied
his orders to mere youthful enthusiasm.

But, upon more careful reflection, it might be something
else. Something far more dangerous. Hence the link with
Dostoyevsky.

The slow descent into the inferno of Raskolnikov, a murderer who seeks redemption without repentance, only to come
at last to the conviction that there can be no redemption without repentance. That parable had the power to leave him deeply
uneasy. Nothing like it had ever happened to him before. He'd
gotten away with things many times before, and he'd never felt
even the slightest twinge of remorse. The possibility of an alternative path disturbed him. It troubled him that someone like
Dostoyevsky should have written it. It meant that this alternative
really did exist. That there were people willing to throw their
lives away in order to follow a path that was so . . . so senseless.

Repentance! Redemption! And in the end that son of a
bitch, the investigating attorney Porfiry Petrovich rubs his

hands together and sends the young man off to Siberia. That was definitely the wrong finale. People like Raskolnikov should be murdered in their cribs. He adored Dostoyevsky. A great romantic who had known czarist prisons, and who had passed from a revolutionary youth to the far right. Taking into account the differing contexts, a life story not all that dissimilar from his own.

But what about Sebastiano?

If he had unleashed a war as a desperate, final assault . . . in order to court defeat? To bring down the ultimate and final ruin? The Ragnarök of the Nordic sagas. In the end, he'd emerge dead. Or else free. Free and cleansed.

He still had too little evidence to base a conclusion on, and that was why it was absolutely necessary to regain his liberty.

Fabio Desideri was still on the loose, and at this point there were no margins. The job needed to be done. If prison hadn't entirely demolished his intelligence, well, then he was capable of reading his protégé's mind.

Sebastiano would finish up his game with Fabietto, and then he'd leave him. For good.

Forever alone.

The problem was certainly a serious one.

# XXII.
## APRIL 20TH
### *Saint's Day: Pope St. Anicetus*

SWITZERLAND. CANTON TICINO. IL CARDO NURSING HOME.

His nurse, a magnificent blonde with big hands and long, tapered fingers, gently finished massaging his neck with an ointment of mineral essences and whispered into his ear that the morning therapy was over now. Facedown on a massage bed lined with organic cotton sheets, Danilo Mariani nodded slightly, feeling for the first time in a long while the sensation that he possessed a body. And therefore, a skin, a smell, blood in his veins. It must be the effect of the sedatives he'd been stuffed with for the past three days, he decided. Or maybe the first of the cycles of self-donated blood transfusions, which were done by that machine they'd hooked him up to the very same night he'd arrived. A silent centrifuge in which his own blood was replenished with oxygen, so that it then could reactivate collapsed synapses, deleted desires, senses inhibited by years of heavy narcotics dependency.

The first twenty-four hours had been horrible. The hallucinations had followed one after another in a terrifying psychotic sequence that had featured the faces of Sebastiano, Samurai, and Malgradi. In the middle of the night, he'd been awakened by his own screams, convinced that he was, first, suffocating under an avalanche of cocaine, and then buried alive under the mechanical mole of the construction site of the metro C line at Piazza San Giovanni. At dawn, in the bathroom of his suite—a barren rectangle decorated with pastel hues and with a large French door looking out upon a forest of fir trees stretching out into the distance—he'd wept bitter tears, convinced he could no longer locate his cock between his legs, no matter how hard he looked for it.

But now, in fact, he really did seem to be awakening. For the first time, that morning, he'd even been able to eat. Some marmalade and organic honey spread on boatloads of whole-wheat biscuits. And even the herbal teas that he'd been pre-scribed were starting to taste good to him, all three liters that he was brought on a daily basis.

The nurse gently caressed the back of his neck and then wrapped him in a feather-soft dressing gown of some white yielding material. She explained to him that, for the first time that day, he'd be allowed to leave the spacious grounds of the clinic and venture down toward the lake for a stroll.

"Alone? Can I go alone?" asked Mariani.

His fräulein shook her head, indicating he could not.

"I guessed not."

"No," she replied, in that mountaineer's accent that the Swiss Italians of the Canton Ticino had. "Not alone. But maybe with your friend that I met down at the reception desk a short while ago. He asked me to tell you that he's waiting to see you."

"What friend?"

"He said that he comes from your city, from Rome."

Danilo was shot through with rush of adrenaline. Who was this man who'd come to see him? And above all, how the hell did he know he was here? Only Sebastiano could know that.

"Is he a handsome young man?"

The young woman smiled uneasily.

"I couldn't say, handsome, perhaps. Though, actually, not really handsome. And maybe not young, either."

He instinctively decided to refuse to see whoever it was.

"I don't feel much like going out. Maybe it's not a good idea. Ask your colleague to find out who it is. And say that I appreciate the visit, but that I'm just not up to it. I'm still feel-ing very weak."

The nurse picked up the telephone and dialed the extension for the front desk. She spoke a few words in German. Then she turned to speak with Danilo.

"Your friend insists. He says to tell you that Sebastiano sent him."

Danilo felt his throat go tight.

"What's his name? Ask the name of this friend of mine, please."

That Italian really was a character, thought the nurse. But at Il Cardo clinic, they were not only paid to ask no questions about their guests, their history, and their pasts. They were paid especially to make sure their guests' every whim was satisfied. And so she turned back to the phone and further questioned her colleague at the reception desk, speaking in German.

"On the passport he gave to my colleague, the name is Temistocle Malgradi."

Mariani felt a sudden surge of relief.

"Oh, all right. Tell her that I'll take ten minutes to get ready, and then I'll be downstairs."

"So you feel better now?" smiled the nurse.

"Definitely," Mariani agreed.

Malgradi gave him a vigorous hug.

"How are you, good friend?" asked Temistocle, slapping him on the shoulder and looking him up and down, from the top of his head to his shoes.

Danilo made an uncertain face.

"Better, I'd say. Let's just call it a long road ahead."

"I know. I know. Deep down, even though I've forgotten it myself, I'm a doctor and I understand the problem."

Malgradi locked arms with him. Danilo greeted a small knot of doctors at the front door of the clinic with a brief nod, assuring them that he'd soon be back, and then the two men ventured into the park, heading for the trail that cut through the woods and led down to the lake.

For a while they walked in silence. Danilo took deep breaths of the warm early afternoon air, the intense scents of the underbrush, a bouquet of moss and wood, while his gaze wandered toward the peaks, still snow-capped, that surrounded the valley.

"And to think that I've always sort of hated the mountains," Mariani said at a certain point.

"You can say that again," Malgradi piled on. "Plus, in the mountains, zero pussy."

"As far as that goes, I've had to change my mind about that, and fast," he replied, thinking for a moment about the deep cleavage of his fräulein in a white smock.

They went on walking without exchanging any other words. Until Malgradi pulled a pack of Marlboros out of his jacket pocket and offered Mariani one.

"They warned me not even to take a single puff."

"What are you, in middle school? I'm a doctor and I can tell you if something's good for you or bad. With all this fresh air, how do you think a little carbon monoxide is going to hurt you. It'll just bring back the taste of home. Go ahead."

Danilo took two greedy puffs and felt a sense of bewilderment, followed by a slight vertigo.

"Better, right?" smiled Malgradi.

They'd emerged from the woods and now their feet were sinking into the water-soaked grass along the edge of the lake, which stretched out before them: a cobalt-blue mirror in which the mountains were reflected. Danilo stopped and, without turning to look at Malgradi, came straight to the point.

"Why are you here?"

"To say hello and see how you're doing."

Mariani turned to face him, abruptly.

"Temistocle, I'm a cocaine addict, but I'm not a complete

idiot. Why are you here? Did Sebastiano send you to check up on me?"

"I'm not Sebastiano's sheepdog."

"Then what are you doing here?"

"You need to know the truth, Danilo. Because that's the only way you can go back to being the man you once were and still deserve to be. To conquer an addiction, you need to be strong, confident. And in order to be strong, you need to love yourself. And in order to love yourself, you have to be willing to know, you can't be afraid of it."

Danilo was stunned. He'd known that animal Malgradi for years, and it had never occurred to him that he might be able to speak in a language any different from that low-life criminal vulgarity and obscenity that only politicos who haunt the Capitoline Hill know how to wield. Either Malgradi was reciting a role that he'd memorized, or else he was face-to-face with some strange revelation. In any case it was worth his while to ask Malgradi to show his cards.

"What truth are you talking about, Temistocle?"

"It would be best for you to know who's behind this hell you've plunged down into. Why you're in this prison. Why you can never set foot back in Rome."

"Who is it?"

"Adriano Polimeni, the extraordinary delegate for the public works of the jubilee. That Communist appointed by Giardino. Let's just say that Polimeni had and still has an excellent understanding with Chiara Visone, that tremendous slut who's been fucking Sebastiano. It was Polimeni who convinced her that, without you in the way, the jubilee would have a nice clean face. And the slut, who now controls the party, asked and obtained your head on a pike from Sebastiano."

Danilo stared at the surface of the lake; a light breeze had started to ruffle the flat mirror of water. He took a deep breath.

"Why should I believe you?"

"I could just tell you that you have to believe me because you have no alternative. Because by telling you what I've just told you I'm risking my hide without getting anything in return for that risk. But instead I'll tell you that you have to believe me because you're an intelligent man and, if you put together all the pieces of what's happened to you in this past month, you'll conclude that what you've just listened to could only be the truth, pure and simple."

Danilo took a short walk along the lakeshore, leaving Malgradi behind him. A hundred feet or so away, a fisherman was quickly landing a fat brown trout, bringing it in with deft, fluid, whirling movements of the rod. The fish was thrashing violently, flailing against the surface of the water, twisting in the agony of the hook that had penetrated its gills, struggling in vain to regain its respiration and its freedom. Until, at last, following one last decisive yank, the man pulled the fish onto shore. The fisherman's left hand immobilized the fish, pressing it against the ground. The right hand grabbed a rounded club, hoisting it into midair. The blow hit the big fish between the eyes, launching a jet of vermilion blood, the distinctive hue of fish blood, charged as it is with oxygen. Just like Danilo's blood was now.

The trout lay motionless, in the rigidity of death.

Danilo turned to look at Malgradi.

He smiled.

Now he'd understood.

He knew what remained to be done.

Malgradi smiled back at him. He'd dropped the bait in the water. Now there was a good chance that the fish would take the bait.

Polimeni and Giovanni were strolling in the Botanical Gardens. At the edge of a field of iridescent irises, Adriano felt as if he were appreciating the irresistible perfume of springtime for the first time in his life. He filled his lungs with air, and finally made up his mind to open his heart to Giovanni.

He told him that he felt uneasy about the surreal calm that reigned on the Capitoline Hill. After the terrible week of Easter, when everything seemed on the verge of tumbling over the brink at any moment, and there were even those who were calling for a state of emergency and the invocation of martial law, the waters had suddenly grown still. The attacks on the mayor had ceased. The organization of the jubilee was proceeding in an orderly manner. Malgradi had stood aside. Sebastiano Laurenti had vanished from the scene. In place of the completely unpresentable Danilo Mariani, the Consortium of Builders had chosen a young technician from the Ciociaria area, just south of Rome, a new face and, according to all the information that could be gathered, squeaky-clean and above suspicion.

"Then what are you complaining about, Adriano?"

"It's all too easy, Giovanni. It smacks of a Mafia truce. You know, when an old system has been eliminated and it's being replaced by a new one. It always takes some time to realize what's happened, and in the meantime the new power structures stabilize, and by the time the problems emerge, it's always too late to do anything about it."

His secret fear was called Chiara Visone. By now, she held the Roman party firmly in her grip. She had saved Martin Giardino. She was the secret mastermind behind the peace. Chiara had taken his advice and had lined up on the side of the "good guys." But he didn't have any illusions about Chiara. She'd played the game that way because it had been to her advantage. She'd given Martin his jubilee but, when the time came, she'd return to the charge. That, however, wasn't what left him uneasy. That was politics. There was something else that was troubling him.

All that peace.

That some kind of deal had been struck was evident. He'd tried to draw Chiara out on the point. But she avoided the line of questioning. Was there some new deal? And with whom, if not with Sebastiano Laurenti? Was the reconquered rule of law the new face of corruption?

"We'll stand watch together," Giovanni consoled him, after listening to his outburst, "you and me."

"Who? The two of us? Don Camillo and Peppone, two-point-oh?"

"Well, those movies weren't actually all that bad."

"I hated them. The priest was a sly dog and the Communist was an idiot. Anyway, I don't know, Giovanni, I just don't know. I really feel like handing it off to someone else."

Their stroll had led them to the Japanese gardens. The gentle noise of the little waterfall that slid over the little rocks irregularly arranged along the walking trail was a bright Asian symphony. A few large carp swam placidly in the little pond.

Behind them, a couple materialized. The man might have been in his early forties. The woman, a little younger. He had short, graying hair; he wore a pair of shorts, hanging down to mid thigh, and a pair of trail runners with short ankle socks. He had a belt around his waist with a fanny pack attached. She wore a skimpy, flowered dress, brunette hair, freshly shampooed, high high heels, an aggressive perfume. *Borgatari*, hicks from the outskirts of town.

"Look at that yellow one! Look how big it is!" she shrieked, all excited, pointing to the carp in the pond.

"If it's yellow, it must be Japanese," Polimeni commented, ironically.

The man came over, with something helpful and didactic in his voice with its heavy Roman accent.

"You're right! It's called a 'Japanese carp,' and precisely because it's yellow! It's a very rare fish, and in fact, at the Trigoria lake, when you catch one, you have to give it back. They put them back in the water, and in exchange, they give you a pole."

"Well, don't just say pole," the woman jumped in, helpfully. "A fishing pole, honey."

"Okay, anyway," the man cut the conversation short. "Let's go, we're bothering these nice gentlemen."

Adriano tracked them with his eyes as they moved off. He watched as they exchanged a brief kiss. How much did he really know about the Italian people he'd been pursuing all his life?

Later, he and Giovanni exchanged a hug. The bishop was expected at a private audience with His Holiness. Adriano had a few tasks to take care of in his office on the Capitoline Hill.

They had no way of knowing they'd never see each other again.

CAPITOLINE HILL.

His meeting with Giovanni and, to an even greater extent, the vision—yes, vision, because that is exactly what it had been—of that couple at the Botanical Gardens had convinced him once again that the time really had come to return to that cone of shadow from which he had been yanked. Or, perhaps, it would be more accurate to say, from which he had enthusiastically allowed himself to be yanked. As he made his way up the long climb of the *cordonata*—half lane, half staircase—of the Capitoline Hill, Adriano Polimeni felt an urgent impulse to stop and stare at the Senatorial Palace and the bell tower that, like a mirage, slowly emerged from the perspective of the grand staircase designed by Michelangelo Buonarroti, guarded on either side by the two statues of the Dioscuri—Castor and Pollux.

That Palace was empty. Irremediably empty. That Palace, by now, was just a hollow shell.

The Capitoline Hill no longer needed him. But, more importantly, he no longer needed to offer his face and his political past to a new coalition of power about which he knew nothing, but about which he sensed much, to his deep misgivings and trepidation. As for what the right thing to do might be, he could sense that in the relief he felt, a wave of consolation that had immediately swept over him at the mere thought of making that decision.

He turned, looking down at the Piazza dell'Aracoeli,

Palazzo Venezia, the slow stream of Saturday morning traffic. And in the teeming crowds of tourists, he paid no attention to the man who stood thirty feet or so below him, motionless, staring up at him, along his same line of sight. What's more, the man was bundled into a raincoat that was completely out of keeping with a warm spring morning.

If it hadn't been for that glaring trench coat, in fact, no one would ever have noticed Danilo Mariani. He'd lost almost forty pounds, a neatly trimmed beard shaped his taut face, and he wore sunglasses under a baseball cap, out from beneath which tumbled long but neatly combed locks that made him look at least ten years younger.

Motionless at the center of the staircase, Danilo stared at Polimeni until he could start climbing again uphill, toward the equestrian statue of Marcus Aurelius and the center of the piazza atop the Capitoline Hill.

In those endless moments, Danilo tried to guess what thoughts might be going through that bastard's mind. The man who had ruined his life for good. The obsession he needed to rid himself of, not in order to even the score of a game he had long since lost. But in order to start living again, as he had finally understood on that mid-April afternoon on the lakeshore, with Malgradi.

At the very instant Polimeni started climbing again, Mariani took off his sunglasses and slipped them into his pocket. He lowered his right hand beneath the hem of his trench coat and caressed, for a few scant seconds, the butt of the tactical cross-bow hooked to his belt by a light harness. He whipped it out and leveled it, laying his eye against the sights. He aimed at the back of that man's neck, the man who had turned his back to him, the man who was fifty or so feet away and whose pace had seemed to accelerate, as if he were seized by some sudden sense of urgency.

He wouldn't call out that man's name.

He wouldn't give him the time to think, or even to look death in the eyes.

No one had given him that opportunity when he'd been judged and found guilty.

He took a first deep breath, then another. His forefinger squeezed the trigger. He felt the 180 pounds of thrust release the aluminum arrow and send it hurtling toward the target.

The back of Polimeni's head exploded in a porridge of bones and blood. His body crumpled face forward onto the stairs.

Mariani hung the crossbow back in its harness inside the trench coat, put his sunglasses back on, and without turning around again, while a few people standing next to the victim's body began to call out for help, he trotted down the short stretch of the long staircase toward Piazza dell'Aracoeli, and there he climbed onto an oversized scooter. He was already far away by the time the helicopters rose into the sky and dozens of squad cars sealed off the Capitoline Hill and Piazza Venezia.

Danilo was standing at the check-in counter, booking a flight for Malpensa, when Chiara Visone learned that Adriano was dead.

Malgradi grabbed his cell phone and called the mayor. Martin Giardino was sobbing.

"A terrible thing, Martin, incomprehensible. An immense loss for Rome, for all of us. I'll be right there. You can count on me."

And so—he thought, as he selected a dark suit and a tie that went well with it—and so the lure that he'd tossed into that little Swiss lake had actually resulted in the death of the biggest fish. There could be no doubt about the identity of the assassin, not to his mind, seeing that already the first websites were staring to mention the "anomalous weapon." Danilo Mariani's crossbow had hit the target that he had suggested to him. Now he'd have to deal with the wrath of Sebastiano. Poor old Danilo.

With cold clear logic, there were excellent reasons for wishing for that death. It wasn't about the jubilee. Something much more profound demanded the elimination of Polimeni. With a mayor you could play a refined game, but not with people like Polimeni. Men like him were dangerous because they could serve as the foundation for a reconstruction of that damned holy alliance between incorruptible officials, the Franciscan church, honest cops, and let's even throw in the good judges. The hurricane that cyclically bore down on public life. Nor could Chiara Visone, with all her alleged modernity, or Sebastiano, with his grip on the street, or even Samurai, a great general and strategist, certainly, but still just a renowned thug, hope to control the tempest all on their own. Only someone like him, Malgradi, could do it. It was a question of nobility, if you like. The nobility of the *arcana imperii* constantly threatened by the hordes of the various Robespierres that come along and vanish. "Communists" was too bland a definition, because with many Communists sooner or later you could come to an understanding. Moralists. There, that's a term that renders the idea. Moralists. In short, it was for all these reasons that Polimeni had to die.

Before leaving, heading up to the Capitoline Hill, Temistocle Malgradi dictated a brief dispatch to the ANSA news service:

> The barbaric assassination of Adriano Polimeni deprives Rome of one of its finest and most resonant voices. This is an injury inflicted on the entire city and upon me personally, because I was a friend to Adriano.

Chiara Visone swallowed the umpteenth tranquilizer. Her eyes were stinging from hours and hours of unbroken weeping.

It had been a struggle to get out of the bed in her residential hotel, where the news had caught her unawares, and where she had desperately clung to the idea that no, it couldn't be true. In the darkness, in that bed whose sheets she had pulled and clutched at until she'd torn them, she'd shouted that name—Adriano—first as a plea, and then as a lullaby, a nonsense rhyme. Chased by the ghost of herself, by the phantom of Sebastiano. She'd unsuccessfully tried to call him on the phone. She couldn't even remember how many times. Thirty, fifty, a hundred? Then, in the early afternoon, she'd made up her mind to go over to the apartment house on Via Ludovisi where the former Future Consulting had its offices. The only address where, perhaps, someone might be able to tell her something about him. Because she had to find him. There was just one question she had to ask Sebastiano: Was it you?

When she rang the buzzer on Via Ludovisi, a male voice replied and, without even asking her who she was, invited her up. She found herself face-to-face with a handsome, very young man, with short black hair, who politely waved her in. Given the furnishings and the sheer quantity of papers and files, it looked like the offices of a company doing booming business. Though the company itself no longer existed—as documented by the traces of a plaque that had recently been removed from the front door—and there seemed to be no sign of staff, except for the young man. And not because it was Saturday, but because the desks were bare and clean, the cleanliness that usually denoted abandonment, and the air was stale, the way it usually is in premises that are seldom if ever aired out.

The young man welcomed Visone into a large conference room and walked over to a Bose stereo to lower the volume of the music.

"Wagner, right?" Chiara asked.

The young man looked greatly surprised.

"How do you know my name?"

"Actually, I was referring to the music you were listening to."

"Ah, *The Flight of the Valkyries* . . . great, isn't it? But Wagner is my nickname. My name is Luca. Luca Neto. But now, let me guess. You're Chiara Visone, right? The Honorable Visone."

"Exactly. Maybe you recognized my face from the pictures in the papers, I imagine. Even if this isn't much of a day for it."

Wagner observed her in that moment of coquettishness, explored the beauty of her body and her features. He perceived in her an instinctive hardness. Images surfaced in his head of crystals and fury, diamonds and volcanoes. Who could say where those thoughts even came from. It certainly wasn't anything he'd picked up in Casal del Marmo. It's just that with all the time he was spending with Sebastiano, he was starting to resemble him a little. He'd even started to think about reading a book or two, and he'd tried a few, and would go on trying out others.

By now, Kessel was feeding the worms. They'd caught Ring immediately, because where his twin was, he was too, and with a hole in his shoulder, too. But he was a tough kid, a solid one, and he kept his mouth shut. Fabietto had proved to be a straight shooter too: he'd picked no one out of the photo gallery, a week in the clinic, and then he was gone. Sebastiano had given orders to search for him; this chapter had to be dealt with, settled, and shut down.

Sebastiano was always in a bad mood, harsh, brusque. He just kept saying: Find him, this last hit, and then . . . He wouldn't finish the sentence. There was something of the living dead about him, he'd dwindled away till he was thin as a beanpole. Every time they met, Wagner got the shivers, worse than when he'd huffed glue as a kid.

Chiara grabbed him by the arm, impatiently.

"I don't want to waste any more of your time. Let me get to the point. I need to get in touch with Dottor Laurenti as urgently as possible. I was hoping you had a phone number for him. Or that you could tell me where he is."

"I'm afraid I couldn't say. Dottor Laurenti went away several weeks ago, and since then, I haven't heard from him. If I can be useful to you in any other way . . . "

Chiara stared into the boy's face. She was capable of spotting a lie from a number of details, many of them seemingly insignificant. And she knew that that Luca, or Wagner as he called himself, was lying. She was certain of it. But if he was lying, then it no longer even made sense to ask the question that had been tormenting her since the moment she'd first learned of Adriano's death.

She thanked him with a quick handshake and walked out the door.

She heard Wagner's voice from the landing, wafting down after her as she descended the stairs.

"If he were to call, should I give a message of any kind to Dottor Laurenti?"

Chiara didn't reply. There was no need.

Sebastiano was behind that murder.

"C.V. just came by."

Wagner's text message reached Sebastiano on the cell phone with a Swiss SIM card as he was putting yet another signature on the Hertz car rental agreement at the counter in Linate airport. He took the keys to the Mercedes convertible, and set up the GPS device. He looked at his watch. He was right on time.

In the café of Il Cardo clinic, with its large plate-glass windows, Danilo Mariani gulped down a bracing, revivifying celery-and-carrot smoothie and decided to go for a walk down by the lake. While he waited for a sunset that the spring season had pushed much later. He'd just returned from Rome, a few hours earlier, and he had done his best to insulate himself from any and all news about the Polimeni murder.

He'd gotten rid of the crossbow, he'd shaved his beard, and he'd trimmed his hair.

He was starting his new life. His latest exams showed that he was now completely clean. In his blood and in his head. They were going to release him inside the week. The pact with Malgradi was that he'd start again, in Zagreb, Croatia.

Mariani reached the lakefront in a heartbreaking spectacle of light. The red of the sunset was fading into pale hues of purple and pink that lightened the dark blue sheet of the water's surface. The air was still and sweet-smelling. He picked up a few smooth round rocks and started skipping them along the water, counting the splashes as they bounced. Like a little boy. Happy as a little boy.

He heard someone calling him from behind.

"Ciao, Danilo. You look absolutely marvelous."

He didn't need to turn around, he recognized that voice. Sebastiano.

Mariani stood frozen in place for a few seconds. As if a giant, invisible hand were slowly crushing him in on himself. From above toward the ground. Emptying him of all strength, and taking his breath away.

Until he heard Sebastiano's voice again.

"What's the matter? Aren't you going to turn around? Aren't you going to give me a hug? Aren't you happy to see me here?"

This time, he had the strength to turn around. But what he saw terrified him.

Sebastiano's face was twisted in a grimace of ferocity that he'd never seen before. His eyes were glassy, expressionless. And in his left hand he held a velvet bag from which poked something that resembled the grip of an antique dagger.

Sebastiano answered his fears.

"Do you want to know what I brought you?"

With his right hand he extracted the stiletto and took a few steps toward Danilo.

"This dagger is called 'Mercy.' It was a weapon they used in the Middle Ages to finish off the wounded on the field of battle, those too badly hurt to be transported. The men for whom they could do nothing more than to entrust them to the judgment of God. Normally, at the end of a battle, the bishop would kneel over the poor wretches, impart last rites and extreme unction, and then, with a nod of the head, he'd order them to proceed. The blade would go in near the top of the sternum and split the heart in two. A single blow. A 'mercy,' in other words. Here it is, I've brought you what you deserve, Danilo."

Danilo gulped and sensed a sudden dryness of the mouth, while his arms, reaching back, tried to imagine any object they could seize.

"Listen, Sebastiano, you wouldn't think that . . . Polimeni, I mean, I . . . "

Those were his last living words.

Sebastiano stabbed him right at the center of his throat, severing the carotid in one blow.

Danilo clutched at his throat with both hands, as he slowly drowned in his own blood. He collapsed onto his back. His face looking up at the sky, fiery with sunset.

Sebastiano stood there, panting, contemplating Mariani's death throes. He rinsed the weapon in the crystal clear lake water and put it back into its velvet bag. He turned to look one last time at Mariani's dead body.

"You didn't even deserve to be stabbed in the heart. You never had one."

# XXIV.
## Epilogue

Politicians and ordinary people. Old comrades, resigned, and young men and women, indignant. All Communist Rome was there, Communists now or one-time Communists. There was all of secular Rome.

They're all here, in the Little Egyptian Temple, down in the depths of the Verano Monumental Cemetery.

It's the Rome that refuses to surrender.

There are even three aging anarchists with a faded banner with the A in a circle: who knows in what moment of their pasts they ran into Polimeni, and what mysterious paths created who knows what affinity. There's no saying. But they're here. Here to bear witness. And maybe they too are thinking, along with the long snaking line of people walking slowly under a driving lunar rain, behold, behold, the sky is weeping for a Just Man.

Malgradi moved away from the annoying correspondent from who knows what left-wing radio network—did they still exist? Just unbelievable—who had managed to worm his way onto the dais prepared for the final farewell to Polimeni. That young man's rhetoric irritated him. But this was not the time to display such emotions as disgust. Better to maintain a rigid, sober demeanor, as befits a man who represents the democratic institutions. Malgradi stepped aside, and settled back to enjoy the show.

Martin Giardino was there. Shaking with sobs he simply

couldn't control. Chiara Visone was there, pale and dignified like a widow of bygone times. The grief that she displayed looked for all intents and purposes to be authentic.

Chiara Visone in mourning was a tremendous hoot. Maybe she even believed in the show she put on. After all, hadn't she and Polimeni been an item, once?

The loudspeakers that, up until that moment, had broadcast the heartbreaking notes of Bach's *Cello Suite No. 4 in E-flat major*, fell silent. Someone handed Martin Giardino a microphone. The mayor shook his head no: he wasn't up to it. From the crowd arose a sincere burst of applause. The microphone wound up in the hands of Chiara Visone. The Honorable Visone uttered a few impassioned words: "Adriano Polimeni wanted to change Rome, and he was succeeding. A murderer's hand stopped him. But we will continue in his footsteps." More applause, but with palpably less conviction.

Quite the performance, thought Malgradi appreciatively. And he drew close, to shake her hand. But Chiara avoided all contact and fled, with a rapid, indignant step.

You'll come back, oh, you'll come back, Malgradi sighed. And you'll come back too, sooner or later, Alice Savelli, because you feel a little uneasy and you're starting to ask some serious questions about politics. And about yourself. Excellent, go on asking those question. Because sooner or later you're even going to have to give yourself some answers. And that's when you and I will have it out, the two of us.

A man in his early fifties stepped forward, dressed in a black suit. Ah, this was the priest who was such a close friend of the dearly departed. Now let's hear what he has to say for himself.

Don Giovanni grabbed the microphone.

"Wealth devoid of generosity makes us believe that we're all-powerful, like God. And in the end, it deprives us of the best thing there can be: Hope. Blessed are the poor in spirit.

We must rid ourselves of our attachment to wealth, and we must ensure that the riches that have been given to us are spent for the common good. The only way. Open your hand, open your heart, open the horizon. But if your hand is closed, your heart is closed, like that man who held banquets and wore luxurious clothing. Then you have no horizons, you can't see the others who are in need, and you will wind up like that man: far from God. With these words, dear brothers, Your Holiness Pope Francis . . . "

A rumble arose from the crowd. The bishop ran a hand over his forehead and nodded.

"You are right, all of you. I ask your forgiveness. If Adriano had been here beside me, my good friend Adriano, he would have told me to go soak my head. And he would be right. Forgive me. You are secular humanists, your faith . . . this word that I really can't do without . . . your faith is very different, and Adriano was like you. He didn't believe in an afterlife. But I do, I believe that there is an afterlife, and that it is ready and waiting to take in even those who have spent their whole lives here on earth denying its existence. I am talking about the good and the just, and Adriano was both good and just. And I am about to commit, here, publicly, what constitutes for those like me who hold our faith, a sin of pride: But I swear to you that Adriano Polimeni has already entered that afterlife of the good and the just. And if it hasn't happened yet, I promise you that I will make very sure that it does."

Giovanni dropped the microphone and abandoned the stage, his head low. They watched him go in silence, the crowd opening to let him through.

Malgradi watched him go for a long time. The bishop stopped for a few seconds in contemplation of a grave with a yellowed inscription. Mauro P., 1976–1983. A child. Who on earth could ever have decided that the temple of secular ceremonies should lie cheek by jowl with the area of children's graves. A terrible idea, Malgradi reasoned.

Children are innocent.

Politicians have nothing to do with the innocent.

Nothing at all.

Then the ceremony resumed. Malgradi, with a gesture, pushed away the microphone when it was offered to him. As Samurai had once said, enough is enough, and too much is too much.


Chiara was wandering down the Via Tiburtina, holding tight to her umbrella and her last memories of Adriano. When she felt herself seized and hustled into the shade of an apartment house door, she put up no resistance. Sebastiano stared at her with a manic glare that was unusual for him.

"It wasn't me, Chiara. And it wasn't us, either. Think. Polimeni's death was of no benefit to any of us. We had a pact, and now everything's blown sky high. Who ever killed him did it to damage us, not to help us."

"Are you done?"

"You have to believe me, Chiara.'

"Does it matter, Sebastiano?"

"Nothing else matters to me."

Chiara shook her head, unconvinced.

"Okay, I believe you. It was a madman, a serial killer, someone from Mars. Okay? Can I go now?"

Sebastiano clenched his fists.

"I loved you, Chiara. I should have told you so before this, but I hoped . . . I believed that with you, it might be possible . . . to change . . . "

"You? Change?"

"Yes, me. Change. The jubilee would be the last maneuver. And then . . . "

He was humiliating himself. He was playing the emotional

card. Chiara felt the rage rise within her. She lunged at him, scratched his cheeks, pounded him with her fists. Sebastiano let her. She placated herself eventually.

"Sure, I believe you, Sebastiano. For you it was all a matter of convenience, of self-interest. We, them . . . but he was Adriano. It shouldn't have happened. No one should have laid their hands on Adriano."

"I've already taken care of that."

Suddenly she felt helpless. She gestured vaguely, as if to say, "I believe you about that, too," and nodded.

"Sure, sure, you've taken care of it. Of course you have. People like you never change."

Sebastiano went online to purchase his plane ticket to Rio de Janeiro. The flight departed early the next morning, at seven o'clock. He had a fair amount of cash, and from Brazil, with no particular hurry, he could shape up his accounts. It would take him a few days to calculate his exact share of the whole amount. He didn't mean to take a single penny more than what was due him. He'd get Alex to help him, on the more complex operations. And from Brazil he'd write Setola, explaining the reason for his irrevocable decision. Setola would report to Samurai, and Samurai would arrange to appoint a successor. But he wouldn't recommend Wagner to him. Over time, he'd grown fond of that feral child of the streets. He'd watched his progress, he'd appreciated his constant efforts to better himself. And so he wouldn't hand Wagner over to Samurai's tender mercies. He wouldn't push him into the slavery that he himself had lived through. Samurai might very well have guessed already. The signals that kept coming to him through Setola were unequivocal. The race was at an end, it was time to turn over a new leaf. He checked his passport one last time, then he went to his appointment with Wagner.

At first, he was clear and laconic with the young man. The war was over. The army was being disbanded.

"What about Fabietto?"

"That's none of my business now."

"And Samurai?"

"No longer any of my concern."

"Are you turning your back on everything, Sebastia'?"

"On everything. And without regrets. Actually, I do have one regret: I waited too long."

Then he ordered two beers and opened his heart to Wagner.

"Things are going to happen in the next few days."

"Such as what?"

"Such as everything collapses. Things grind to a halt on the public works of the jubilee. The supervising contractor's company gets shut down. Samurai's sentence is confirmed in final appeal by the Supreme Court, and they throw away the key. Such as Fabietto becomes the king of Rome. Such as utter ruin, Such as the bitter end. And roughly speaking, I'd also say that the government will appoint an Extraordinary Commissioner for the Great Public Works of the Jubilee. Maybe a High Prefect, therefore, a cop. I'll tell you something else, after the death of Polimeni, I think we're going to see the German tiptoe offstage, too. But that's no longer a problem that concerns me, I'd say . . . "

"Sebastia' . . . "

"Don't interrupt. So there's a little money for you. You'll get it in the next two or three days. It's up to you to decide what to do with it. You can keep your crew and go back to beating up negroes and gypsies, if anyone comes and asks you to do it, that is. You can go, in my name, to the lawyer Manlio Setola and put yourself at Samurai's service. You can throw yourself at Fabietto's feet and pray that he takes you on. Or else . . . "

"Or else?"

The young man was hanging on his words. Sebastiano took a long drink of beer. He stood up and laid a hand on Wagner's shoulder.

"Or else I can give you the keys to my house. You start studying, you find an honest job and a girl who loves you. And you turn your back once and for all on this shitty life."

"Sure."

Wagner saw him leave, his back bowed, and understood that this was goodbye forever. And he wondered how it could be that someone like him, a boss, could have fallen so low. But it had been because of that woman, the Honorable Visone, or maybe because things hadn't gone right with Fabietto, or both things, or else Sebastiano had simply changed, and you tell me whether changing means going forward or back.

In any case, the money would be arriving, and that was a sign of friendship, as well as a piece of good news. He ordered another beer and drank to the health of his lost friend, the Master who had abandoned him and bestowed such benefits upon him. Now, as for what he ought to do with the money that was coming . . . Wagner considered for an instant the option of normality. Start studying, find a job. Where he came from, the ones who studied left quickly, and the ones who stayed, even if they had a job, were considered just a step above the losers, the failures. And even Sebastiano, who had studied and had maybe even had a normal job, at some point, wasn't he a wreck himself now? Work and break your back and maybe raise some kids, spend the weekends at Ostia. And so . . .

There was another choice that Sebastiano had forgotten. Peddling drugs, but on a serious basis. After all, even the mythical boys of the Magliana gang had gotten their start that way. They'd pulled a robbery, and invested the money from the take. He, Wagner, had ideas, he had men, and he had many, many years ahead of him. Why not take advantage?

As he was heading back to his scooter, Sebastiano's sage advice and his grief already seemed to him like a fading ditty.

He started the scooter, whistling "The Flight of the Valkyries," and lost himself in the evening that was scented with cheesewood blossoms.

By the time Sebastiano headed home it was the middle of the night. Along the way he'd stopped in a couple of bars, said hello to a few old friends, treated others to whiskies, and accepted offers of whisky from others; in the back of a restaurant in San Lorenzo he'd smoked a really kickass joint, and it had taken him a good half hour before he recovered a little. But nothing mattered now. He was a free man. Lightness and euphoria accompanied him on the last Roman night of his life.

He leaned against the parapet of the Ponte Sant'Angelo. He looked up at the silhouette of St. Peter's. As if lost, the seagulls whirled in the white light cast by the headlights against the banks of the river below.

The cold pistol barrel came to rest on the back of his neck.

Fabio Desideri's voice rang out mockingly.

"Good night, my friend."

*Rome, June 24, 2015.*

NOTES ON THE TEXT

The verses on page 198 are taken from the song *Testarda io* by Cristiano Malgioglio and Roberto Carlos, as sung by Iva Zanicchi. The quote on pages 286–87 is from *Crime and Punishment*, by Fyodor Dostoyevsky, translated by Oliver Ready, Penguin Books, New York, 2014.

## About the Authors

Carlo Bonini is a writer and investigative journalist. @carlobonini

Giancarlo De Cataldo is an author and magistrate. He writes novels, essays, and screenplays for TV. He lives in Rome.